ATROYEL

ATROYEL

ROGUE ANGELS
BOOK ONE

LILITH DARVILLE

eBook ISBN: 978-1-998127-21-4
Paperback ISBN: 978-1-998127-22-1

Cover Design by Atra Luna Design (www.atraluna.de)
Editing by Maggie Morris, The Indie Editor (www.indieeditor.ca)
Formatting by Kate Tilton's Author Services, LLC (www.katetilton.com)

FRIEND & FAMILY ALERT

Yes, indeed, this is for my evangelical and otherwise sensitive loved ones . . . especially those of you who tell me you're wearing your knees out praying for me. I'm already overwhelmed with guilt—not really, but that's the polite thing to say. If you went batshit crazy over my spanking scene, this series would make you certifiable. *evil grin*

This story is my ~~breakdown~~ fantasy, so I might as well imagine that Brad Pitt and I walk off into the sunset just like in the movie . . . but before we do. . .

In the unlikely event you stumbled upon this book by accident, remove it from your Kindle immediately. Don't hesitate; do it NOW! I can't deal with any more guilt over causing arthritic knees.

There are some things you should know before you dive into this book. Although all of the sex depicted in this book is consensual, there are references to abuse the heroine suffered. If any mention of abuse is a trigger for you, this may not be the story for you.

Put judgments aside, and get ready for a fantasy ride . . .

BLACK ROSE AND THE THREE PRINCES

Once upon a time, an archangel named Syrael was the Sex Angel Lord of all the realms. Syrael, a vain and wicked archangel with great power, possessed a magic mirror. Every morning, Syrael asked his magic mirror, "Mirror, mirror, on the wall, who's the most powerful sex angel of all?" The mirror always told him he was the most powerful, which pleased him to no end because the mirror never lied.

But the day came when the magic mirror told Lord Syrael that there was a more powerful sex angel, and the large golden eyes of a beautiful Nephilim stared back at him. She was plain and unadorned; her beauty needed no enhancement.

One of the Nephilim race had survived.

This damn near shocked Lord Syrael into a chronic case of erectile dysfunction. All the Nephilim had been hunted down and destroyed during The Thousand Years War. The sex demon lords had removed their scourge from the universe. Yet there was no disguising the divine light shining from those eyes. The power of the Nephilim sexual appetite was legendary, and the moment he saw her, Syrael knew she had to die.

It wouldn't be easy. Instead of the usual tears and supplications, this Nephilim wore a shield of rage and determination, hiding her fear and vulnerability from the world. But her silent screams from years of abuse drove daggers of delight straight into Syrael's heart. Her pain appealed to his baser instincts. Her determination made him want to break her. He wanted her to suffer before she died. As he looked into those large chestnut-brown eyes, his heart hardened into darkness that started to consume his divine light.

Furious, Lord Syrael summoned three princes of the realm who were bound to him, the sex angels Cassiel and Atroyel and Tristan, and he dispatched them to kill the lovely Black Rose. As proof of her demise, he demanded they bring him her heart so he could consume it and gain her power . . .

1

———

ALEAH

Every cell in my body screams for his touch, a touch that will never come. My Troy is gone. I'm so very alone without him, but life must march on. So, I wall off my shock and swim in a moat of numbness. But every Saturday night, our date night, I sit here for hours and bleed my sorrow into a bottle.

I'm perfectly content . . . That's a lie, but we won't go there right now . . . having my weekly vigil in our favorite private dining room at Maison Raul. Well, it was *ours*. Now it's just mine. Troy died. And for the six months since, I've been coming here, trying to recapture the feel of his oh-so-clever hands on my thighs and between my legs. They were some of our happiest moments, and many were in this very room. We were best friends, and there were not enough words to describe the depth of our love, so we'd used our bodies to speak the truth instead.

Even during the pandemic, while everything had been shut down, Raul, the owner and maître d', had graciously met me at the restaurant and let me occupy the space until it was time to pour me into an Uber.

Earlier in the week, my editor called, begging me to

3

return to work, enticing me with an assignment. Now I have to make up my mind: resume some semblance of life or continue to wallow in my grief. But it's more than that. Whether I'm ready to return to work or not, I'm just not sure about this assignment. My confused thoughts have a firm hold as I try to make sense of what's bothering me about it. As a journalist, not every assignment turns my crank, but I don't usually feel any emotional connection with the client even when one does. This time I have.

I'd agreed to a video conference call with the mysterious Cyrus Stone, and something about him nags at me. While I could put part of it down to my grief, there's something more—something dark and possibly dangerous. Or I'm letting my overactive reporter's imagination run away with me. Let's face it, I haven't been able to think past the crushing pain in my chest that started when Troy died.

"Greetings, my dear, it's time for Name This Wine," Raul says as he places a large glass of wine in front of me. He straightens and waits for me to do the swish-see-smell-sip thing with the rich red wine. I've come to know the restaurant owner pretty well during the past six months. He prides himself on his "psychic" ability to match the right wine with a patron's mood, and it's become a weekly game with us. I look up at him and force a smile. "Baco Noir?"

"You got it in one." Raul's voice is filled with a warmth I can't help responding to. "Glass or bottle?"

"Bottle." My answer is his cue that he'll need to load me into an Uber in an hour or two. Since Troy died, I've genuinely come to know the meaning of "drowning my sorrows."

"Chef has whipped up a beef stroganoff with your name written all over it, or would you prefer to see a menu?" Raul smiles as he wraps a napkin around the neck of the wine bottle before placing it in front of me.

"That sounds awesome. Beef stroganoff it is. Thank you, Raul." I give him another smile that doesn't reach my eyes. Eating, like everything else since Troy died, is no longer a pleasure; it's a necessity. Without food, I'd die, which might not be a bad idea, but I'm not the suicidal type. As if he can read my mind, Raul pats my hand before leaving my private dining room. Before the pocket door slides closed, I catch a glimpse of golden eyes that seem to glow. Warmth floods my body as the light reaches me, and I'm hit in the gut with memories of Troy. But then again, I see Troy everywhere.

I take another sip of my wine as I let my mind wander down memory lane to when Troy had given me an explosive orgasm while I sat on this very spot. I let my head rest against the wall while closing my eyes, letting the memories flood in. The feel of Troy's hands as they pushed apart my thighs and his fingers found my clit. I know I'll only have those experiences in my mind from now on, and I'm having trouble embracing my future as a celibate.

My cell phone rings before I get too far down Pity Party Lane and into the pit of pain that makes up my life these days. My editor Daisy's brilliant smile appears on the screen.

"Hey!" I try to force some cheer in my voice as I pick up.

"Hey, you. Is everything okay? How'd it go?" I can almost feel Daisy crossing her fingers as she waits for my response.

"It went great." A lie. "I was just about to call you." Semi-truth. I *was* going to call her once I figured out just what to do about this contract offer.

Daisy breathes a massive sigh of what is no doubt relief. "This calls for a drink."

I can't help but smile at her enthusiasm. "Don't get too excited. I'm not sure I'm the best person for this job, hon."

My headphones pick up rustling sounds, and I imagine Daisy settling back on her leather sofa, crossing those shapely legs and taking a sip of wine. "Spill, girlfriend, and don't leave out one tiny detail." Daisy is one of those beautiful women you'd love to hate, except she's so damned nice, you can't help but love her.

I close my eyes again and think about Cy Stone, for once thankful I don't think in pictures. Tall, dark, and very French, the billionaire's presence had overwhelmed me from the moment he filled my computer screen. A presence so imposing, it was almost as if he were in the room with me.

"I look forward to developing a close working relationship with you." Cy's voice had been deep with an undertone of sinister that matched his brooding looks.

I sink deeper into the well-padded booth. Cy's words keep playing in my head, along with the heat from eyes that held mine far too long to mistake his meaning . . . and the flicker of interest it sparked in me.

"There's not much to tell that you don't know, Daise. He said the call confirmed that he wants me to do the series, and he'd contact you with the details, including a list of reading materials for research and a list of the places where I'll conduct his interviews. I told him I'd look over his proposal and let you know my answer. He gave me twenty-four hours."

"Let me add a little incentive. Cy's offering the magazine five million dollars to run a series of five articles on his clubs and lifestyle. His contract will keep us in the black for several years, never mind the hefty portion that comes to you." Daisy sighs. "Not that you care about the money, I know. But we sure could use it." The wistful tone in her voice tugs at my heart. And I can't hate her for that, either, because, with Daisy, there's no subtext to the message. She's not trying to manipulate me at all. If I say no, she'll accept it without malice. But her sigh and tone let me know just how important this is to her.

So I refrain from telling her that I was more than a little

put-out at his controlling attitude. *Or that his penetrating gaze made me aware there's still life in my lady bits.* He'd made it clear he'd be calling the shots, and that just isn't how I work . . . Assuming I want to go back to work at all.

"I'll think about it, Daise. I know how important this is to you. I'm just not sure I'm ready to go back to work yet." I slowly rotate my head, trying to ease some of the perpetual tension I carry in my neck and shoulders.

"Ali." Daisy's voice is warm and gentle. "You're going to have to join the land of the living sometime. You'd be the first one to kick my butt if you saw me hurting myself. You know you would. So consider this your kick in the ass. I think you need this. Let me know what you decide."

"I'll text you tomorrow. Be good." I ring off before we can do our usual "but bad is better" exchange.

I squeeze my eyes shut as I let grief, my constant companion, wash over me. Since the day the doctor and I told Troy he only had four to six months to live, I haven't cried. Not even at his funeral. Oh, I started to. Two tears rolled, one down each cheek. Then the funeral director hauled my ass off to sign more papers.

I wish I could cry. Maybe that would relieve some of the weight from the mountain of grief sitting on my chest. The grief makes it very difficult to think past the deep sense of loss that consumes me. But think I must. If I'm to give Cy Stone my answer, I have a lot of research to do, not to mention figuring out the physical reaction I had to this man—I refuse to acknowledge it's a spark of physical attraction.

My nerve endings start simmering when two of the most exquisite-looking men I've ever seen invade my space and jolt me out of my alcohol-induced reverie.

"May I help you?" I squint at the two hunks staring down at me.

"We have a message for you from your Troy. May we sit?" Tall, dark, and very handsome asks.

My adrenaline surges into overdrive at the mention of my deceased husband. The love of my life. Message? It would be just like him to find a way to send me a message from the great beyond, the one he was sure didn't exist. That thought barely has time to form when my rational mind reaches through the alcohol fog. Shit like this just doesn't happen. Not in real life, anyway. This kind of thing only happens in the Netflix shows Troy and I binged on as we coasted through his last months. There had been two requirements when choosing the shows: there had to be magic, and either good had to triumph over evil, or there had to be a happily ever after.

No, you cannot sit, asshole. Have you lost your mind? I give them both the once-over while I get my racing pulse back under control. How dare they invade my privacy? My heart continues to hammer although I have no idea why.

I should be afraid. Lord knows with my history of abuse, being confronted by two strange guys should have vaulted me into protection mode. But I feel nothing but the weird hum, that simmering feeling. I'm perfectly safe, and I'll have to get used to talking to strange men if I take this assignment. Besides, all I have to do is yell, and Raul will throw their asses out posthaste. And there's something familiar about them. I wave my hand as if I'm a frigging princess allowing them a royal audience. It won't hurt to hear them out.

The two men sit, and a hum starts warming every cell in my body and intensifies as a breath of air caresses my cheek, drawing my attention to the men. The one sitting to my left is the epitome of tall, dark, and handsome but in a very different way from Cyrus Stone. While Cy reeks of European nobility, this man reminds me of an Israeli prince. Thick, curly black hair frames a sculpted face holding molten gold eyes. On my right sits a drop-dead gorgeous blond god. Certainly, someone so perfect must be Apollo or even Zeus himself. I rack my brains for the names of other gods while I examine them. Both have smooth olive skin and look at me with undisguised attraction.

"Okay, let's hear it." Not my most polite welcome, but these guys have a lot of explaining to do.

Gorgeous blond gives me a wicked grin and holds out his hand. "Forgive our intrusion. I'm Tristan Adams, and this is my brother, Cassiel." Magnetic blue eyes capture and hold my gaze, making me feel more than a tad as if I'm slowly being reeled in. The instant our hands meet, a jolt of electricity zings through me. Those are the closest words I can find to describe the strange sensation—one I haven't felt since the moment I met Troy.

Cassiel's hand replaces Tristan's, and a similar bolt strikes. I can't conceal the shudder that rolls through me.

"What's the message?"

2

ATROYEL

I sit beside my beloved in all my incorporeal glory. Just as I guessed, Aleah's made it a tradition to visit one of our favorite haunts. Looking at her, memory after memory of her inner beauty floods me—her strength, her resilience, her determination. Yet here she sits, motionless, in a pool of melancholy like a boat without a rudder, and it's my fault. Those exquisite brown eyes usually alight with life are dull with grief.

The depth of her pain shocks me. Aleah's always been the bravest person I know, and nothing ever got her down for long. She battled chronic illness that brought her pain and misery, insisting we keep an "attitude of gratitude." Despite her pain, she'd made it her mission to ensure my comfort and dignity during the awful months while my body slowly deteriorated. Something about the depth of her care and commitment had taken my love for her to a level I can't describe. And here she is. It's been so long since I smelled her sweet scent, tasted her tantalizing flavor, felt her satin skin. Seeing her again brings me to my knees, and if I had a body, I'd sink to them.

Now that I'm near her, I feel the shock, the numbness she uses to wall off the pain. The depth of her sorrow, her loneliness, almost knocks me back to Bardo. I hadn't realized it until it was too late—I had been her rock, her anchor. It's the only selfless thing I've ever done, protecting her. I hadn't known why, but I'd been driven to her.

I curse as my hand goes right through her when I brush her cheek. Her shiver lets me know she felt me. I want to scream in frustration that I can't touch her, can't soothe her, can't make it all better. But there's no time to linger on romantic thoughts. When Syrael sent us to find Aleah, he thought we'd be obedient. We weren't. For reasons I won't get into now. But that bastard knows Aleah is on Earth now, and it's only a matter of time until he finds her. If he hasn't already. Since he's been cast out as an archangel and made a sex demon lord, he's more dangerous than ever. The Oracle had warned us that he thrives on torturing his victims, prolonging his evil pleasure until the victim's body gave out. She'd warned us that if Syrael meets her, he'll use his dark magic to trick her into becoming his slave before he kills her. My brothers and I simply will not allow that to happen.

The stillness in Aleah's body and her clasped hands don't fool me. It's as if I have a telepathic link with her now that I no longer occupy my human vessel. Her mind and soul are a cauldron of swirling emotions, but a spark of interest breaks through. That's all I need to see. I give my brothers a penetrating look. *Get on with it.*

"He said to tell you he made a deal with the devil," Cass says.

Aleah gives him her side-eye look. "He wouldn't say that." She forces additional challenge into her voice, letting Cass know she's not one of those bimbos who melt at the first sign of attention from a handsome man.

He's having none of it. He simply stares back at her. "What would he say, then?"

"He wouldn't say anything because he's dead." The sorrow resting under the challenge in her voice almost makes me break. "Or are you telling me he's sent a message from the great beyond?"

I'd warned the two of them. My Aleah's intellect marches ahead of her like a beacon. She takes almost nothing at face value. She's far too analytical for that, and this sparring could go on for hours, knowing her. I clear my throat, knowing only Cass and Tristan can hear me.

"Tell her I'm sitting beside her and need her to shut up and listen." I instinctively try to drum my fingers. They slide through the tabletop. *Fuck!* I hate being mist while the gods figure out what to do with my body. Cass repeats my words to her.

"Now that does sound like something he'd say," she says.

"And what would he say about you letting your life pass you by in a wine-induced haze?" Tristan uses a gentle tone that would make even the most belligerent person compliant.

"He'd say something like don't be an idiot. Get out there and enjoy yourself," she says.

"That's precisely what he said," Cass says. "You need to listen to us." Despite his intentions, Cass sounds like a sergeant major giving orders. He can't help himself; taking control of a situation is as natural as breathing to him. As expected, my beauty gives him one of her intense stares while she tames the curses that are her automatic response to any male trying to control her. *Fuck you, mister. I don't need to listen to you, asshole.*

She taps the tabletop in front of Cass with her index finger. "No, you need to listen to me. You two invade my space, my privacy, without a by-your-leave, and ask me to listen to some unbelievable story about my deceased husband. Give me one reason why I shouldn't have Raul throw your asses out of here." Now that sounds like my Lea. She'll demand proof. But her mind will already be spinning because she feels the neural humming that started the moment I drew close to her. It's just too unsettling for her to dismiss, even with her strange health history. She's too aware of her body. And judging from her physical reaction when my brothers touched her, she feels a connection with them as well.

"We don't have time to waste with this nonsense. Tell Aleah I can prove she's having a real psychic experience if she lets me." It's at moments like this that I miss my corporeal body because my drumming fingers would be all the signal needed to remind them of the urgency of our mission.

Cass gives me a penetrating look. My spirit form stares right back at him.

"What are you looking at?" Aleah asks as she follows the direction of his gaze and sees nothing. But she senses something, me. I can tell.

"Troy says he can prove you're having a genuine psychic experience if you'll let him." Tristan gives her one of his Mr. Charming grins. My Lea doesn't respond; she simply stares back at him.

"And how precisely will he do that?"

"Remember the movie *Ghost*?" Cass asks.

She nods slowly, turning that around in her head. She wants to believe.

"Just like that. All you have to say is yes." Tristan gives her another encouraging grin.

"How is that even possible?" My Lea is not an easy sell; I warned them. Tristan looks at me and raises a brow.

"Atroyel, Troy, carries a piece of your soul in his, as you

do his in yours. You are bound for eternity." Tristan always was the romantic of the three of us.

Suddenly, the room's atmosphere shifts, signaling that the bastard Syrael's mirror eye is sweeping the area.

Aleah grabs the side of the table as if it's moved. "Did you feel that?"

"Feel what?" Tristan asks. Cass meets my eyes as we feel the psychic energy of the sex demon lord. We're out of time.

"Could be an earthquake," Cass says, then cuts in before Aleah can draw breath, "Do you trust Troy?"

"Yes, with my life," Aleah says.

That's all I need, her consent, so I'm not tearing the fabric of time. I slip into Aleah's body, essentially stealing her motor functions and senses. She still has control of her mind, although it would take a mighty mental thrust to push me out of the spotlight. I give the fingers of her right hand a quick drum, taking a split second to enjoy the relief of physical movement.

"Beauty, listen up. We don't have much time before you pass out." At least I remember that much from the condensed training session they'd given me in Bardo.

I ignore her mental squeak of protest that reverberates through my mind. "Yes, it's me. There is an afterlife, but we don't have time to get into that here. Nutshell version, I'm an angel, and these are my brothers. You and I have some unfinished business, so the gods allowed me to come back and see you. But for me to stay on in the Earth realm, I need to be near a portal." This version of the truth will have to suffice until we get Aleah to safety. "Will you come with us so we can explain? My essence is already fading. You can feel it." This is a bit of a gamble, but I'm pretty sure my spirit is snatching the essence from her body.

I focus inward and catch her mental whisper. "I can't stand this burning tingling, Troy. I'll go. Just make it stop."

Her body collapses onto the banquette as I leave it. Tristan leans forward and takes her carotid pulse before giving a quick nod and gathering Aleah in his arms. Cass tosses a few hundred dollar bills on the table, ignoring the maître d's frantic yelling as we rush into the waiting limousine.

ALEAH

I slip into slumber, and Troy drops into my dream. I sense him first as I had in the old days. He quietly pads up behind me, and only his soft breath on my skin tells me he's there.

He slides his warm, full lips down the side of my neck, flesh barely touching flesh. Desire skitters over my skin as he uses his strong hands to smooth away the anticipation goose bumps that break out all over my arms. He wraps long fingers around my wrists, fingers that bring me great pleasure . . . if I'm patient. But I already feel the heat building between my legs as beads of arousal collect between my thighs.

"Want to tuck me in?" He keeps his voice neutral, calm, but I hear the need behind the innocent code words for a blow job. Something he rarely asked for. Usually, his entire focus is on satisfying me first, making me come until he's pulled every last thread of tension from my body. Then and only then would he sink into me and fuck me into oblivion.

But occasionally, he lets me pleasure him first. Lets me suck that magnificent cock.

"I sure do," I say before I drop to my knees. Such is the stuff of dreams.

I look up, trying to drink in his face, but a glowing light blurs his features. I focus instead on the beautiful hard cock I haven't seen in over two years and almost weep. Every part of me wants to suck him deep into my throat until he's buried balls deep in my mouth, something that isn't humanly possible in our waking life—he's just that big.

I grasp the base of his pulsing cock with my small hand and welcome the shudder that runs through him. He's missed me as much as I've missed him. When I flick my tongue across the tip of his cock, his sigh brings a trickle of arousal rolling down my naked thigh. Despite my eagerness to devour him, I pull back so I can make this dream last. I take my time, feeling his steel heat as I lick and lap my way up, down, and around his shaft.

I tickle his balls with the fingers on my free hand and coordinate my hand and mouth movements until Troy strains and arches his back. His hands grip the arms of the chair as he fights the urge to thrust hard into my mouth. I still until his harsh breath evens out. I'm not ready for this to end yet. Then and only then do I suck him deep into my mouth, showing him with each slow contraction of my lips just how very much I've missed tasting him. I make love to him with my mouth, savoring the scent of his heavy musk, reveling in each clench of his muscles as he joins the battle to make this time together last.

I startle half-awake as his spent cock softens in my mouth. The ambient light from the almost-full moon illumi-nates the large room where I lie . . . alone. If it weren't for the tingling in my engorged lips, I'd think it was only a dream. I won't let the feeling end by waking. I slip back into sleep as the tingling warmth reminds me of just how very much I've missed making love with him.

This time when I wake, it's no fucking dream. I'm lying on the left side, my side, of a huge bed with a warm hand gripping my wrist. I jerk away and try to sit as my old panic instinct ratchets into high gear. My heart tries to jump out of my chest.

A second later, the pain of a migraine nearly blinds me. I fall back on the pillow gasping . . . I'd almost welcome death to stop this horrific head pain.

"Shhh. You're okay. You're safe. I'm Tristan, remember? Take this. It will help you feel better." He clasps a warm hand behind my neck and breathes on me. It feels as if I'm breathing in fairy dust that makes me feel a bit better—I have that kind of imagination. I shake that nonsense out of my head and immediately regret it as another jolt of pain shoots through my head.

"This would be easier if you'd let me kiss you."

I open one eyelid a slit and glare at his smiling and absolutely gorgeous face.

And there it is. Mention of sex. It seems to always come around to that with men . . . even the drop-dead gorgeous ones. I squeeze my eyes shut and battle to push aside the pain so I can think. Thoughts dance through the pain. Angels. Troy. Wings. Horrible tingling numbness. Danger. Brothers.

Despite the hammering of my poor heart, I don't feel as if I'm in any imminent danger. But I need to figure out just what the fuck is going on. First, I need to get this pain under control, and then I can figure out where the hell I am.

"May I have my purse please?" I need my meds.

A warm hand grabs my wrist, turns it, and places a pill in my palm. "Is this what you're looking for?" The warm baritone makes me open one eye a crack. I bring my palm up close since I don't have my glasses on and I can't see a frigging thing. It's one of my pain meds. "Thanks." I dry swallow the small pill.

"It would work a lot faster if you let me kiss you." The humor in charming guy's voice almost makes me smile. Tristan. I remember the electricity that sizzled through me when he touched me.

"How do you figure that?" I dearly wish I could give him the look I've perfected, the one Troy calls my side-eye, but all I can do is blink against the light.

"I'm a sex angel. Remember? We told you last night." He shoots that grin that makes me want to drop my pants again. Speaking of pants, I do a quick inventory. Thank gods I'm still dressed. If they want my body, they're taking their sweet time about it. Odd thought, given my vulnerable situation. I blame my migraine.

"You did not tell me you're a sex angel." I take the offensive while I rack my aching brain for precisely what had been said. "How exactly does that explain you needing to kiss me to heal my pain?" At the moment, that wouldn't be a bad idea. His lips look an awful lot like Troy's.

He doesn't seem the least bit disturbed by my bitchy tone. "I can heal or repair any bodily damage by having sex or using sexual energy. A kiss gives stronger energy than a thought."

Troy will no doubt be apoplectic if I start dishing it out with his brothers. I look around for my glasses. My shield.

"Looking for these?" Tall, blond, and handsome hands me my glasses. I shove them on my face and look around.

"Where's Troy?" One thing I sure as hell remember is the feeling of him taking over my body. Assuming all of this isn't a psychotic break, he's come back to me. I struggle to sit, and Tristan helps me to a semi-seated position as the pain eases enough for my brain to start functioning again. Flashes of memory sift through my head as I try to get a fix on what's happening. A beam of light hits my eyes, and I slam them shut again.

"Take it easy. You'll be okay soon." Tristan grabs my hand. No sooner are the words out of his mouth than a wash of heat reduces the pain.

"Where am I?" I open my eyes halfway, and Tristan takes my pulse. Either I'm experiencing a real psychic phenomenon, which is highly unlikely, or I'm locked up in a psych ward somewhere, given the delusions I seem to be suffering from. So there's no point in delaying the inevitable. "What hospital is this?"

"We're on an island." That rich tenor voice makes this pronouncement, confirming my worst suspicions. We're not in Toronto anymore. Dark blue eyes sparkling with humor and lust look down at me. On instinct, I pull the sheet up to my neck despite being fully dressed.

"Troy said you'd freak out if we undressed you." Tristan rakes his eyes down my covered body as if he'd like nothing better than to see me naked. Nothing is threatening in his tone or demeanor, making my usual bitchy put-down seem a little over the top. While I contemplate the right one-liner, the dark-haired guy from last night walks into the room bearing a tray. The smell of baked goods makes my mouth water, reminding me I haven't eaten since yesterday at noon.

"You're awake. Good. Let's get some food and your pills in you." Cassiel sets the large tray across my lap, then steps over to the entire wall of windows through which I see nothing but water and trees. I glance around the room. If I'm in a hospital, it certainly isn't one of our public institutions. It was more like the private hospital where I'd had surgery years ago in the US. There'd been two super cute anesthetists there who'd taken Troy's place in one or two wet dreams.

I drag my wandering brain back to this reality. Something is definitely very wrong with me, not because my mind skips merrily from rabbit hole to rabbit hole but because it has never done it when my life or body could be in mortal danger. I look around the room as I take stock of whether I've lost my mind or stepped through some sort of supernatural portal. I don't sense any danger, but it's all too much like a fairy tale. For some reason, this guy going to the trouble of dispensing my morning meds in the same plastic cup I use at home makes me feel all warm and squishy. As if it's not the first time two gorgeous men and an exquisite ghost have looked after me.

"I'll ask again, where am I?" I put every ounce of bitch-goddess into my tone that I can muster.

"I told you, we're on an island," Tristan repeats.

"You'll have to be a bit more forthcoming than that." I let the implicit threat of my silence hang in the air, although truth be told, I'm more intrigued than frightened. And that's more than I've felt in months. More importantly, if there's a way I can be with Troy again that doesn't involve eternal damnation, I'm all in. I give both of them my sweetest shark smile. "Start this story from the top."

ATROYEL

"Start this story from the top." Aleah flashes her piranha smile before paying close attention to uncovering and examining the food on the tray before her, all seeming nonchalance except for the tension simmering below the surface. My wonder woman is back. My brothers won't know what hit them.

Her synapses are firing like a supercharged high-performance sports car engine. For several glorious moments last night, my favorite fantasy had come true. When I'd taken possession of her body, I'd been able to feel what she feels and see how her mind works. Even that quick glimpse fascinated me, as this woman always has. I have no doubt she always will.

While Aleah pours a cup of steaming hot tea, Tristan and Cass exchange glances. Tristan, the one of us with the devil in him, gives a wicked grin and says, "Once upon a time, a century or so ago, there was—"

Aleah holds up a hand, her impatience barely contained. She may be appreciating every square inch of his body, but she didn't trust him. It would take more than Tristan's charm to earn it. "Perhaps we can start with something a little more current. When did Troy give you this message?"

That's my beauty. As expected, Cass took over. "Troy tells us you're familiar with the concept of Bardo and the afterlife." He waits until Lea gives him a slow nod. My woman is cautious. She's not threatened, but she's on full alert.

"When Troy, as you call him, died, his soul ascended to Bardo for processing. Although he's an angel, he'd ascended through a mortal vessel, so he had to be cleared before he could return home. Any questions?" Cass raises an eyebrow at her. She looks steadily back at him while she takes a sip of her tea.

"Not so far." Oh, she has questions all right, but I know my Lea. She doesn't have enough information to start her cross-examination.

"Problem is, Troy's spirit, his essence, is still attached to yours, so he feels the depth of your misery and refuses to ascend. The gods called us forth to talk some sense into the asshole." Cass starts spinning the misdirection, shielding our real purpose, to protect Aleah while finding the key to undo Syrael's curse. Lord Syrael had buried a strand of dark ether deep within Aleah's soul. That strand will lead him to her. With the use of powers I hadn't known I had, I'd woven protections around the dark ether, immobilizing it. Lea's exceptional willpower had done the rest. As expected, her face becomes a study in concern.

"We'd calmed him down. Then something happened this week that troubled you. So asshole that he is, he almost tore apart the processing center trying to get back to you."

I give Cass a glare that he pointedly ignores and plant my thought in his head. *Enough with the* asshole, *asshole.*

If the shoe fits, he replies. My asshole brother continues. "He can thank his damnable good luck that the queen of the gods has a soft spot for him."

"Women always do," Aleah murmurs. Aha, even in the afterlife, she remains under the allusion that I'm all that and more to women. She refused to believe me the numerous times I told her otherwise.

"Yeah, but he never knew it. He only ever had eyes for you," Tristan says.

"Why would the gods call you to come to his rescue?" Aleah focuses on Cass.

"We're his brothers," Cass says.

"We're triplets." Tristan puts on his helpful face. He points at Cass. "He's firstborn. Troy's second, and I'm the runt of the litter."

"So, you're all angels?" Aleah asks.

Cass nods.

"Go on," Aleah says.

"Long story short, Troy talked his way into coming to Earth to find out what's bothering you and to help you to accept his death. He refused to take the time to finish the processing to release his mortally bound spirit, so his spirit remains incorporeal. They sent us as his anchors. As angels, we're able to bring his spirit through the portal and hold him here." Cass reaches over, plucks a strawberry from my Lea's tray, and pops it into his mouth.

By this time, Aleah's making her way through a warm croissant with orange marmalade spread over it. "I'm a little hazy on all this angel stuff. Help me understand why you think you're angels." Despite her attempt to keep her tone neutral, her skepticism leaks through.

Tristan takes the bait and leaps up. "Babe, we don't think we're angels. We *are* angels." With that, he steps into a clear space in the large room and unfurls his enormous wings.

I watch her with a fascination I never lost as her eyes widen, just a little. The only sign of surprise she shows. In a succession of quick movements, she shifts the tray off her lap, throws off the blankets, and walks over to Tristan. She circles him slowly, bending from time to time as she tries to figure out whether it's some kind of trick.

"Now, put them away." She gives her command a second thought because a beat later, she says, "Please."

"Happy to oblige, ma'am." Tristan bows his head and retracts his wings. He waits until she circles him once more and stands in front of him, and then he ejects them again. "Want to feel them?"

Bastard. Only he can make asking what should be an innocent question suggestive of a sexual act. She doesn't answer. She reaches up and brushes her fingers over them. Then she takes one of the feathers, running her thumb and index finger from shaft to tip. With another, she gives a quick tug.

"Careful," Tristan says, "you'll get me all turned on."

Aleah snatches her hand away as if he touched a blow-torch to it. "Sorry." She takes several quick steps back. I want so much to hold her as she turns things over in her mind.

"Let's assume I believe you're angels." She frowns as Tristan grins at her. "And the jury is still out on that." She presses those gorgeous full lips together as she tosses around her next question. "Is Troy here?"

"Yes. He's lounging on your bed, looking longingly at your body right now," Cass says.

Aleah tries not to look pleased. "What do we have to do so I can see him, talk to him?"

Oh, I wish I could kiss her. Instead, I need to focus on the other million reasons I love her so I can keep my mind off my damned cock. She has no time for the trivial details and blasts right through to what she needs to know. Cass gives her a veiled look, but I know she's caught his interest, some-thing that's very hard to do. He'd had brotherly affection for her as a child in the forest. Now it's as if he's sniffed her scent and it calls to him.

"That's two different questions," Cass says. Aleah gives him her best fuck-you look.

"You can talk to him right now. He can hear you, and we can hear him. So, say what you have to say, and we'll tell you what he says." Cass gives her a grin that reminds me of a hunter sighting prey. "And while you can't exactly see him, you can feel him if he possesses one of our bodies. As you can see, our bodies are almost exact replicas."

"Or you will see if given a chance." Tristan gives her a wicked wink. "Cass is right. If you want to fuck him, he has to possess one of our bodies just like he did yours, but there's a condition." Tristan gives her a look that says the price will be steep.

5

———

ALEAH

"Can I have a freebie, a trial run?" I feverishly search for ways to be with Troy that won't involve having sex with one of these men. I'm attracted to them, but I can look without touching. I don't do casual sex, I don't do the multiples thing, and I especially don't do brothers. Troy and I explored the emotional ramifications of expanding our sexual horizons at length in our Double Diary.

One thing I pride myself on is my self-awareness, and I knew the moment I laid eyes on these two that I'd jump their bones in nine-tenths of a second. And now there's an added complication, they're Troy's brothers, for Sully's sake.

"What does that mean, a freebie?" Cass asks. Already, I can see I'm not going to get much past him. Tristan, on the other hand, has the same devilish side as Troy without the cautious side. I bet he'd try anything. All I have to do is figure out whether I want to pay the price.

I give Cass the look I give reluctant interviewees. "It means I'd like you to show me how this works without activating this condition, whatever it is."

Each of them has a version of a wolfish grin that tells me neither one falls for my innocent act.

"I'll do it for a kiss, but it has to be a duplicate of whatever kiss you give Troy," Tristan says. "You are beautiful." He looks me up and down, taking in my casual clothes.

The burning heat on the tips of my ears is the only way you can tell I'm blushing, and those words coming from that smoky voice set them on fire. Angel or not, the man must need his eyes examined. My body is on the smallish side, although the roundness of middle age in all the wrong places gives me a curvier look I never had in my youth. I could give him a list of faults with my body, but he seems oblivious to all that as he takes in my small breasts, big butt, and tawny skin.

I try not to lick my lips as I consider his proposal, but I have too many questions not to give this freebie a try. "Okay, but one kiss and one kiss only." I look at him pointedly. The bastard winks back at me.

Moments later, warm chocolate-brown eyes shimmering with an eerie light beam back at me instead of blue ones. Troy! I shut my eyes and let the aroma of his fresh male scent wash over me. He cups my cheeks and tips my head back. I know he's taking that moment to study me while he bends his knees to lower himself to my height. My Troy is thoughtful like that. Putting my sexual needs first is one of his great strengths . . . and greatest weakness. I pull myself out of that rabbit hole. I will not miss one second of this moment.

"Troy." I let his name escape on the smallest of breaths, afraid that any movement will make this vision disappear. "Is it really you?"

"You tell me." His soft, full lips meet mine, and I almost expire with need. For the first time since he died, emotion trickles past the state of shock I've been in. I've missed this man and his wicked ways so much.

The instant our lips meet, he starts to tell me what I need to know. How much he's missed me. Taking his time, he explores my lips before deepening the kiss, letting his tongue tease and torment me. He lets me know the depth of his everlasting love, demanding there be nothing else between us. I push aside my grief. I forgot all about the agreement with Tristan. I don't hold back when I answer. I wrap my arms around his neck as I drink from the well of his love. Only a lack of oxygen breaks us apart. He touches his forehead to mine.

"Gods, how I've missed you," he breathes.

We stay that way, unmoving, as oxygen makes my brain cells start firing again. If I kiss him any longer, I'll tear his clothes off. The hunger in his eyes tells me he'll do the same thing. Now is not the time to go there. But he's here, with me. A ghost is inhabiting an angel's body. Where the fuck does one go from here? My mind races, and seconds later, words tumble out like rapid fire from a submachine gun. I try to drink in those eyes as my rational mind puts the brakes on my treacherous libido.

"Where did you go? What's it like?" I narrow my eyes. "And what took you so long to visit me in my dreams? I told you there was an afterlife."

He gives that chuckle reserved just for me. "Babe, if you're going to use our time having an I-told-you-so moment, let's at least get comfortable." Taking my hand, he pulls me to a chair he sits in before pulling me onto his lap.

I narrow my eyes at him again as I remember what it was like when he possessed me last night. "Are you going to pass out? How long do we have?" I press back the panic as I remember that I don't know the supernatural's rules. "Why are you here?" I ask when everything in me screams against asking. If he tells me, we'll find a solution, and then he'll have to go. Because solving problems is kind of my superpower, and I believe the angels that Troy's spirit is stuck to me. I know with absolute certainty that I'm the only tie strong enough to bind Troy's free spirit.

"I won't lie to you, beauty. I'm not sure how much time we have before Tristan's body needs recharging. I suspect it's a lot longer than we had, given his angel physiology and our genetic link." He holds my face, and it's Troy's warm brown eyes that I see. "But your instincts are right on." His pride filters through me like pixie dust. "Every minute I'm in Tristan's body, I'm sapping his essence. We've probably got ten or fifteen minutes. As to why I'm here." He pauses a moment, and his gaze focuses on some distant thought. The look is so intense I can't help it—I turn my head. I wouldn't have been shocked to see a portal open to another universe. Instead, I look into the strange glow coming from Cass's golden eyes and catch a glimpse of the portal into my future—one that includes Cass.

For several intense seconds, I can't move. I'm not sure I breathe. This magic stuff is just too fucking weird. I swing my gaze back to Troy.

"It's a lot to take in, I know. For several reasons we can get into later, I don't have all the answers to why we're here. One thing I do know for sure is that you're in some kind of mortal danger, and we're here to save you. Of that, I'm certain." A strange, intense light seems to illuminate Troy's brown eyes.

I almost drown in the sense of déjà vu that hits, a moment just like one we'd lived before. A moment when we knew we were on the crest of something big, something life-changing coupled with that sense of fatality that confirms we're where we're destined to be. The first time I'd felt it was twenty years ago when Troy finally declared his love for me. We'd lived together for five years as friends with benefits when the big moment came, and it was anticlimactic. Now, the same man asked me to suspend belief in all that we knew to be logical in favor of a supernatural he'd always scoffed at. I should scoff right back at him, but instead, I want to give a fist pump for the confirmation of something I'd believed all along.

6

TRISTAN

"You're in mortal danger, and we're here to save you."

I watch this woman intently as Troy makes his pronouncement. It's fascinating how much a part of him I am as he possesses this vessel called a body. I stare into warm brown eyes, eyes sharp with intelligence, eyes through which every thought passed like frames from a movie. Her irises are like fine brandy with shards of black that spray like rays from her pupils. The finger of her mind hovers over the remote as she decides whether she'll settle on tragedy or happily ever after.

"How long before I have to let you go?" Sorrow flashes through Aleah's dread-filled eyes as she pulls back and studies my face . . . or does she see his face? Such finality rests there as if happily ever after is beyond her reach. Now that Troy's taken over my body, I feel the deep bond between the two of them, the depth of her pain. I itch with the need to grab her, hold her, show her there's no need to despair. But we're a long way from that moment.

"I don't know, beauty. This is all new to me, too. There's

so much to tell you, I don't know where to start," Troy says. The two of them make more goo-goo eyes at each other.

My deltoid starts to burn. *An angel mating brand.* That thought pops into my mind out of nowhere. It's wishful thinking, but I take a moment to coast on that happy thought. Angel mating brands, marks binding angels' souls, rarely happen, although legend suggests it's more common among angel sex lords. Perhaps our promotion to sex lords makes us susceptible to this ultimate love magic.

It was more than filaments of energy that flew between us the moment I touched Aleah; it was the certainty we belong together. Not just as friends and protectors as we'd been all those years ago in the forest. Last night, I'd held my sex lord physiology responsible for the intense lust that passed between us the instant I laid eyes on her. That was undoubtedly part of it, but now I know something else entirely happened. Something that just added a layer of complication we don't need . . . but I welcome. To confirm my theory, I need to see whether Aleah has a brand. I try to give my moon-gazing brother a kick in the ass.

Let's move things along, Troy. I'm dying in here. I use our telepathic link, making my impatience clear.

Fuck off, Trist. I'll take the time I want. Our Troy is one stubborn and somewhat selfish bugger. At least he doesn't pass me off as a pretty boy with no brains, a cross I have to bear in silence.

And find out what's causing the pain in my deltoid.

My facial muscles move into a grimace. Troy feels it, too.

"Babe?" Aleah's large oval-shaped eyes widen with concern. "You okay?" She rubs her left deltoid as she speaks.

"I'm okay, but what about you? Why are you holding your arm? Let's have a look." Troy rolls the sleeve of her T-shirt, exposing the tattoo on her delt, an intricate black rose with a faint red triangle shimmering behind it.

Aleah grabs her biceps and twists her shoulder to examine it. Troy traces the red triangle. "When did you get that? And why?"

"I didn't get that." Aleah frowns. "It just appeared, and it sure as hell feels like a fresh tattoo, only worse. It burns like hell." She frowns again. "Did you guys do something to me while I was sleeping?"

"Of course not, beauty. Why do you always think the worst? You know I'd never do something like that without your consent." Troy says this with absolute conviction. "What kind of burning?"

She studies him for a moment. I can almost feel her mental eye roll, but she decides not to take the bait. "It's like when the tattoo artist used that tiny needle to outline the rose. It burned as if he was searing the flesh, which upon reflection, he probably was. But how did it get here?"

"I have a faint burning pain in the same place, but I don't know if it's my arm or Tristan's I'm feeling.

Suddenly, they both dive for my polo shirt. Aleah makes short work of the two buttons and slides one side over my shoulder. However, there's nothing to see, but both of them stare at my shoulder as if looking for some microscopic fungus.

"This is urgent, beauty. You're in danger. I know from having been inside you—"

"Seriously, Troy. You're going to talk about sex now?" Humor shines from Aleah's eyes despite her scolding tone.

"Even after all these months, that's your first go-to?" Troy puts on his best self-righteous tone. "I know from having taken possession of your body last night that you have a healthy degree of skepticism about being in danger. Have you ever known me to exaggerate about anything serious?"

She shakes her head slowly.

"Right. I'm dead serious about this. And it would take

something major to have me leave the comfort of the blissful afterlife to come back to this existence, would you agree?" Troy asks.

Ouch! A wince flashes over Aleah's perfect features, and the realization hits me. This woman may not be perfect, but she's perfect for me . . . And I want more than to be her friend.

She nods, but she doesn't look happy.

Troy gives his short now-we're-getting-somewhere nod. "You're in danger. I need you to stay here with my brothers until we figure this out. Give me your word, and we can take it from there." Troy's grip tightens on Aleah's arms, but my body's losing strength.

"Please, Aleah, beauty. I don't have much time, but I'll be back. We'll figure this out. Just promise me." The intensity of his desperation, his fear, snatches another handful of my quickly dwindling essence. I pull on reserves, buying a precious few seconds for Troy.

Aleah must feel it, too, because she grabs my shoulders and looks deep into my eyes. "What's going on? It feels like you're slipping away." Her panic pulls another thread of my low reserve of essence. Darkness filters around the edges of my consciousness.

"Promise me!"

She tightens her grip on my shoulders. "I promise. I promise but—"

With a deep sigh, Troy slips out of my body, and I slip into unconsciousness.

7

CASSIEL

Tristan's wings unfurl as he slips into the deep, restorative sleep that simulates unconsciousness. I react without thinking, using my mind to snatch Aleah from Tristan's lap before his wings maim her. With a second thought, I tip his body back, keeping his head free of his wings.

"Fucking amazing." Aleah looks from Tristan's inert form back to me, wonder on her face, eyes glowing. "That was so cool."

That jolt of electricity we all felt when we first touched her races through me again. Her hammering heart sounds like a chime in my head. Those brown eyes pierce through mine as we both realize she's in my arms, her arms thrown around my neck. It must have been an instinctive reaction on her part because she snatches them away the moment she realizes. Every single cell in my body goes on alert as the full force of my sexual power rises within me.

Godsdammit.

I curse under my breath as my cock springs to attention. I shift her a little higher in my arms.

"Thank you. You can put me down now." She pats my chest awkwardly.

I set her on her feet, turn away, and straighten my clothes while I pull my libido under control. I wait for the inevitable reaction of females when they've caught a glimpse of my powers. I'll have to find a way to reject her advances without hurting her feelings, not my best skill. Tristan and Troy were the smooth talkers in our family. I'm the responsible one.

Coming to Earth to babysit the girl we'd refused to kill for our former boss all those years ago was not my idea. There are too many risks for my brothers. As the eldest, I take my job very seriously and taking protecting my brothers is my first priority. Our absentee parents charged me with taking care of things. They didn't have the time or patience for Atroyel's emotional sensitivity or Tristan's empty head. Thank gods the boy had looks that charmed the gods themselves.

I stare down at the girl turned woman staring back at me and almost fall back from the force of a realization: it's patently clear from the curious gaze taking my measure that this woman is oblivious to my powers, although her heartbeat tells me there's more than a flicker of interest. My sudden, savage hunger takes me by complete surprise. I shut it down.

She steps away from me and goes over to the electric teapot sitting on the butcher's block. Troy had made sure we found a place outfitted with only the best. "So, what happens now? How do we find this Lord Syrael?" She asks as she measures a tablespoon of the lemon syrup Troy insisted she needs for her tea. She tips the spoon's contents into the delicate mug she chose, takes a small sip, and holds it in her hands while she leans against the counter, examining me. Her heartbeat slows a few beats a minute. Godsdamn, she's stunning. Absolutely stunning.

What happens now? Good question. I'd warned the brothers we needed a solid plan, but there was no holding Troy back the moment he recognized his beloved was in danger. "We don't find Lord Syrael. We're here to protect you from him."

I step over to the espresso machine and make busy work preparing a triple shot instead of my usual latte. It brings me in closer proximity to Aleah, which, in turn, strengthens the emotional impulses I'm picking up from her. I hear her heartbeat and pick up random pulses of feelings, similar to but weaker than those from my brothers. Our angelic genetic bond automatically links us empathetically.

I have no fucking idea why I'm detecting her emotions, but despite her outwardly calm appearance, I know she's wound tighter than a two-dollar watch as these humans say. The urgent need to protect her and care for her winds its way into my hardened heart. I push it away, drop back the triple shot and make a latte. Her gaze sends trails of heat where it rakes over my body. I stop fiddling and turn to face her.

"Why don't you tell me about that tattoo of yours?" I need to determine whether I've made the correct assumption, and the innocent topic should serve to relax her.

"Isn't it gorgeous?" She rubs her shoulder, and her eyes beam with the special meaning behind the symbol. "I got my black rose tattoo for our tenth anniversary. Troy calls me his black rose. He's not much of a romantic, but every now and then he surprises me." She pauses, then continues. "Not that I'm criticizing. I thought it would be a great idea if we got matching tattoos. When the big day arrived, I went first. Knowing he was watching every movement, I'd put on my stoic face and toughed through the pain."

I know what's coming next. "Let me guess. Troy decided

to think about it when his turn came and denied ever having agreed to your plan."

"Yeah. Chickenshit." She grins and gets lost in the memory for a moment. I wait until she returns to the present.

Her eyes fill with tears, and she tightens her grip on the mug and bites her lip, but she doesn't break our gaze.

"Why do you keep torturing yourself that way?" I instantly wish I could pull back those words, but I hear their insensitivity a hair too late.

She shudders. "Because I'm a fucking idiot and a sucker for punishment." She gets the mug onto the block, followed by her glasses, then grips the counter edge so hard the veins almost break through the skin on her hands. Then the first sob breaks open a flood of erratic breaths interspersed with breath-holding. Sobs tear through her until the force of her muscle tremors takes her to her knees. She hugs herself as she tries to suppress the gasps she's making. I sink to my knees beside her. Although she doesn't raise her bowed head, a small hand shoots out, stopping my instinctual reaction to comfort her. So I sit beside her as she comes apart, letting her grief and fear bleed into me.

The picture of the young girl she'd been all those years ago flashes into my psyche. Aleah had built walls around her psyche, her heart, to protect her from the abuse life had heaped on her as a girl. Walls that made her push away and shut out anyone offering love and comfort because it usually turned into abuse. The girl who wanted nothing more than to be accepted and loved. The girl with whom we'd spent the happiest years of our lives.

I open my angelic empathy to the emotions she's hiding and find what I need to do to relieve her of some of this pain. But her walls are like those on a fucking fortress, almost impenetrable. So, I do the only thing I can; I do what I should have done then, something Tristan tried to tell us.

I pull her stiff body into my arms. It's the responsible thing to do. She struggles, trying to push me away, but the force of the sobs weakens her. I hold on tighter until she stops fighting and lets me hold her.

As her sobs subside, I pat her back awkwardly. She remains curled in a tight ball, and the only movement she makes is the odd sniffle. I flick my finger and bring a box of tissue to my hand. I nudge her arm with the edge of the box. A small hand uncurls and grabs a tissue. She spends a couple of minutes mopping up, but my senses tell me she's using the time to pull her thoughts together.

She clears her throat. "I'm sorry, this is most unlike me." She keeps her gaze trained on the soiled tissues in her fist.

"Since we're in this together for the foreseeable future, and we're family, let's do away with the apologies, shall we? Now, what is this all about?" I leave no doubt from my tone that I expect an answer.

I know from what Troy's told us she'd argue, so I'm surprised when she sighs and says, "I'm not sure it's worth analyzing. Typically, it's something small that makes the dam break. I haven't cried like that since we first heard Troy's terminal diagnosis. I'm probably just spinning. I need time to figure out what to do about all of this." She gives a small shrug and seems to realize where she's sitting. She gives me a weak smile.

"Okay, fair enough. Why don't we refresh our drinks? Figure out what will make all of this easier on all of us." I get to my feet and hold my hand out to her. She grabs it, and I pull her to her feet. We stand motionless for several beats, less than a foot apart, the increasing voltage of our connection holding us captive.

A bite of heat in her left deltoid brings us to reality. She grabs the hot spot, gritting her teeth.

"Let's have a look." I wait for a beat for her nod of approval, then roll back her sleeve, revealing the artistically crafted black rose in full bloom. It looks like it had earlier, except another small, very faint triangle flickers below the first triangle. As I examine the fresh wound, a corresponding sympathy pain flashes in my biceps. I study the mark closely and confirm my original suspicion; it's an angel mating brand. I can sense it . . . more strongly than I should. My heart gives a leap as the ancient lore about mating brands scrolls through my mind. They're rare. They only happen between souls who are destined to be together and are the physical representation of a deep unconditional love bond.

I suck in a breath as she looks up at me. She's unbelievably gorgeous in an understated way, petite, almost girlish but with curves that mark her maturity and amplify her femininity. In that instant, I want her. Just like that. Despite the added wrinkle that will add to our already complicated situation. That's a wrinkle I simply can't afford to indulge. I tuck it away with all the other fantasies that will never see the light of day.

"What the hell is happening to my tattoo?"

8

ALEAH

I look down at my tattoo in horror. When the first red triangle shadow appeared this morning, I'd thought it was some sort of reaction. Something that had probably come on in my sleep. But the addition of the new outline and the burning pain growing in my shoulder feels more like a surgical incision. Whatever is happening, I'd lay bets it has to do with this hallucination that has such a firm grip on me. My foster mother had been schizophrenic, so I have first-hand experience with altered reality testing.

The moment the guys mentioned Bardo and I'd realized Troy's ghost was for real, a plan starts percolating in the back of my mind. There's no doubt these guys are terrified of this demon lord who's coming after me, but he may very well be the answer to my prayers. Now that I know Bardo is for real, I know what I need to do—find the bad guy and let him blow me to kingdom come. I'll be reunited with my Troy, and we can fuck our way into the great beyond. All I have to figure out is just how I'm going to do this because it's patently obvious that if I spring my plan on the guys, they'll go all knight-in-shining-armor on me and try to stop me.

I look into the golden eyes of the man holding me. The gorgeous man with wavy black hair drifting over his ears with long strands feathering over his high forehead. Thick, slightly shaggy eyebrows shield his deep-set, long-lashed eyes. He reminds me of the dreams I had while my foster father pumped away on my teenage body. Dreams about three princes keeping me safe and a cabin in the forest. Judging from the disapproval wafting off of this Cassiel, that's all it is, more of my crazy dreams.

I pull on every bit of control I have so I don't react to his warm breath on my shoulder. There's no doubt about it; I feel a strong connection to this Cassiel . . . Not as strong a bond as I have with my Troy, but it's so tangible I can almost cup it in the palm of my hand. Goose bumps break out on my arm as he traces my tattoo with his index finger. None of this is helping with my plan.

"I'm not sure what's going on with your tattoo, but if I had to guess, I'd say it's an angelic mating brand," Cassiel says. "Atroyel's—Troy's—deltoid was burning as well, so I imagine something about your reunion triggered the brand. I have no idea why it's changing."

I have the distinct impression he has a theory, but I don't push him on it. I have more important things to do, like hiding my reaction to this man and determining whether I'm having a psychotic breakdown.

"Do I know you?" I know it sounds crazy. I would remember this man if I'd met him.

"Met a lot of angels, have you?" Those gold eyes sparkle, and that eerie light flashes deep within his irises. He drops his hand but doesn't move. I'm riveted on the fine dusting of dark hair peeking out from the open buttons of his white dress shirt. Like Troy, he has just enough to highlight the beauty of his muscular chest. My fingers take on a life of their own, itching to run my hand across those perfectly defined pecs. It would take nothing to lift my hand and brush it across his chest. Nothing to trace my finger over his Adam's apple through the slit—

Are you out of your mind, Aleah? He's Troy's brother, for fuck's sake. I pull my eyes back up to meet his penetrating gaze.

"Ha ha, funny guy. I could swear I know you," I say.

"What makes you say that?" Cassiel studies me with those clear eyes that remind me of honey.

Oh, gods, not another one. He sounds just like Troy. This time I hold his gaze, trying to get a read on him, but like Troy, it's impossible to penetrate his shields. He's an angel, idiot. He's an angel with superpowers, and you're an ungifted human. One thing I do know for sure, I'm not going down the rabbit hole of why he feels familiar.

And because I'm the master of distraction and misdirection, I say, "I want him back."

He studies me for a moment longer before rising to his feet in one fluid movement, so graceful yet profoundly raw and masculine. While I contemplate the least inelegant way of getting my ass off the floor, he holds out a hand and pulls me to my feet. Right into his chest.

"We're here to figure out how to make that happen or at least to find a way to put you two out of your misery." His sensual lips turn up at the corners just a little bit. "What are your plans for the day?"

Another dash of that heat that I'm ignoring goes straight to my folds. If Cass is anything like Troy, or maybe even worse, there's no use avoiding his question.

I take my tea over to the table and sit. "Mostly, I don't do much but relax on Sunday mornings and putter around." *Try not to think or feel until enough unendurable minutes and hours tick by while I try to find ways to quiet the noise in my head.*

"So, you avoid dealing with your grief and drink yourself

into a coma on Saturday night to avoid your grief further." He makes it an indisputable statement of fact.

I open my mouth to argue and immediately shut it. There's no point in arguing, so I ignore his uber rude comment. "I plan on gathering together my research. I wish I had our Double Diaries."

Ever since I woke, I've had the urgent need to re-read our diaries. They definitely have something to do with all the strange stuff going on, and maybe there's something in them that will help me figure out a plan.

9

CASSIEL

Another wave of grief washes over her as she mentions their Double Diary, but I focus my attention on the sudden increase of her heartbeat when she says the word *reading*. Then, as if a curtain drops on one stage and rises on another, her attention shifts. She sets her cup down and looks around as if getting her bearings.

"I'd better get to it. Time to settle in." She lasers those chestnut eyes to mine once again. "How long are you locking me away for?" The look in those eyes makes it clear she intends to get to the bottom of this. I watch the determination Troy warned us about surface. No longer the somewhat compliant child, Aleah marches determination and drive ahead of her like twin beacons heading into battle.

"Troy and Tristan know more of the details, but I imagine we're here for a few weeks." I can't lie to her, but I can obscure my meaning. The truth is, we have no idea how long it will take to find Lord Syrael and figure out how release Aleah's powers. Keeping Aleah out of the sex demon lord's clutches means keeping her true identity from her. Her magic will alert Lord Syrael's mirror the instant Aleah taps into it. It had taken our combined magic to save Aleah from him last time. Even the powers we gained with our promotion to sex angel lords might not be strong enough against his enhanced demonic powers. That's why we'd brought her here to this fortress, an island created by magic and surrounded by its protective powers. A sanctuary to give us time to heal our charge while we figured out how to bring her back to Atroyel. *To us.*

Her mention of the Double Diary gives me the opening I need if I handle this just right. Time for me to get my head on straight instead of acting like a besotted teenager. Time to remember my priorities and our calling as sex angel lords. Time for me to do what needs to be done. The three of us agreed that, as Atroyel's mate, she was part of our family, part of our bond. That made it our responsibility to protect Aleah from all harm. I rake through distant memories for the things I knew about Aleah as a child, things that may have changed. But some traits are too entrenched to change.

"How about I give you a quick tour and let you get cleaned up." I stand, assuming she'll follow my lead. "This, as you can see, is the kitchen." I sweep my hand around the oak, granite, and stone kitchen and breakfast nook. "Although it's more Tristan's domain than mine. He's the cook in the family."

She follows me as I wind my way through the myriad of rooms designed as part of the landscape as a nod to one of Atroyel's favorite architects until we arrive at a desk tucked away in a far corner of the house.

"Oh my gods, this is gorgeous." I have no trouble identifying the skip in Aleah's heart rate this time as one of joy. "If I could have chosen my dream writing retreat, this would have been it."

She slides that cute round, firm ass into the ergonomic chair Atroyel insisted she needed and runs her hand over her folded laptop, almost reverently. She adjusts each of the other items—her cell phone, a notebook, and a cup filled with her favorite pens. She presses her thumb on the phone. I expect her to ask who turned it off, but she says nothing.

Gazing out the wall of three-quarter length windows set atop concrete block and overlooking the woods behind the house, Aleah leans back in the chair and sighs. "This is perfect."

Now that I've given her something to relate to, she's latched on for all she's worth. "I guess I'd better get some work done." She bends over the laptop and slides her fingers along the edge, but I stop her before she opens it up by placing my hand on the lid.

"Let's finish the tour first," I say.

When she picks up her phone, I walk past the desk to the window bench built into the small corner at the end of the curved wall. "Here's a reading nook for you." I move to the side as she steps beside me. A breath of her signature fragrance drifts by, so subtle yet it makes me rock hard. She gasps as she sees the stack of books sitting on the cushioned bench.

She slides the phone into her pocket. "How did these get here?" She snatches up the diaries and hugs them to her chest.

"Troy insisted we bring them. He said something about us needing to read them aloud to release the magic."

She connects the dots before the words finish leaving my mouth. To read with Troy, either Tristan or myself—or both —need to be close. She gives me a we'll-see-about-that look, snatches the books up, and marches back down the hall. I lag, ogling her fine ass. Ogling is generally something better attributed to Tristan, but the word fits like a glove in this case.

"Shall we finish the tour then freshen up before lunch?"

She nods and doesn't say another word as she follows me throughout the twists and turns of the house built right into the natural landscape of the peninsula. Most would have oohed and aahed at how the architect incorporated the stone, waterfall, and brook with concrete and the rich grain of mahogany and oak, but Aleah simply takes it all in. She occasionally pauses to run her hand over a surface or take in a view.

She hesitates outside of Tristan's bedroom and looks at the empty bed. "How long will he be out? What should we expect when he wakes up?"

Perceptive. My respect for her goes up a notch. "He'll sleep through the afternoon and be up and almost back to normal in time to cook us a late supper."

She frowns, intelligent eyes searching my face. "What does *almost back to normal* mean?"

"It means he may have a few remaining side effects, but nothing you won't be able to heal." I pause and, using my powers, project the heat of Tristan's desire. From what we knew from the ancient readings, possession left a sex angel lord with a power depletion that could only be wholly refilled by intercourse.

Her large nipples harden beneath the knit sweater she wears . . . without a bra. Unusual in my experience. She pushes her glasses up on her nose and brushes loose curls behind her ears. Regret flashes through her eyes, but she can't take back the habitual action that reveals her perfectly sculpted ears. Her ears are that delicious shade of red that makes me want to lick the heat away.

She turns on her heel and flees down the hall, waggling a hand in the air. "See you in a bit."

But she can't hide that heartbeat from me. Things are

shaping up to be a lot more interesting than when Hera first sent me down here to help my brother. A lot more interesting, indeed.

10

CASSIEL

Aleah's hands are bound high above her head with a braided cord that matches the black silk blindfold covering her eyes. My breath catches as I gaze at her naked beauty. I'm completely in love with the splendor of her petite curves, the soft folds of her pussy just inviting me to lose myself in the rapture of her arousal. I stretch out beside her, tracing my fingers down the sensitive skin of her neck, before leaning in to kiss the slight dip at the base of her neck. My cock stiffens as she trembles in anticipation, and a deep-rose blush highlights her tawny skin. I ignore my cock's insistence, intent on enjoying every second basking in her arousal.

With the tip of my tongue, I draw a line from the base of her neck to her right nipple. I flick the engorged bud with my tongue, alternating with a slow circling of her areola. I plump the small globe in my hand, and her nipple stiffens further in a cry for my attention. I answer the call, sucking the fullness of its nub deep into my mouth. She whimpers and arches her back. I relax the suction until she falls back on the bed.

I worship each of her breasts in turn. Aleah cries for

more, rolling and moaning in her urge to have me move to the epicenter of her desire. I feel her struggle, confident that if her hands were free, she'd be pushing my hand to the wetness hiding between her thighs. I trail a finger down the soft, smooth skin of her abdomen, content that I've made the right choice in binding her wrists to the headboard. I'm the teacher; she's the pupil. I'll make love to her like she's never experienced before.

I smell the perfume of her arousal as she writhes and begs for more. Using fingers and tongue, I pay homage to each part of her perfection—the dip of her cute little belly button, the gentle slope of her stomach, the curve of her waist. I inch my way down to her cunt. I pause. Everything about her fills me with longing. I thank the gods for giving me such a gift.

I slide my finger over her mound into the slick folds of her labia. The head of her clitoris stands at attention, begging for release. She widens her legs, unleashing the beautiful fragrant musk that's distinctly her own. I inhale deeply, certain I've never smelled anything so enticing, so fresh, so feminine. I gently part her full brown lips and gaze, stupefied, at her sweet cleft. Again, I'm awestruck at the beauty of this woman who opens herself before me. I lean down and blew gently on her button of bliss. She rears up as if hit by another surge of electricity. I close my lips around her dark pink clit. A low, deep moan escapes her as she goes perfectly still.

As I torment, tantalize, and tease her with my tongue, her muscles start to vibrate with pent-up tension. Relentless in my enjoyment of her hunger, I take her to the edge of the cliff then bring her back. There. Back. There. Back. I lose track of how many waves I make her ride. I keep her on the edge until I know there's nothing else in her world except for me and the sensations I pull from her. I close my lips over her clit and suck with deep, long pulls, reveling in the taste of her exquisite nectar. She screams as release jolts through her and then she sinks, shuddering, onto the bed.

I stand, rubbing my fingers along the hard thickness of my shaft, giving myself one last moment before I take what I've waited so very long for. I bend and give each nipple one more long pull, releasing another set of post-orgasmic tremors in her. Desire sweeps through me like a river rushing toward white water rapids, and my cock grows ever harder. I plunge into her tight channel. My balls and anus tighten as the first familiar pulsing of my orgasm hits the base of my member. I still and work to regain control. I will make this last.

I inch my big cock out to the surface of her pussy, then slowly submerge. In. Out. In. Out. Nothing has ever felt better in my life, Nothing. I grab a handful of her ass to help distract me from the pulsing demands my cock makes. Aleah rocks her hips, matching my thrusts as her sheath tightens rhythmically around my shaft.

"Fuck me, Cassiel."

With those three words, I explode into a frenzy. I ride her fast and hard. Each thrust drives me closer to the edge. Her pussy clamps down hard around my cock, and the spasms of her orgasm push me over the precipice. I explode…

Gasping, I stand under the shower stream while the fantasy fades, and I return to my right mind. I throw on some clothes and head to the kitchen, determined to get things back on track.

I barely have time to set an array of food on the butcher's block when she arrives. As she approaches, I don't need my empathic powers to tell me Aleah's determined footsteps mean I'm about to be interrogated. Atroyel had warned me to expect a confrontation, except he was supposed to be here to help out. Both of them are. I shouldn't be surprised. It isn't the first time my brothers have changed the course of things with their impulsive behavior. Typically, Atroyel is the careful one of us, but something about this little Nephilim makes him forget his natural responses. So, now it's up to me to try to put Aleah at ease without revealing anything that might put her in harm's way.

She stops on the other side of the butcher's block, and I slide the glass of red wine I decanted in front of her.

She smiles politely and slides it back to me. "Thanks, but it's a little early for me."

So far, she's behaving exactly the way Atroyel predicted. Despite her attempt to direct attention away from her sexuality, the combination of elegant casual clothes does the exact opposite. I study her for a moment, my empath powers on full open and run right into the vast wall she's erected to protect her feelings. I smile inwardly because I know from centuries of experience with Atroyel that there's always a crack in that wall. But first, I'd need to distract her.

I slide it back in front of her. I give her my most charming smile and add just a little bit of supernatural power. She stares back at me with those wide eyes, and her heart rate remains steady, no reaction at all. Usually, I'd have great power over anything sexual; however, Aleah possesses the power of Indomitable Will. That willpower may be blocking my sexual powers.

"Surely, you can share one toast?" I pick up my wine glass and tip it toward her. Flash another panty-dropping smile.

While she considers my request, I send threads of empathic power through her psyche looking for the cracks in her defenses. I dive under the wall of her Indomitable Will, through the glimmer of hope peeking through. I bob and weave around the cages holding her anger and agony at bay. I dig and search until I find the fortress holding her terror . . . terror that almost shatters me with its force. *I have no one.* The fortress hides the shattering of her soul from the world. She has no one to care for her, no one who gets her, gets that she's special although she has no idea why. Something powerful rises within me. Something I can't think about. I pull back my power and study those inscrutable eyes. As I do, they widen. The toast?

Right. I'd better think of something right quick. "To reunions."

Instead of raising her glass, she asks, "Whose?"

Ours. I shut down the impossible thought. "Yours and Atroyel's, of course."

."We're a long way from being reunited." She snorts. "Let's toast to possibilities."

"To possibilities." I raise my glass an inch higher but don't do the clink thing.

She raises the glass to those luscious lips, tips her head back, and sips. I go rock hard. That won't do.

"Why do you call him Atroyel?" She focuses that intense stare on me again, but she keeps her hand wrapped around the stem of her glass.

"That's his name. What do you call him?"

"Troy." She takes another sip of the wine. "Atroyel." She rolls it around her tongue, deciding whether the flavor suits her. Her grin transforms her face and bathes her with her grace. The divine energy infusing her is a bluish-white mist that reveals she's a Nephilim. "I can just imagine your mother scolding him. Now, Atroyel, you know it's not right to swear. I'll stick with Troy."

"We call him Troy, too." I can't help but return that smile. I tip my glass at her again. "Troy, it is."

We both take another sip. At this rate, we'll be half in the bag before we eat. I put my glass down and turn on the gas burner. Tristan's the cook in the family, but I make a mean omelet. I appear to lose myself in a whirlwind of breakfast-making activity, giving her time to settle in. As I'd hoped, she takes a seat at the island where she can watch me.

"Do you prefer Cassiel or Cass?" she asks.

"Which do you prefer?" Not that I care. Master is the only word I want to hear from those lips. Fuck, I've got to get a grip on myself.

"One thing you should know about me is that answering a question with a question drives me batshit crazy."

"So I've been told." Before she can retort, I add, "Unlike Troy, I'm asking because I'm curious, not to be a bastard."

"Can you read minds?" Aleah asks. So she's still the curious little minx she'd been in the forest . . . Only now she is of age.

"No, but Troy can when he's in angel form. I read emotions. We all share complete lordship over anything sexual." I slide an omelet and a couple of slices of buttered toast onto the plate in front of her. I hold a knife and fork out to her.

She takes them. "Thanks." She takes a long, slow inhale. "This smells divine. I'm starving." She dives in, fork in her left hand and knife in right, English style. Efficient.

She inhales several more mouthfuls, not even attempting to do the sexy tiny-bite thing most women I've met do when trying to impress me. It's sexier than hell watching her eat, watching the way she takes the tip of her tongue and lifts away any crumbs. She waves her cutlery in the air. "You didn't answer my question. Don't think I didn't notice." She takes a healthy bite of toast. Smiles gratefully at me when I place a glass of orange juice and her pills beside her plate.

"Who do I have to thank for pulling my stuff together?"

"That would be Tristan, for the most part, under Troy's rather demanding direction."

She smiles at that comment. "So, tell me more about your powers. What does it mean that you have lordship over anything sexual? Are you some kind of Dom or something?" Despite her attempt to appear knowing, that slip reveals her naïveté. Atroyel had warned us about that and her intense curiosity about anything sexual. Curiosity she tries to hide, sometimes even from herself.

11

ALEAH

He full-out smiles this time as if I've delighted him, and he's so frigging gorgeous I almost faint. Pass out right there on the spot. My heart rate rockets past one hundred as if someone's put the peddle to the floor. I turn my attention back to my food before I embarrass myself more than I already have. For some reason, I'm starved, and for the first time in months, eating is feeling *really* good.

"I prefer Cass, casually," he says, "and yes, I'm a Dom as certainly as you're a sub."

My heart skips. I pull on my willpower to bring it back under control. Cass turns back to the stove, but I'd swear I see a bulge in his dress pants—very tailored dress pants with knife creases, just what I love—as he turns. What's happening to me? Why am I having this reaction to this man? He's Troy's brother, for gods' sake. I shouldn't need to keep reminding myself of this.

I push my glasses up and tuck hair behind my ears and drop my mask of professional nonchalance in place. But I'm curious. My need for knowledge vaults into overdrive.

"Well, that's a topic best left for another time. What do you mean you like Cass, casually?"

Those golden eyes give me a look I instantly recognize because it's identical to Troy's. Few things fluster me, but talking about sex is one of them. Which isn't great for a journalist about to do a series of interviews with a guy who made billions of dollars from sex. Cass's going to play with me. He knows he shouldn't play. I know we shouldn't play. Troy's trapped in some kind of dead zone, hovering between this realm and the next. I am a kink neophyte, although a well-read one. Sure, we'd dipped our toes into a bit of kink, but the only things I know about the lifestyle are what I've read. Since Troy wasn't a role-playing kind of guy, it wasn't a question for us. He was a control freak, but he hadn't been that kind of control freak.

Cass turns and faces me, tented pants deflated. Not that I'm looking. I snatch my eyes back to his. He caught me looking.

"Same topic. Are you sure you want me to answer?" The gleam in his eyes tells me he knows he's poking the lioness.

Heat bolts to my ears again, and desire skitters over my skin. I want to say no, but I want to know everything when it comes to stuff about sex. At least I had when Troy was alive. It was one of the things he loved about me when he wasn't chuckling about my rather prudish boundaries. Boundaries that were constantly warring with my sexual curiosity. Curiosity won. When it came to sex, it usually did.

"Yes." I hold his gaze, but I fight to do it to keep from dropping my eyes. Something about him makes me want to submit. Then, a thought occurs to me—maybe he's using magic. He's a sex angel, after all, and they've proved magic exists. I narrow my eyes, ready to dig in.

"I prefer my subs call me Master Cassiel." The challenge is clear.

Curiosity and will go another round or two in the ring. Then it hits me. I can use him as a credible source on my assignment. It could save me a ton of research time, and there's nothing like the real thing. I'd interviewed a few slave types for an article, but I'd never talked to a real Dom. "Do you have a lot of them?"

He raises his damned eyebrow in the same irritating way Troy has and no doubt for the same reason. "Them?" Yup, same reason. "Isn't that a little vague? I'd have thought a journalist would be a bit more precise."

"Subs." I snap the word out as if he's stepped on my last nerve.

"I think you know what I'm talking about." Cass is having none of my attitude. He leans forward, resting those beautiful forearms with their dusting of fine black hair peeking out from the rolled sleeves of his dress shirt, and locks eyes with me. "Aleah, that's no way to talk to me if you want my help." His deep voice is soft and leaves me feeling as if I've been scolded and any further infractions would lead to a spanking. And I swear to god that if he says my name like that again, I will swoon.

"What makes you think I want your help?" I get all righteous as I do when trying to deny the growing heat between my legs.

"Don't you?" Light flickers in his eyes as if he's daring me to deny it. He's getting a kick out of this, just like Troy. I give him my best side-eye.

"Fine. Have you had a lot of subs?"

"Aleah." He says my name again, and I swear there's another little shot happening between my legs. "I'm a sex angel. That makes me an expert on all things sexual."

He says this as if he's a frigging superhero or something, except he's not smug about it, just confident.

"So, if Troy's your brother, then he's a sex angel, too,

right? How come he isn't an expert on all things sexual?" I want to die of embarrassment the moment the words leave my mouth. There I go again with the heat rising. I swear I must be perimenopausal. Hot flashes, that's it. "Not that I'm inferring there's anything wrong with Troy's, um, performance."

Cass outright laughs as I choke out that sentence. "Even in his human vessel, he no doubt outshone most."

This is true. Troy had been the best lover I'd ever had; there was simply no comparison. Cass's eyes flash with that mysterious fire that makes me feel as if he's reading my thoughts. Time to change the subject.

"What do you mean by *human vessel*?"

Cass regards me as if he's deciding how much to tell me. As a journalist, I've seen that look before. I give him another side-eye. *Don't dare lie to me, buster.*

"We've been looking for our bonded mates. When we travel to another realm, we have to inhabit a vessel to be compatible with the culture." He hesitates as if there's more, but he's said enough.

"What happens to the person who owned the vessel in the first place?" I sound prickly; I can't help it. I've watched too many horror movies.

"We take over a body at the moment of death, change places, if you will. The family thinks it's a miracle cure and blames any tiny differences on the near-death experience. The rest is magic." He winks, and another shot of joy juice trickles between my folds. "Now, let's talk about how my expertise can help you."

I rub my left shoulder again, very aware of the heat building there. I'm adjusting to it, just as I became part of the pain, reducing it to an almost pleasant burn while having the black rose tattoo colored. It feels as if the tattoo artist is working on another layer, but my eyes trick me when I look.

One second, a 3D triangle hovers under the rose, the next, two, then nothing. I shake my head and pull my attention back to Cass. His attention is laser-focused on me in a way that tells me what I say has to matter. Makes me want to tell him the whole story.

12

CASSIEL

Aleah examines me with that look of speculation again, only this time, she's deciding just what to tell me. That part of my DNA connected to hers tells me the best thing I can do to get her talking is to give her something else to focus on at the same time. Taking care of her is the best way to do that, so I slide a dish of fresh sliced fruit in front of her, then busy myself making her a latte. That block of ice around her heart is still solidly in place, but her intellect has started firing, and that's the next best way to break through to her. Yet I have to tread carefully because if she reveals her power too fast, she'll be a homing signal for Lord Syrael's henchmen.

"I'm not sure how much you know about me. You know I'm a journalist, right?" She watches me make the latte and add a healthy shot of coffee liqueur to it.

"I do, but assume I know nothing. I could listen to your voice all day." I love the sound of her slightly husky voice. Troy warned us it's one of many things she's sensitive about, and he'd no doubt never told her just how spectacular it is.

She instantly looks down, but she can't hide her pleasure

and confusion from me. She clears her throat and pops a blackberry in her mouth.

"I'm a senior contributor for a magazine called Mosaic that relies on contracts from high-end clients who want to promote their businesses subtly. The magazine's been struggling since the pandemic hit, despite our online presence." She snags a slice of banana and slides it off the fork onto her tongue, utterly unaware of just how sensual she is. "Daisy, she's the editor-in-chief, says it didn't help that I took a leave of absence. My sizzling exposés are popular. Hits went down exponentially when my blog pieces stopped."

I slide the doctored latte in front of her and prop my elbows back on the bar to show I'm actively listening. The skip-a-dee-doo-dah her heart does betrays my ulterior motive.

She licks her bottom lip and pushes those damned glasses up her nose. Glasses I want to rip off so I can see those eyes glitter without their shield.

"I'm assuming you took leave to take care of things after Troy's death?" It's not like me to tap dance around an issue, but I choose the indirect approach, unsure of what will trigger the grief. She surprises me.

"I took a leave because I completely fell apart when Troy died." She picks up her latte and cradles it. "And because it was easy to shut out the world and go into hibernation."

"Didn't you have friends and family to check on you?" I'm mystified how someone who sheds love the way she does can be so alone.

She gives me a sad smile. "There are a couple of faithful friends, but most drifted off during Troy's illness. There's nothing like a good cancer diagnosis to get folks running from their mortality." She looks thoughtful. "The majority of my friends are used to me being the mover and shaker, so it's easy for them to use the excuse of waiting for me to contact them."

"And the faithful?"

"There's something about the grieving process, especially during a global pandemic, that makes it easy to blow folks off. They usually check in by text to ask if I'm up for a call. So far, I haven't been." She squeezes her left delt again. As much as I want to take a look, now is not the time. She's relaxing a bit, so best to keep my distance . . . for now.

"So, what's changed? Has the pandemic ended, making it necessary for you to restart life?"

"No, the pandemic's still going strong. That's part of the problem. It's caused a major economic crisis for many industries, including media. Mosaic's been offered a huge contract to run a series of articles about a sex tycoon, but there's a catch. He insists I be the one to write the article or no contract, which is strange." She gives another heavy sigh that makes me want to take her in my arms and show her it will all get better, but her last sentence raises my hackles.

"Why is that strange? I understand from Troy that you're an award-winning journalist. Maybe he just wants the best."

Her smile reaches her eyes this time. "As good as it is for my ego, I'm not that good. My only experience with the BDSM community is a short piece I wrote a couple of years ago on the psychology of a submissive. We have a couple of outstanding reporters who live the lifestyle." She pushes back her stool, tucks her left knee against her chest, and leans her chin on her knee.

Every movement is graceful yet efficient, like the dancer she yearned to be. But this is not that girl who jetéd across the forest floor. Now, there's a definite sexual undercurrent to every movement, something she seems completely unaware of. Something I'll have to teach her. *Focus, Cassiel!*

"So, why insist on you?" I ask.

"That's what I need to figure out. I had planned to research Cy this afternoon, but you guys happened."

"Well, what's stopping you now?" I ask. "I'm surprised you haven't checked your phone. Connected, isn't that what you call it?" I don't bother to try to hide my technological ignorance. She'd lived with our Luddite, so she'll take it in stride.

She beams me that grin again, and more of her grace drifts into the air, and I can't risk it escaping while Tristan recovers.

"You. One doesn't want to be rude, does one?" She claps her hands over her cheeks. "God, it's been so long since I smiled, my face is starting to ache." Her expression sobers. "When I saw one of you had turned off the phone, I decided to leave it off for a bit. There'll be seven hundred messages from Daisy, and she'll know the instant I read one of them." She lets out another sigh, something she seems very used to doing. It's now a mission for me to change those sighs to smiles. Damn, I'm beginning to sound like Tristan.

"She'll call instantly, demanding an answer. The problem is, I don't know what that answer is."

"So, that's your priority, then, researching this tycoon." I push up my rolled sleeves. "Shall we get started?"

She doesn't move, just tucks that lower lip between her teeth. Sighs. "I've got another priority, and it's something you can help me with." She drops her gaze to the floor.

I lean forward and tip her chin up. "And what might that be?"

The hope radiating from her eyes almost brings me to my knees. "Help me figure out how I can be with Troy . . . Be with him without having to take over one of your bodies."

"Oh, I know how to make that happen, but first, the research. We need your mind free and clear when we share the secret to Troy's corporeality." I turn as her mouth opens to protest and walk out of the kitchen, praying Tristan knew what he was doing when he put the computer protections in place. Now, I'm the one smiling.

13

ALEAH

You can bet I got my ass off of that stool and beetled after him. He simply lengthens his stride, outpacing me. *Bastard.* He probably has something like angelic speed to boot. But the vision of that angelic ass as the material of those fine tailored pants rides across the cheeks of his ass makes me shimmer with heat. Of course, it's because it's identical to Troy's fine ass, and the reminder draws my attention. That's my story, and I'm sticking to it.

He leads the way to the writing nook they set up for me and points to the desk chair.

"You told me earlier there's something I should learn about you, Aleah. Well, there's something you should learn about me. I don't like repeating myself, but I will this once. We're going to research this tycoon and whatever else we need for you to make your decision despite the fact you've already made it. Then, you'll let Daisy know your decision. Tristan and Troy should be awake by that time, and we'll discuss how our magic works." Cass's tone leaves little room for discussion on the topic as he pulls a chair beside me.

"Yes, sir." Despite how his masterful tone seems to tickle

my libido, I throw every ounce of sarcasm I can muster into the two words. I flip open the lid of my laptop and wait for it to load.

"Now, you're getting the idea." The glee in his eyes lets me know my sarcasm is lost on him.

I click on my email program and am not surprised to see several hundred new emails in my inbox. At least ten of them have the Urgent flag, all from Daisy. I sigh inwardly. I'd better get back to her before she has an apoplectic fit. But what the hell do I tell my editor and friend? *Hey Daise—I'd love to take one for the team, but I won't live long enough to finish the series. I'm pretty sure I'm about to meet my doom.* Right, that'll work. She'd send a flock of men in white coats to lock me in the security of a padded cell.

Before I can move, Cass slides my cellphone toward me. Instant electricity runs through me as our hands touch when I reach for it.

"Thanks." I focus on pressing the power button and staring at the black screen as if, by looks alone, I can make the thing load faster. But he's so close, and it's been so long since I've felt the heat of another human being . . . Or in this case, angel. My body pulls in the heat generated by this man and pulls it to my core as if trying to melt a block of ice there. Now that I think of it, I relate heat to the dark side. He might be an angel, but there's something a bit dark and dangerous about Cass. Something that yanks a particular chain in my libido. As the heat of his gaze keeps my eyes glued ahead, a shiver runs through me.

My phone starts pinging. I pick it up and stare at the screen. Sure enough, there are thirteen text messages from Daisy, and I can almost feel her franticness growing with each text.

Daisy @ 11:27 a.m.: You awake, Ali? What did you decide?

Daisy @ 12:22 p.m.: Come on. I know you're there.
Daisy @ 1:12 p.m.: Ali, I'm starting to get worried.
Daisy @ 1:15 p.m.: You're not reading these. Now I'm really starting to get worried.
Daisy @ 1:20 p.m.: If you don't answer me right now, I swear—

And so they go until just a few minutes ago. A pang of guilt washes over me at worrying my dear friend and editor. She's one of the gentlest and most caring souls I know, and I feel terrible about notching up her anxiety. Even if it was unintentional. Shit.

"What's wrong?" Frowning, Cass leans forward to look at my phone. I swipe it off the desk; I'm not sure why. It's not like anything is revealing about Daisy's mini panic attack.

"Nothing. It's just my editor. I haven't checked in, and she's worried." And she wants to know my answer. The problem is, I'm not sure yet. There's something in my gut telling me that taking this assignment will be a mistake. But maybe Daise is right; maybe it's just me refusing to let go of Troy's memory. Now that he's here, I don't have to let go. Or, if I do, that's no longer a consideration on the table about this job. Whether or not I'll be on this earth long enough to finish it is.

I hold the phone against my chest while I figure out what the hell I'm going to tell her . . . while I try to keep my breathing nice and steady . . . while I resist the urge to lean into the hard male body that's just a little too close for comfort. And oh, what a comfort it would be. I mentally slap that thought right out of my head.

Aleah @ 3:42 p.m.: Chill, girlfriend. I'm here. Give me time to type a message . . .

Three dots appear on my screen, alerting me that she's there and typing frantically.

Aleah @ 3:43 p.m.: I'm fine. I slept in. Stop typing and let me tell you the story.

I risk a glance at Cass. His lean, muscular body appears relaxed, but I can feel his intensity burning underneath the facade. He's a bit better at hiding it than Troy, but he's watching my every move.

"Where are we, exactly?" I ask.

"An island on Georgian Bay. We helped Troy arrange this Airbnb rental before he died. He knew you wouldn't be able to grieve in the South of France in a pandemic, so he decided this would be the next best thing." Cass delivers that little speech as if it's wholly plausible, but there are one or two holes that I'll be sure to explore later. Like why they waited six months to come to get me.

Aleah @ 3:44 p.m.: Troy's brothers arrived last night and whisked me off to a retreat for a month. I'm on an island in Georgian Bay in a gorgeous house. One of the brothers, Cass —I pause for a moment, trying to remember whether I've ever told Daisy Troy's brothers' names. I take out his name— just cooked me a late lunch.

Daisy @ 3:46 p.m.: Read your email. Cyrus Stone wanted our answer by noon today.

Annoyance flashes through me. I don't like pushy clients. If they get pushy before we begin, it's never ended well, in my experience. *He can damn well wait.*

Aleah @ 3:47 p.m.: Seriously! It's the weekend, for fuck's sake. What's the big rush?

Daisy @ 3:48 p.m.: **Read your email.** He's treating it like a tender process.

Whatever that means. I've never heard of articles being assigned by any tender process, but I stay away from the management side of things. Nothing good happens when I go there.

"What's going on?" Cass's tone is friendly enough, but there's something in it that compels me to answer. This compulsion, in turn, makes me *not* want to answer. I don't want to examine why this man makes me act like a spoiled brat.

"I missed a deadline. The guy contracting the magazine wanted an answer by noon." I have what people call "the tone" in my voice, but I can't help it. All of this stuff has me out of sorts. I'm much better when I know what's going on, when I'm in control of my situation. Right now, I'm spiraling.

"Ah yes, the tycoon who insists you write the series. Let's have a look at his terms, shall we?" Cass gives my arm a reassuring squeeze. I immediately start scrolling through the multitude of email alerts from Daisy while a little voice in my head asks me what the fuck I'm doing. This man, this supernatural being, is family and has superpowers. Therefore, my reasoning mind continues, there's no point in hiding anything from him.

14

———

TRISTAN

I wake, instantly alert as always, and filled with joy. I'm connected with Aleah. It's not the same as my connection with my brothers where a piece of their grace, their essence, links us almost telepathically. With her, it's physical, as if my ability to read sexual brain activity links with her cerebral cortex. But this is very different from when I read activity with others. As her brain triggers a sexual response, the corresponding physical reaction happens in my body. Our joining had triggered some kind of chain reaction.

When Troy's spirit took possession of me, I'd felt his angelic grace, the energy that infuses us angels, pour into her, seeking the link to his destined mate. The deep love she holds for Troy allowed him to break through the walls protecting her angelic grace. Flashes of divine light streamed through my body, merging with hers for one intense moment. An image of her angelic brand had dropped into my psyche, like a brilliant canvas—an intricately drawn black rose flanked by three deep red triangles, giving it an almost 3D effect. Now more than ever, I know for sure that she's ours.

I shrug on a black T-shirt, comfortable white cotton pants, and a pair of deck shoes before checking on Troy. He's still out cold, but his essence is still firmly in this realm. He'll find us when he wakes. After masking my power to avoid detection from Lord Syrael's ever-seeking eye, I make a quick circuit of the island we've created to ensure the magic dome cloaking its existence is firmly in place. I repair and strengthen a few cracks caused by us using our magic, glad to see our combined spell casting withstood Lord Syrael's seeking eye. I take another couple of circuits to stretch my wings before heading back to find the others. By now, I expect that Cass has ensured Aleah's needs are met, and she's in a receptive mood for a good meal, one of my specialties, and a long chat about many things magic.

I've got the first three appetizers for our dinner well underway when a laughing Aleah leads Cass into the kitchen.

"What'd I miss?" I ask as I slide a plate of stuffed mush-rooms in front of them. I'd had to guess what foods might appeal to Aleah based on the somewhat sketchy list of her favorite foods from Troy. Aleah takes a stool at the butcher's block, making it easy for me to keep working while we chat. Cass wanders over to the dual-zone wine fridge and ponders the reds through the glass door.

"Cass says I'm the first person he's met who's more of a control freak than he is." She laughs as I widen my eyes in surprise. "I know, right? I haven't known him long, and even I can see he's a total control freak. These smell delicious." She picks up the small tongs and slides a couple of the stuffed gems onto the small plate in front of her. I puff up just a little. Cooking soothes me, and there's nothing better than cooking a good meal for an appreciative audience. Even better, I've hit on one of her favorites with the first pitch. Just as Troy had warned us, our little goddess is far too small, having lost even more weight since he died. As I watch her pleasure consuming the delicacy, I make it my mission to put more pounds on that tiny body.

Cass comes back with a bottle of wine and three glasses, uncorks it, and pours us each several ounces. He takes a seat beside Aleah.

"You are more of a control freak than I am." Cass's stern appearance and our connection tells me he's not content with where things are at with Aleah.

"Why do you dislike me so much, Cass?" Aleah asks.

The directness of her question surprises Cass. I hide a smile and pretend not to watch while he tries to hide his discomfort.

"What makes you think I dislike you?" Cass takes the offensive.

"Every time I'm near you, I get the distinct feeling I'm a supreme pain in your ass, and you think I'm not good for your brother," Aleah says.

"Don't take it personally, beauty," I say, "Cass treats everyone that way. I've been trying to get his approval my whole life." I clamp my lips shut. I hadn't meant to let that nugget of information slip.

Cass frowns at me then turns his attention back to Aleah.

"Being a sex angel isn't a job, it's a calling. One that requires our commitment, and we can't be split between to masters. Being here with you takes us away from our mission. It's nothing personal. Why does what I think of you matter to you?" Cass asks. I glance over in surprise. My senses tell me he's taking this quite personally.

"I'm tired of people disliking me for no reason, that's all. If you prefer not to have me around, let's figure out a way Troy and I can carry on without you." She looks thoughtful while she takes a bite of the mushroom. Determination radiates from this woman. She looks at me. I wink, hoping to convey my admiration for her. I've never seen anyone stand up to Cass this way. His frown deepens, but he says nothing.

She closes her eyes and sighs as she chews, making it clear this particular discussion is over. "Oh my gods, these are so good. What's in them?" Her chestnut brown eyes beam pleasure at me.

I laugh. "So many questions, *mon chou*, but then Troy did say you're an amazing cook. They're baby portobellos baked with olive tapenade stuffing, asiago cheese, and a layer of prosciutto."

"Amazing. I usually don't like olive tapenade, but these are great." She pops the rest of it in her mouth. After a swipe with her napkin, she says, "Why did you call me a cabbage?"

"My darling woman, *mon chou* is an endearment meaning *my favorite one.*"

She keeps those eyes trained on me and says quite seriously, "You barely know me." The buzzing in her brain tells me she's gone on alert, looking for whether this is a sting, a scam from a sweet-talking man, or an actual compliment.

"Not true. I've known you long enough to know you're my favorite mate-in-law." I step away from those probing eyes and slide a board of smoked salmon bites from the fridge. I never lost the comfort from cooking no matter what realm we occupied, but the choices available here made it a delight.

She laughs and helps herself to a few of the bites. "You get first place for being the charmer in the group." She raises one of the bites in the air and salutes me. "And if you keep cooking for me, you'll be my *mon chou*, too." She pops it in her mouth, but a smile beams from her eyes.

"So, what's up for the rest of the day?" I assemble the fixings for a salad, thankful my brother, mister fussy, is a ghost at the moment. Including his finicky appetite limited my options. Cass will eat anything as long as it's well cooked.

"First, we had to set priorities. Then we had to do the research, so I had enough information to make an informed decision. Then I had to give Daisy my answer and set my to-do list for tomorrow." She draws in an exaggerated breath. "And then, I had to decide what my priority is for this evening."

"I hope it will involve coming up with a plan to keep you safe from Lord Syrael." I add a bit of angelic speed to my prep, and the knife flies through chopping the veg.

Aleah's eyes are fastened on my hands. She holds her breath and only lets it out when I stop. "That is so cool. And frightening."

I flash her my panty-dropping grin. I feel the flush of heat flow through her, but it's as if I run into a brick wall in her mind.

"Our priority is to find out how I can be with Troy in the flesh." Her tone makes it clear this is not a subject for discussion. It's the brick wall of her will. I've only encountered this once before in my travels. It was with the head of a religious order who'd used his will to deny all need for creature comforts to help those considered the bottom feeders in any society.

Cass raises his hand, and the small tray of bottles sitting on the counter glides through the air and settles in front of Aleah.

Show off. I send the thought to Cass.

Takes one.

Brother banter is fun, but we've got to figure out how to release Troy's soul.

"We'll do just that as soon as Atroyel gets here. Meanwhile, let's get your meds into you." He places the tray and a medicine cup in front of Aleah. One thing about Cass, even if he hates you, he'll do the right thing. "Atroyel tells us you must take these medications consistently. We don't want to miss another dose."

I expect annoyance, but there's a tickle of activity in her cerebral cortex that signals humor. "No, we most certainly do not." Despite a tone that's hard to read, her eyes dance with laughter. She drops her gaze but not before I catch a glimpse. Cass gives her a stern look.

Troy's ghost shimmers into the room, going in and out of focus. Aleah jumps to her feet, clutches her left shoulder, and looks around frantically. Her brain activity goes into over-drive, trying to figure out what's happening as adrenaline surges through her body.

With a burst of speed, I catch her before she hits the floor in a dead faint.

"I'm fading," Troy gasps before his divine light winks out.

ALEAH

My heart hammers in my chest as something yanks me back to consciousness, back from the black hole I've dropped into.

I've lost him again. He's gone. The dream has turned into the nightmare I knew it would. I can't feel this pain again. It's taken me months to lock the terror behind bars that make it tolerable. Then my godsdamned mind tricked me into believing he's still with me.

He's gone . . . without me.

The pain is too much. I sink into blackness. Except it's not black; it's nothingness. As if I've been dropped into a sensory deprivation chamber. I try to sink in deeper. At least I can't feel anything here. Not feeling is good. Nothing else matters. I'm determined to get the best of this situation, but something keeps pulling me back.

Fuck off. Stop taking pieces of me.

"Aleah, get your ass back here right now." A man's voice snaps the command as a beam of light breaks into the void. "You will help us bring Atroyel back."

But I'm too tired. I can't do it anymore. I can't fight. I don't even know what I'm fighting for. I've lost the only person who loved and accepted me for myself. I'm suffering from hallucinations. My body is breaking down with something rare, an obscure diagnosis where the only thing they know for sure is that it's progressive. I just don't have the strength to do it all on my own. To do it without the one person who made me love life. Maybe if I go into the darkness, I'll find him.

Far, far away, I hear voices.

"Stop that. If Syrael's found us, we haven't got much time." This voice is soft but filled with urgency.

Time. What is time? I have a vague sense that it's something I want to stay far away from.

Something warm seeps into the void, and a faint light shimmers in the distance. It's as if I'm hovering on a precipice. If I step off, life as I know it will be over, but I'll have peace.

"Oh no, you don't." A blast of light drops into my chamber, blowing away all that wishful thinking. I squint against the blinding light and see a man . . . with wings . . . wearing low-slung jeans . . . who looks just like Brad Pitt in the movie *Meet Joe Black*.

"You're Joe Black, the angel of death."

"I get that a lot. My name is Bob. Now tell me, Aleah, to what do I owe this rather inconvenient call?"

I narrow my eyes and send him my best asshole look. "I have no idea what you're talking about."

"She's right. You do huffy like the best of them." Bob leans against something invisible and crosses his legs at the ankle. "I'm talking about your attempt at a premature death. Why are you trying to run from your destiny?"

Only I would have a delusion with a madman who looks like Brad Pitt. "I'll bite. What destiny would that be, and who is *she*?"

"You're destined to be reunited with your mate, and *she* is our wife, Tate. She's the Chief Justice of Bardo, and she said to tell you she's not about to let you into Bardo before your time. Although she takes a more romantic view of all this, I agree with her. We did too much work to return your Troy to you. He seems to be willing to tear the universe apart to be with you. Are his feelings misplaced?" Bob raises his left eyebrow and extends his wings.

"You have no idea what I'm dealing with." That damned eyebrow lifts even higher. He probably knows exactly what I'm dealing with, but I decide to ignore that for now. Once I've got something to say, nothing will stop me from vomiting it out.

"I'm on my own in a system that swallows people like me," I whine. I can't seem to hold back the self-pity leaking out of me. "Besides that, you have no idea what it takes to help your husband die with dignity in the middle of a pandemic. But I gave him my word, and I did it." Right about now, I wish for my body back so I can pace. This moment is definitely a pace-worthy one. "But now that he's gone, I'm all alone. There's nobody there for me, and I'm sick, too. I'm just so tired." I let out a long, dramatic sigh. "And now I've gone off the deep end, and I'm not even on good drugs. The fact that you're here is proof positive I'm caught up in some kind of psychotic breakdown."

Bob straightens up and tucks his wings in. At least, I assume that's what he does because they disappear. "Maybe Tate's right. You need to get laid so your brain can engage again."

Ouch. The rebukes sting even if they are close to bang-on. I am wimping out. Who can blame me after what I've been through? But the criticism gets my hackles up . . . Which was probably the point, but that doesn't stop my motor mouth from engaging. "Who the fuck is this Tate, and where does she get off criticizing my love life? And why do you call her *our* wife? What has all this got to do with my death, anyway? You are here to take me to heaven, right?" I don't have a pity party often, but when I do, I make sure it's a frigging event. I might as well play along with my demented state until the drugs kick in. Oh gods, maybe I've had a frontal lobotomy, and that's why I'm floating in this sensory deprivation chamber. I give a mental eye roll. That's a little dramatic, even for me. But since this is my breakdown, I might as well imagine that Brad Pitt and I walk off into the sunset just like in the movie.

"Ahem." Bob interrupts my death dream. Of course, he does, just when I'm finally getting to a little sizzle. I have every right to be a bit bitchy, and it has nothing to do with my hormones.

"I see what caught her attention. Tate is the Chief Justice of Bardo, which is—"

"The realm between realms where we go before we're reincarnated. I know all about it. I wrote an article about it." Oh yes, I'm on a roll, telling the angel of death who probably rules Bardo that I know more about it than he does. The look on his face says that in spades. "Sorry, continue." I think a semi-sheepish grin his way.

"She *gets off* criticizing you because she's chief justice of all things dealing with sex and love, and your Troy asked for her help. I call her *our* wife because I'm one of four mates."

I've never been so glad of this nothingness stuff because it hides the expression that springs to my face. I gape. There's no other thing for it. A hundred or so questions spring to mind. Bob puts his hand up, stemming the flow before it can get started. I snap my mouth shut.

"You can find out about the lifestyle when you go back. As for your death, it's not your time. One of the demon lords is trying to snuff out your light prematurely, but it's not his decision to make. Do I have your attention yet?"

No need to get pissy. I know he's trying to kill me. That's the point.

Bob gives me a look. I nod but keep my mouth shut.

"You need to learn to believe. First in yourself, then in the magic. Let the magic lead you."

"And just how am I going to do that?"

"That's easy. You're going to look beyond the wall of rigid rules you have and let the angels guide you. The spell you need to release the magic is in your Double Diary. You don't have a lot of time to lose because your Troy is somewhere in the void beyond our reach. Let the angels read it to you and free yourself, body and soul." He extends his wings again. "And for gods' sake, get laid."

With that, Brad's lookalike disappears. A very different bright light replaces his. And heat. The line from *The Wizard of Oz* springs to mind. I'm not in the void anymore. I open my eyes and stare into brilliant blue eyes that look a lot like those on the Bob guy.

"Oh, Ali." Tears spill out of Tristan's eyes. He makes no attempt to hide his fear or the fierce determination behind it. He clutches me to his chest, and a warm flushing sensation spreads through me. Fingers of heat similar to the effect from contrast dye used in CT scans take away my usual pain. He lowers my shoulders to a pillow. I immediately try to sit up and wish I hadn't as nausea rolls through me. Then the migraine hits. The blast of nausea curls me into a ball and gives a split-second warning of the crushing pain that follows. The kind of pain that would make me blow my brains out if some fool put a gun in my hand.

Hands clutch at my shoulders, presumably trying to make me stretch out. Not a fucking chance. Go away. I just want it all to go away. There's nothing there but the pain. Make it stop. But something is stopping me from passing out. Something I have to get out.

"He said to read the diaries. You have to read the diaries."

There, I did it. I let go and slip into blessed darkness.

16

ATROYEL

I punch the gray curtain separating me from Aleah but don't even have the satisfaction of that relief. My incorporeal fist barely causes a ripple in the strange barrier. I've run into a lot of curious things since I died, and that angel took me to Bardo, and here was another. It's as if I'm watching Aleah and my brothers from inside a large aquarium. Their hazy images ripple in and out of focus. The sound of their voices drifts through, soft and indistinct. I have no idea what caused this latest problem, but none of that matters now. There's a lot I can't remember, but a couple of things are apparent. My beloved, my only reason for living, is in danger; her life is in danger. Somehow I'd weaved magic into our diaries that would unite us if we were separated. These angels, my brothers, are part of the equation. At least I could feel them before. Now, this fucking curtain took that away. It will take all of us to save my Aleah. I have to find some way to get back to her.

I slam both fists against the gray curtain as she slips into unconsciousness. "Read the fucking diary!" The force of my silent scream ripples the curtain. Troy shakes Aleah's limp form and says something to Cass. Cass's mouth forms the word "fuck" loud and clear. He snatches up the first journal and starts reading. *Finally. Thank gods.*

Double Diary
Troy on Tuesday, August 21

The Double Diary is not a new concept but unique considering the traditional diary is usually a one-person endeavor that offers the benefit of personal insight and/or a record for historical reflection. A two-person diary provides the opportunity for so much more.

I intend to use it, and it is my hope that you will, too. Why? Well, depending on how long we utilize the process, and that remains to be seen, it would be an interesting personal and historical perspective of our relationship in years to come. One day, it may be a very interesting and emotional read. A reflection of the day-to-day, week-to-week, month-to-month relationship of two people's lives, thoughts, concerns, needs, wants, etc. But, most importantly, our shared love!

This is, of course, the long-term perspective, whereas the true essence of this diary is the day-to-day notations of private thoughts to be shared by you and me. There should be an attempt to make notations of a personal nature, which, if you think about it, really opens the door. Also, notations do not have to be every day, every week, or every month for that matter. It would be good to sign and date notations made. This helps to maintain a chronological perspective.

Importantly, this diary does not preclude any other form of interaction from verbal to your sticky notes. I like those, which is a good example of my intentions for this diary. Sticky notes are not left every day. Sometimes, not for months. But when it strikes you, you share your thoughts. This does imply that your diary notations are always positive. In fact, I'm sure you remember how much easier it is to deal with issues, sometimes, some issues, on paper. It gives you that arms-length protection, giving time for considered thought.

Thoughts on sex is another great example. Just think of the possibilities. Stories, short or otherwise, to stimulate. Fantasies to excite. (Yes. Yes. Just another word for stimulating as I guess that's the point of sex.) Insights into our sexual activities. Such as: "Oh, I liked this," or "That was different." Of course, I would write back, asking for elaboration and perhaps share thoughts from my perspective. So many possibilities! To reiterate! Why I believe I'm getting excited just writing about what we could write about.

In any case, I'm sure this could be a viable medium to express those things that, at the time, would only disrupt that languid aftermath. After having you, I can only feel good, and I wouldn't usually want to dissect the activity. The next day, we could talk, but time and life circumstances sometimes supersede the opportunity. But again, that is not to say we shouldn't talk as I certainly enjoy that as well. But this provides another great outlet for insight into the pursuit of perfection. I'm not sure how you could get any better, but I'd love to try.

Sex. Sex. Sex is not by any means the exclusive focus for this diary. But, as I indicated to you, it was the catalyst. Can we take another step, through this diary, to even more hidden desires and new experiences? Perhaps. At the least, even sharing and recognizing your sexuality excites me with anticipation. Another form of foreplay if you will. Anyway, a diary provides an outlet for fun and insight when other methods of communication just don't work or become awkward for various reasons.

As previously mentioned, and as life cycles, so would the use of this diary. I would probably keep it in our bedroom. Possibly in the headboard for easy access for us. If and when I write something, I would tell you or hand it to you. Just trying to facilitate the ease of process, confidentiality, and privacy for us.

End of Intro overview. —Troy.

17

ALEAH

Something blasts through the pain and yanks me out of the darkness. *Shit.* I squeeze my eyes tight to shut out any light and huddle into the warmth of the arms holding me. *Breathe. Breathe. You've been here before. Embrace the pain.* Yeah, right. The fucking genius that came up with that idea should see how he feels about embracing the pain. Only a man would come up with something like that.

But something warm is seeping through me. Oxy. Thank gods. The guys found my Oxy. I relax a bit into those arms and wait for the drugs to take me to a place where I can think rational thoughts again. The few thoughts I have drift away as I snuggle deeper into Troy's arms. I drift into dreamland as he reads me a story that sounds very familiar.

Double Diary
Aleah on Tuesday, August 21

Well, it certainly is a welcome and stimulating idea. I like that it's open and affords me the freedom I need, given my life circumstances—balancing love, life, and work. And I'm loving anything that moves us in our exploration of our sexuality. I feel almost ashamed of how I'm reveling in your love and our growing exploration of sexuality. Sometimes, I fear you'll be bored, so this certainly presents a way to add a different dimension to that exploration.

And yes, it can serve as a way to explore other aspects of our emotional life together. Right now, I suspect that will mainly be positive for me—I don't think I have the need anymore to express difficult emotions through the written word. I'm much stronger and have come to prefer the verbal sparring if need be. So, for me, it will likely be about sex and love. :-)

—Aleah

18

ATROYEL

The gray curtain dims, and the words Aleah wrote all those years ago come at me loud and clear. I barely have time to drink in this woman I miss more than life itself as she lies in Tristan's arms before the veil drops as Cass reads the next words from my entry. *Godsdammit!*

Double Diary
Troy on Wednesday, August 22

As this is my first installment, I'll keep it easy. Just a simple comment, no response required . . .

You mentioned yesterday that although you wished you had more time to spend with me, you're working and very busy. Being my own boss allows me more freedom, and I do, at this point anyway, have more time to recognize you. I assure you I understand, and I don't expect you to be overly reciprocal, so don't worry. In fact, if I'm being overly distracting, just let me know. It won't be easy, but it's not your fault that you look so good. It shouldn't be a problem to be more aware of those times when it isn't appropriate, and I can simply up the masturbation factor. All you have to do is try and not look so good. Kidding, of course. Love you. —Me :-)

PS: Damn, it's muggy today!

PPS: It's still Wednesday but now nighttime. I'm back from golf. You're fresh out of the shower, wearing only a nightshirt. You do excite me. However, it's late, and you need to get to bed. Not only do I understand, but in a twisted way, I relish the feeling of my excited anticipation for Saturday nights. I seem to take perverse pleasure in imposing a delay in actively participating in any sexual encounter with you. It's almost like I take pleasure in torturing myself with prolonged foreplay to the point of a painful need for release. In some twisted way, the pain is what I want.

I so love the feeling of wanting you; it's like a drug or more likely an endorphin release that I need to maintain. The longer the foreplay, the greater the sexual hit will be. Here's an example you might find amusing. Understand that it's totally self-serving at best, to pump those endorphins. However, I pause as I'm not used to revealing myself this way . . . You know how I love thinking of you, seeing you, when you're sexually aroused.

I'm downstairs and hear your footsteps creaking across the floor. I know you're going to the bathroom, but my endorphins immediately suggest I can take pleasure in this. My mind conjures up the image of your being so sexually aroused that you are quietly opening the bedroom door to see if you can hear me masturbating. The thought of you so excited as to attempt this makes me smile, and I wish it was so, so I could pretend I didn't know you were there and put on a show for you. And I do this because it excites me all the more, thinking of you. What an insipid hedonist I've become! I blame you, of course.

Five minutes later, I have an afterthought. Being a voyeur who loves to watch you masturbate . . . Is this just projection?

Time for bed. —T.

Double Diary
Troy on Friday, August 24

Friday night. Watching *Predator* with you. I wanted to grab you and take you to bed. Too late and both you and I are too tired, so we should wait for Saturday. That's the smart thing to do. Oh well. I still get more endorphins.

It's getting late, and I should go to bed, but I wanted to write down a few thoughts. Sooo, I'm into it at this point. The writing is getting easier having gone through the initial trepidation. I hope you went to bed and masturbated. One of my favorite fantasies. Of course, there are more, and I may write to you about some, sometime.

Speaking of self-pleasure. I'm really quite curious:
- How often do you masturbate?
- What is the best time?
- Where, or does it matter?
- What gets you to that state?
- Do methods vary?

Etc. Etc. Etc. . . .

I wonder how far you, or me for that matter, have come in being able to reveal ourselves? I'm sure there are insecurities that have not been surpassed as yet. Perhaps these vulnerabilities can be part of taking the next step, and perhaps we will write about them. I like the wild and strange ones the best!

Until then, I'm going to bed and will hopefully have a great dream about you. Maybe, I'll get lucky and the dream will be a little nasty . . .

Troy: I'll always love you, Lea.

Double Diary
Aleah on Saturday, August 25

In answer—

1. I have—once or twice—opened the door and listened for the sounds of you masturbating. You sit in the dark—

2. Writing is obviously much easier for me than you. You're much more likely to hear my inner thoughts—esp. if you ask the right questions.

3. Masturbation: I masturbate once or twice a week. It used to be more often, but now less for two reasons: a) I like to fall asleep just thinking of you, often sexually, and b) Sometimes sleep overrides the hornies, and I'm out before I get to it.

Time: at bed or upon waking, if the situation allows. I'm too involved in the day-to-day otherwise.

Where: Usually bed, but on the couch if you've gone to bed before me. Very occasionally, in the bathroom if you surprise me by coming to bed early and before I've come.

State: You get me to that state. Sometimes it is a difficult battle—The sublime joy of our foreplay and the delightful torture of waiting, versus the need for immediate gratification and the need for you.

Methods: Do the methods vary? Not often. I'm really quite boring. What works, works.

I do want to hear some of your fantasies and thoughts. It's

in my nature to ask to hear all of them—as you've demanded of me. I'm trying to mediate my desires, though.

This will be fun.

You know I love you deeply, forever, always. Even the thought of life without you brings me such pain, I can't explore it often (How's that for a closing? :-D) . . .

The curtain clears as soon as Cass starts reading her words, but this time, I'm ready. My Lea moans in her sleep. Her form, relaxed out of the fetal position, still rests in Tristan's arms. Her body arches as her eyes dart back and forth under closed lids signaling a dream state. I have no idea how this works and don't take the time to figure it out. I give a quick prayer to the universe and dive into her dream.

19

ALEAH

I slip into the familiar dream state that's eluded me for so long, a place where I'm an active participant in my dream despite being fast asleep. When Troy was alive, he'd visited my dreams every night. Sometimes, my dreams were filled with hot and heavy sex with Troy playing the lead role. Most times, he was my protector, my hero saving me from all sorts of precarious predicaments.

During the last couple of days of his life, the dreams turned to nightmares where something stopped him from reaching me, from saving me. I'd awoken drenched in sweat, pulse racing, terror streaking through me, the pain in my chest almost unbearable. When he died, he'd disappeared, and the nightmares took charge as a feeling like Sauron's eye pursued me, trying to consume me.

Somewhere far away, a warm voice very similar to my Troy's reads to me. I let the words pour over me, the words that had come from his heart and mine. I see his beautiful face in the distance and reach out for him. He reaches back, and just when my heart fills with joy at the thought of touching him, he vanishes. He does that a lot lately.

In the back of my mind, I'm aware strong arms are holding me. Troy's? I twist around, trying to catch a glimpse of his face again. Hands cup my cheeks, and hot lips sear mine. I turn into his arms and kiss him with a passion that takes both our breaths away. I wrap myself around him. All that control and security and heat and power that I wear like armor fall away. My Troy finally came to visit me in my dreams.

The magical story he's reading to me plays in the background. Suddenly, he shifts, and his perfect body hovers above mine. I arch to reach for him, but he holds me down. Holding both hands above my head with one hand, he reaches down with the other and pulls my folds apart. Thrusting his cock in straight to the hilt, he rides me. My mind screams as I welcome him. I stare into the light streaming from his eyes, tears filling mine as I reach for the searing heat as his beloved cock claims me. He brushes his free hand over my face, inviting me to close my eyes.

"Shhh, beauty. Don't think. Feel me."

I slide into his commanding voice, dropping into that place where nothing else exists but his body claiming mine.

Instead of his usual controlled pace, he thrusts into me as if running a race against time, gliding his heat out to the tip before burying it deep within me again and again. With each stroke, my clit brushes against his pubis fanning the flames of my passion.

Each thrust drives me nearer to a frenzy so powerful I want to scream. My essence trickles down the crack of my ass, exciting me even more. Nothing else exists except Troy's body moving in mine. For what seems like an eternity, the voices whisper the magic words as Troy fucks me. I lie spread and captive to his will.

I'm exposed and vulnerable as only he's seen me. Somewhere in the far recesses of my mind, I'm aware that someone is watching us. If it had been any other time, I would have resisted. But this is my dream, and if it means being with Troy, I'll fuck him in a stadium. My excitement shows as the wetness oozes from me.

His cupped hand slides between us and captures the full mound of my sex. I push up, sliding through the wetness, saturating the palm of his hand. My mind and body rage with need when he closes his hand in a viselike grip, capturing my throbbing clit between the engorged lips of my cunt. He massages my clit until I'm panting with the need to come, but my orgasm remains elusive. In one quick motion, he removes his hand, grabs my hips, flips me to my knees, and buries his cock deep.

With each stroke, he slaps the cheeks of my buttocks, hard. His hand molds the round globes of my ass perfectly. My flesh shudders under the impact, and I'm sure he's left his brand with a red-tinged imprint of his hand. I gasp as each slap enhances the pleasure of his hard cock. I lose control, completely overwhelmed by the unrelenting waves of plea-sure, pulling me to a climax of uninhibited abandon.

A blue mist merged with a golden light swirls around us as my Troy solidifies in my arms. I fall into the love and light streaming from his beautiful brown eyes.

Suddenly, searing pain blasts my joy out of existence as Troy disappears, and another migraine hits.

As I grip my skull, that terrible feeling like Sauron's eye sweeps over me, and I slip into darkness.

"I will find you!"

BLACK ROSE AND THE THREE PRINCES

The sex angel princes captured the lovely young maiden and took her into the forest. The moment each touched her, divine light passed between them, binding the princes to protect the Nephilim named Black Rose. The princes vowed to keep her safe from suffering and had word sent to the sex angel lord, Syrael that they'd all been killed, torn apart by wild beasts. They hid deep in the forest and built a magic cabin to shield Black Rose from the archangel's mirror.

Years passed, and the princes fell deeply in love with her inner beauty and developed an unbreakable bond of trust and friendship. The princes channeled their energies into the labor of keeping the pantry stocked and cabin repaired. Whenever they left to gather supplies, the princes warned Black Rose to be careful not to leave the cabin lest Syrael catch a glimpse of her in the magic mirror.

20

TRISTAN

Divine light fills the room as my brother Troy's ghost takes form for several seconds. Cass and I exchange a look, confirming we know what needs to be done. Magic released in the Earthly realm drains the essence, called grace, that fuels angels. Although angelic mating brands, a sign of the mating bond, enhance an angel's powers, *forming* the brand uses all of their reserves. Troy and Aleah need to recharge before the remaining fragments of their essence fade into the Void. Once there, it will be almost impossible to gather enough fragments of their grace to pull them back.

As Troy's body slumps forward, Cass uses divine light to grab his vanishing essence and dashes from the room. I look down at Aleah's sleeping form locked in their dream. Her unseeing eyes remain wide for several seconds as if looking at a vision disappearing over the horizon. The divine light disappears, snatched out of the air as the dome of protection I conjured suppresses the force of the mating bond magic. Her eyes close. She curls into a ball and starts shivering uncontrollably. Post-magic hypothermia. I've only seen this once before when the potency of a destined mating bond drained the magic from the mates before their combined energy could replace it. It had taken several sessions of intense lovemaking to restore their powers from . . . That's not an option in this case. The triggering of Troy's mating bond and the pain building in my left delt that signals that my own mating brand may be forming are all the confirmation I need that Aleah is our destined mate. I will not lose her to the Void.

Without hesitation, I strip off my clothes and crawl into bed beside Aleah, pulling the large comforter over us. Consequences be damned. I have to keep Aleah from passing into the Mourning Fields. I'll deal with the fallout later.

Aleah moans as her body quakes. The shivers have such an intense grip on her that I'm afraid her teeth will shatter from the force of them. I touch her clammy arm, using my senses to read her temperature. Ninety-one degrees. Shit. I need to warm her core temperature and stop the shivering. She's slipping deeper into unconsciousness. Covering as much of her skin as possible, I pull her against my chest and wrap my limbs around her. Focusing every bit of my attention on infusing healing ether into each exhale, I cover her with healing breath until I reach the point of hyperventilating. I keep going, plowing through the pain that builds as my reserves grow low. And pray to the gods for strength.

After what seems like an eternity, Aleah's intense shivering stops, and her core temperature rises a degree. She's not out of the woods yet, but I can take a moment. I pull her tighter against me and fight the building fatigue. I must drift off because the next thing I feel is a warm mouth wrapped around my cock.

Aleah's lips, tongue, and mouth pull me toward rapture. Her mouth envelops my shaft and holds it there as if savoring my taste. She trails a small hand up over my stomach, now tight with desire, and moves toward my chest. After several moments of nuzzling, sucking, licking, and grazing, I lose myself in the joy of receiving pleasure. I look down, startled to see the color of her eyes, like dark storm clouds, gazing at me. I grab the sides of her head and hold on gently. She circles the base of my pulsing cock. It leaps to life as she draws me deeper into her mouth, as if she's trying to burn me alive with her passion or die trying.

Ever so slowly, Aleah glides her lips over my shaft. My balls draw up, tight and firm, when she cups them in her hand. She sighs with pleasure as if she's in heaven, exploring and exploiting my pleasure. My low moan spurs her on to take me even deeper into her throat. She works my penis so hard her cheeks must ache. My moan turns into a groan.

She adds her fingers to the equation and circles them around the base of my cock. My back arches and hips thrust forward with a life of their own. *Yes!* Pressure like I've never felt before builds at the base of my shaft in my balls, signaling the most intense orgasm of my existence. I cling to it, all thought of healing magic aside. This orgasm will be hers. I belong to her. The stinging sensation in my left shoulder sings a response, further evidence that my suspicions are true.

Aleah slows the pace and uses her teeth to trace up and down my slick pole. Slow. Steady. Inch by inch. Up and down. She alternates teeth, tongue, and mouth, licking and flicking, making me her ice cream cone. I can't hold still. She keeps the rhythm steady, like a metronome. When my writhing spirals out of control, she stops. Then she starts again, her warm mouth balm for my roiling torment. Slow and easy as if she's getting ready to milk me for every last drop.

I brace my arms against the mattress, arch up, and start to thrust, almost dislodging her. She tightens the grip with her mouth and hand, matching my pace. A few hard thrusts, and

I break. My load shoots down her throat. She holds me captive with her mouth, savoring each pulse of my cock, drinking in the most potent healing essence in the universe. I lie panting as my slowly retreating erection slips past her lips.

Reaching down, I pull her into my arms, planting a gentle kiss on top of her head.

"I missed you so much." She wraps her warm hand around my soft cock and gives it a gentle squeeze. I almost burst into tears despite the depth of her emotion actually being for Troy. It's such an incredibly simple sign of affection the likes of which I've never had before. And one I want to feel again—but meant for me.

I ponder my dilemma. Aleah needed my essence to heal, but she'd thought I was Troy. Should I have stopped her? Will she forgive me for doing what had to be done? Will Troy?

Sustained by the power of my ether, Aleah slips into sleep, her warm breath tickling the hairs on my chest. I decide not to think about the future as I let slumber overtake me.

"How's she doing?" Cassiel, my oldest brother by mere minutes, sits on the other side of the bed. Aleah sleeps peacefully between us.

"Okay now, but it's been a rough night. She had a series of nightmares, and each one made her weaker. It was everything I could do to replace enough essence to keep her conscious. Thankfully, fucking Troy topped up her tank, or I wouldn't have been able to hold her here." I conveniently leave out the part about Aleah mistaking me for my brother and giving me the best blow job of my life. The look Cass gives me tells me he knows what happened, but he'll let it go for now. Just as well because I can live without another sermon on our calling as sex angels. Also, Troy will take me apart when he finds out I let Aleah suck me off. There's also the whole issue of consent to consider . . . Did I just tear the fabric of time by not stopping her? There'd be huge consequences to pay with the Tribunal if I'd done that.

"Time for a break, Tristan. You've done all that you can for now. I'll keep a close eye on her." Cass crosses his arms over his chest and gives me his no-argument stare.

I sigh inwardly. He's right, but I don't want the moment to end. We'd know if I'd changed the time line soon enough, and this may be the only time I get to hold Aleah like this. I return my gaze to the goddess sleeping peacefully on the plush canopy bed and reach down to brush a few curls off her face.

"Syrael's close by. I'd better check the dome for damage after last night's magic." I take in a deep breath but don't move, reluctant to separate from Aleah's body heat, but we can't ignore the threat of Syrael's magic mirror.

"How do you know he's close?" Cass asks.

"I'm telling you, I felt the mirror's eye." The certainty in my tone leaves no room for doubt. Just like Cass can feel Aleah's heartbeat, I can sense the presence of dark sex magic. While sex angel lords are the most powerful of all archangels, we each also have a special gift, and sensing dark sex magic is mine.

"Fuck. We'd better move. How long before he finds us?" Cass runs a hand through his dark hair as worry creases his brow.

"Let me see how much time we have." Regretfully, I wiggle out from under Aleah's sleeping form and get dressed, but my burning shoulder lets me know for sure this emotional bond with Aleah is more significant than we all think.

ALEAH

I snuggle into the warmth of the bed as I slowly wake, trying to hang onto the postcoital sensations running through my body. Heat hums between my legs as I enjoy the feeling of there being nothing else in my world except for Troy and the sensations he pulls from me. The trembling I've always called *quivers* hits as a series of images from my dream flash through my mind. Snuggling even deeper and squeezing my eyes shut, I try to block out the return of reality. It's been so very long since I've trembled—two and a half years since Troy had been healthy enough for a real romp.

Something heavy lands on the mattress beside me, causing a massive adrenaline rush that kills the quiver rush. I scream and startle in the bed. I've never had a problem with feeling disoriented when I wake, and this morning is no exception. My synapses fire as I take in my surroundings, looking for the danger that ignited the adrenaline . . . and find a tall, dark, and very handsome man. He's giving me what can only be described as a sardonic smile and holding out my glasses.

"Looking for these?" He holds my glasses by the frames,

being careful not to touch the lenses. That gives him another check on the thoughtful tally I didn't know I was keeping till that moment. I slide the glasses in place and plaster a smile on my face while I will my heart rate to return to normal.

"Thank you. You startled me."

"I can see that. Why such an extreme reaction?" He crosses one long leg over the other, obviously settling in right here on my bed. I stop myself from shifting over to give him room.

"Why what?" I snap. The raw animal tension coming from this man makes me unsettled.

"Why were you so startled?" Cass's expression makes it clear he's not going to leave the subject alone until he's satisfied.

"I had a rough childhood. I instantly go into fight or flight mode. It's just a knee-jerk reaction. It hasn't happened for a long time." I give him my best persuasive smile. The look he gives me is so penetrating it makes my skin itch.

"What happened? Where's Troy?" I hope to change the subject and get some answers so I can figure all of this out. But now I know one thing for sure; life with Troy isn't done. He's with me . . . forever. It's as if there is a direct connection from my tattoo, the symbol of our love, straight to my heart, making him part of my DNA. That thought shatters the ice that's held me in suspended animation for the last six months. My Troy is with me—that's the most important thing. Now all I need to do is figure out how to reunite us permanently. The mention of Bardo planted the seed that I need to flush out a plan. Problem is, I haven't had one damned minute alone to think.

"He's with Tristan recharging his store of grace. You two drained his reserves when you activated the angel mating brand last night. Seems you two are destined mates."

"What does that mean?" My heart does a little hippity-hop, but I'm too analytical to take this at face value.

"You and Troy have the kind of deep, unconditional love that can't be broken. Because of our job, sex angel lords can only mate with someone who is pure of heart and uses sex as a way to show that love. It seems you're that person for Troy." Cass's voice sounds wistful, but maybe I'm reading too much into it. I don't want to face the dislike I sense from him, so I'm making excuses. What matters is that all my feelings about my love with Troy are real. I've always believed Troy and I have the kind of bond that no man or god can put asunder.

I give a mental fist pump. Although I have no idea what the ramifications are of this brand thing, I know our love. Thank gods I never lost faith. I knew our love would endure beyond the grave. I ignore the silly little voice in the back of my head reminding me that I almost had. *All that matters is the now, not the what-may-have-been.* My personal Yoda's voice rings in my head. "Does that mean we've brought him back to life?"

"I'm afraid not. All we know for sure is that it means the tapestry of fate has determined you two belong together for all eternity. Atroyel remains in some nebulous territory between life on Earth and his natural state as an angel. We need to figure out why that is." Cass looks at me, making it clear his first and only priority is Troy.

"We will." I start to wiggle to the edge of the bed without exposing any of my bits. The nightshirt I'm wearing feels a little on the short side.

"I need a shower." I manage to pull the hem of the shirt over my big, round ass as I slip out of bed. I feel his eyes on my sweet asset as I hustle to the washroom. "I'll meet you in the kitchen in fifteen." I lock the door and take a deep breath before heading to the mirror.

The woman staring back at me surprises me. The dark

circles are gone. A sparkle replaces the dull sheen that's clouded my large brown eyes for so long. I found my Troy. Or he found me. Who the fuck cares? For the first time in months, I *feel* something. I pull the mass of messy curls from my face and examine my smooth skin. Skin Troy loves. Skin I need to clean while I figure out what I need to do to be with Troy again.

I've always believed in Bardo and reincarnation. They're the only things that make sense in this crazy journey called life. Having my belief confirmed only makes me more certain that all I need to do is die to be reunited with Troy. These guys aren't telling me everything, but one thing they've made clear is that this Syrael guy wants my ass for some unknown reason. All I need to do is find him and let him kill me and *bam!* I'm reunited with Troy in Bardo. Whoever makes up the review board will see our mating brands, and we'll ascend to the happy kink playground of my dreams.

I take a quick shower and pad into the magnificent dressing room I've barely noticed, suddenly interested in my surroundings. One of the only things Troy had been willing to spend money on was me. Otherwise, he was one of the world's most frugal men. Just about anything Troy had owned that cost more than one hundred dollars I'd bought.

The neatly laid out dressing room displays all of my favorite clothes arranged by color and type. Troy would never have gone to that level of detail, although he clearly had a hand in making the choices. I slip into one of my signature black T-shirts, and then put on a pair of jeans and an embroidered hoodie. Socks and black Sketchers complete the outfit before I head to the kitchen to pick Cass's brain. No amount of self-talk about not getting my hopes up will dash the joy singing through my heart. I don't know how to explain it, but I can feel Troy sitting right next to my heart. Nothing else matters.

22

ATROYEL

I come to with the sense that something monumental has happened, although I can't quite remember what. Whatever it is, I'm certain it has something to do with my wonder woman. Gods, how I love Aleah.

I'm lying beside Tristan underneath a pile of bedding. He's staring up at the ceiling with his hands folded behind his head. Waves of his internal conflict wash through me as he works through whatever's bothering him. I assemble my incorporeal form in a similar position and wait. Tristan, like Aleah, can't hold in anything that's bothering him for long, so all I have to do is wait. I can use the time to take stock. I wish I could remember more.

I look down at my left shoulder and rub the warm burn. A black rose tattoo that looks exactly like the tattoo Lea got to celebrate our tenth wedding anniversary. I'm not sure what its relevance is, but I know from the soft red glow surrounding it that it's something significant.

I realize I'm at peace. I feel whole for perhaps the first time in my life. It has everything to do with Aleah being part of me. She's part of me, and it's as if there's a chain pulling me toward her. If Cass's babbling about prophecies is accurate, making love to her last night activated our angel mating bond. I want to be with her right now. The pull is urgent, insistent. I can't ignore it. Together, we'll figure out how the magic works to bring me back to my form so we can be together. So I can hold her and tell her all the things I should have told her before. I tamp down my impatience and wait for Tristan's confession. In addition to anchoring my spirit form to Earth, my brothers are connected to my bond with Aleah. And our Double Diaries have something to do with activating the magic. I remember that much, so why can't I remember how the magic works?

"You can't do this on your own, you know." Tristan's soft tenor voice pulls me from my frustration. I keep my mouth shut, knowing more is coming.

I control my impatience by dwelling on just how good it felt to be inside Lea last night. How good it is to feel her. I curse inwardly at my inability to remember how the magic of the Double Diaries works. Why can't I remember how I infused the magic? The guys and gods tried to convince me all will come clear when I go through the Bardo processing, but that process will take me away from Aleah and give Syrael time to find her.

"Aleah gave me a blow job last night." Tristan decides on the direct approach. "I think she mistook me for you and kind of just went for it."

And I bet you fought her off real hard. I push my instinctive jealousy away. Tristan would never do anything to hurt me. Neither brother would. Our bond is virtually indestructible. I might not remember much, but some things were embedded in the fabric of my soul. Besides, something else must be bothering him because he knows I would be able to sense his sexual activity.

"I'll look past it because she needed your healing ether.

Why don't you tell me what's really bothering you?" I prod Tristan the way Lea prods me when I'm reluctant to reveal my feelings.

He slowly brings his arms from behind his head and pushes up his T-shirt sleeve, exposing his left shoulder. "Have a look."

It takes a few seconds before the faint etchings of a black rose appear for a few seconds. No doubt, Tristan feels my heart jump the second I recognize the tattoo. "What the fuck? This angel mating bond stuff is supposed to be between Aleah and me. No one mentioned you being part of the bond." And if Tristan's involved, what about Cass? The three of us are linked through heritage and divine providence. It makes sense that if Tristan's involved in the mating bond, then so is Cass, and I'm not sure how I feel about sharing her.

I get out of bed. "We'd better go find the other two and see if we can figure out just what the hell is going on," I say.

Tristan looks relieved. "You aren't pissed about the blow job?"

I sigh and study him for a minute. "Honestly, Tris, I'm not sure how I feel. Mostly, I'm just so damned happy to be reunited with you two and my Lea; not much else matters. We need to focus on keeping her safe from Syrael. I'm not sure how I know it, but he's getting close, and right now, we have no idea who he is or how to save her. And if I know my Lea, despite the little she's been told, she's working on a plan." I turn and follow the invisible chain binding me to my beloved.

"Do you think we should tell her about my tattoo?" Tristan matches my gait as we head toward the smell of freshly baked bread coming from the kitchen.

"Let's hold off on that for a bit." I have no idea why, but for some reason, I'd rather keep Lea to myself for now, even if it's only in her mind. And even if it's only for a short time.

Besides, she'll want to focus all of her attention on helping us get out of this mess.

"My first priority is figuring out how to be with Troy again." My Lea's voice rings with determination and insistence as I enter the kitchen.

"Our priority has to be keeping you safe." Cass uses his no-room-for-argument voice, and I brace for the barrage I know is about to follow.

"I must have missed that memo. And one can have more than one priority, you know. Besides, you guys told me I'm perfectly safe as long as I'm here on this island. That was the argument, correct? Or was that some ruse? I don't even know why I'm asking. Troy would never lie to me like that. It breaks our vows. So, I'm perfectly safe, and we need to figure out how to bring Troy back. He'll know how to fix this." Aleah's tone holds a finality she expects will end the conversation. I know my woman. Cass has met his match when he goes up against her determination.

"Tell her I'm no Prince Charming about to ride in and save the day. Tell her we need her help coming up with a plan," I say.

"And you tell Troy—" Aleah's eyes widen at the same time as ours . . . She heard me.

Aleah raises her hand and pats the air beside her. "Troy? Is that you? Say something. Anything."

I walk over and stand in front of her upraised hand, letting it pass through the mist forming my "body." Gods, how I want to hold her again. "Look, babe. I want nothing more than to be with you again, but Cass is right. The sex lord demon has his sights on you, and we need to keep you safe from Syrael's magic, for starters."

"I can hear you." Her tone is almost reverent. She looks through me as she turns this over in her mind, then she pats the stool beside her. "Okay. Sit. You're right. Two heads are better than one, or in this case, four. You know I have a ton of questions, but I'll try not to take us down too many rabbit holes. Let's start at the beginning. Why would this Syrael demon lord guy want to kill me? And how do we find him?"

I'm just about to spill when Cass gives me a hard look. We'd agreed that the best way to keep Aleah safe from Syrael until we figure out how to protect her is to keep her in the dark about her true nature. To defeat Syrael, Cass says we need to combine our power with hers. To do that, Aleah has to discover her powers. Cass and the two goddesses had babbled something about an ancient prophecy. Apparently, Aleah is the last of an ancient race called the Nephilim, and this Syrael wants to destroy her power.

According to this prophecy and unbeknownst to me, I'd been put on Earth to shield Aleah from the seeing eye of Syrael's mirror. Blocking each pass of his magic power reduced mine and took a toll on my human vessel, slowly breaking it down. The weaker I became, the stronger the pull of the eye.

They'd told me a story called "Black Rose and the Three Princes" that sounded like a fairy tale. The whole thing sounds crazy, but I don't care. Aleah's life is in danger. That much I can feel deep in my core. Like her, I believe in focusing on the problem at hand and worrying about the rest later. At least that's the theory.

That leaves me with a huge problem. How do I convince Aleah to work with us without alerting her to her true nature? Then it hits me. I know what to do to distract her.

23

ATROYEL

I realize how I might have infused the magic they say I possess into the words of this diary. Whatever my powers, I would have used the words to ask her to reveal her hidden truths. I'd only just begun to unravel the mystery of Aleah's sexuality when the fading sickness had hit. That had been a singular mission for me. Maybe that has something to do with all this sex lord stuff.

"Do my powers have anything to do with the written word?" It's not as if I have any idea what these powers are that my brothers seem so certain I have.

Cass looks at me as if I'm unhinged. "Letter Power Bestowal is your superior power. Why the hell else do you think we're fixated on these diaries of yours?"

"That piece of information would have been good to know," I snap. "What the hell does that mean, anyway?" Clearly, big brother and I have a few issues.

"It means you're able to bestow powers to yourself or others through letters or words," Cass says. I have the strong sense that he knows something more, something that has to do with Aleah, but I let it go. If my theory's correct, I can help find the solution instead of being a useless piece of shit.

"What other powers do I have?"

Tristan damn near levitates off his stool. "Oh, you have all kinds of powers, bro, we all do. And now that we're sex angel lords, we have even more. We haven't even had time to explore all of our powers, but your superior power has always been Letter Power Bestowal. Even humans have a superior power. Most of them don't explore their potential, that's all."

"Pretty boy is correct. Chief Justice Tate said your powers would be restored once you're corporeal again. One more reason we should get back to the business at hand," Cass says.

Despite all Aleah's assurances that I'd made the best contribution to humanity possible—being her rock and loving her unconditionally, truth be told, I'd done little more than I had to. I had little interest in most of the trivialities that other humans pursue. I had few interests, and Aleah topped the list. I'd never been great with expressing my emotions in words—that's something we had in common. But we'd found a way to break through the barriers of my reserve and her abuse and spoken our love through our bodies. And now I find out I have powers.

It boggles the mind, but Cass is right, we need to focus on the business at hand . . . I need to be in the only place I'm completely myself—buried balls deep in my Lea's embracing cunt. Sharing our memories as we explore our sexuality is the next best place. Ignoring my brothers' telepathic messages, I flip through my memories for one of Aleah's favorite fantasies.

"Beauty, find the fantasy about the prison. I think it's near the beginning." I focus on Lea's gorgeous face. "I have an idea, and I want to test it out. Pretend we're getting ready for date night, and this is foreplay. Tristan's going to bring you a glass of wine. Lay your head back and listen. That's all I ask."

She looks a little perplexed, but she trusts me, and her curiosity will win out. She bends her head and leafs through the diary.

What the fuck, Troy? from Tristan.

We agreed to look before we leap, Atroyel.

Aleah opens the journal and places it on her lap. I wait until she takes a sip of wine and puts her head back as instructed. I send a silent prayer to the universe to give us some sort of sign, then I start to read.

Aleah on Saturday, September 1 @ 8:35 a.m.

In my prison fantasies, I'm often taken to the warden's office to pleasure and "feed" him. I never touch him. I'm always a passive participant, so I convince myself I'm not giving myself willingly. He always has me strip. Sometimes he has me lie on his desk and sucks me when he needs to "eat." Sometimes he then fucks me with a phallus. Sometimes he has me kneel on the desk and probes my ass. So you can see why the prison scene turned me on.

In a different version, he gives me to the guards because I've been bad or need training. The guards come into the isolation cell I'm in, one by one. They sit around me as I lie on a high bed that converts to different positions. They take turns while the others watch. The feel of their eyes on me excites me. I know what I said about one person at a time, so this is hard to admit.

As hard as it is, I love that you asked me to write my fantasies. I'm hopeful that we'll act out some of them, at least to some degree (you can skip the riding crop). When it comes to the BDSM-type fantasies, I have some trepidation as I've said, but I want to—no, I need to explore them. It's time to stop hiding from the things I've been secretly thinking about for years.

I'll carry this fantasy with me all day. I'm smiling and thinking wet thoughts. God, you excite me. Intimately yours forever. — Lea

I raise my head as warmth replaces the nothingness that goes along with this misty form. A soft blue-white mist surrounds Lea. There it is, the sign. Even a skeptical bastard like me can't dispute the reality right in front of us. Aleah glows with soft sexual power.

"Open your eyes, beauty."

She obliges, and a soft light matching her grace shines back at me. She reaches for me. I reach back, expecting my mist to pass right though her. Instead, the moment our skin connects, I solidify. Intense brown eyes, alive with life, gaze back at me. I squeeze her arm.

"Good, this time I see some life in those eyes. So, what's the plan?" I ask.

"Holy shit," Tristan breathes.

ALEAH

Un-frigging believable. Troy solidifies the instant I touch him. One minute, he's mist, and the next, he's sitting right beside me, asking me if I have a plan. I press my fingers into his forearms to make sure he's real. It's him. In the flesh!

I open my mouth but all I exhale are shock and excitement. I can't talk, I can't breathe. Despite praying for it every second of every day, I never thought I'd hold my Troy again. And now he's here. I shake his shoulders . . . hard. I hug him and kiss him.

Troy cups my cheeks, and his kiss tells me more than any words can how much he misses me. He chuckles. "I'm happy to see you too, beauty." He gives me another quick kiss then looks at his brothers. "Gods, I'm good. I knew it." He starts to get up, no doubt to start his usual strutting when he's working out a problem. I let go. He disappears. Shit.

"What just happened?" I wave my hands around in the air, trying to connect with him.

"That's what we're here to find out," Cass says, using that dry tone that makes me want to slap his face. He seems to have taken a dislike to me. It's coming off him in waves. Lord knows I've run into this reaction from folks often enough to recognize it. My strong personality isn't everyone's cup of tea. Part of me accepts this, but a huge part of me doesn't want to think about Cass rejecting me.

I can almost feel Troy slide his arms around me. He pops back into view. "About that plan, beauty . . . Have you figured out how this all works?"

I play with my upper lip while I take a minute to roll an idea around in my head and make sure I've figured out all the angles before Troy has a chance to dissect it. We both have a way of zeroing in on the flaws in any given plan. I don't always appreciate the trait in him.

I squeeze his biceps as I prepare my pitch. "I'm working on one, babe. I haven't had time to iron out all the details, but from what I can see, all we need to do is find this Syrael guy. I'll cast myself in front of him so he can zap me—or whatever he does. Then, I'll ascend into Bardo, where we can explore our sex life in private and avoid all this other stuff. And you guys can use your magic to help make that happen." I sit back, confident they'll see that this is the best and most efficient plan. We skip all the pain and torture stuff and head right on into the afterlife to live happily ever after. The angel of death had told me my death wasn't the demon's choice, but he hadn't said a thing about *me* deciding it's my time. This can work.

I'm not prepared in the least for what hits me.

"Are you out of your fucking mind?" Cass's words are so sharp that they slice through me like shards of glass. "That's why you aren't afraid of Syrael? Somewhere in the back of that devious little mind of yours, you think that if Syrael kills you, you'll be reunited with Troy in Bardo. Voluntarily offering yourself as a sacrifice before your time is suicide. Do that, and you sever your bond with Troy." Disgust rolls off him in waves as he heads out of the room.

Troy lets go of me and instantly vanishes. "I can't believe you of all people would take the coward's way out." Troy's anger and disappointment are evident in the tone of his voice, making my stomach turn. He's pissed in a way I've only seen once or twice before and had hoped never to see again. The warm hum I get when Troy's near fades and vanishes. *sigh* We'll have to talk later about suicide as a complex issue unfairly conflated with cowardice, but now is not the time. Fuck. Fuck. Fuck.

Nothing remains but Tristan's sadness.

All this emotion almost brings me to my knees. "Troy's gone, isn't he?"

Tristan nods. That's all it takes to break me, to remind me, ultimately, I'm on my own. Terror bolts through me, and the dam breaks. Sobs erupt with the strength of convulsions. It doesn't help that the sadness I feel coming from Tristan grows stronger; that just adds to the pain.

I tuck my knees under my chin and wrap my arms around my legs, trying to control the muscle spasms, but I can't stop them.

"You need a hug?" Tristan doesn't move or presume, and I can't speak, but my mind offers up a resounding yes. He wraps an arm around my shoulder and pulls me to him. The warmth of his arms is balm to my pain.

"I'm fucked. I'm forty years old. That's too young to be a nun." I snort and gasp around the words. One of my strengths is the ability to think and talk through hysteria, but it's not a pretty sight. I blow my nose, trying to get myself under control, but that train has left the station.

"I was just finding my own sexuality, and Troy got sick. Do you know what it's like to watch your soul mate in pain? Watch him drift away from the man he was and the love he gave?" Another deep sob rocks me. I try to blow my nose between grabbing gasps of air.

"Sounds like you had a perfect life," Tristan says. His warm, thoughtful voice soothes me, and his full lips curve up at the sides. I'd swear he's envious, but I'm too caught up in my personal hell to dwell on it.

"Nothing in life is perfect, but it was perfect for us. Troy was, *is*, the only one who gets me. He doesn't just love me; he *likes* me. He accepts me for who I am."

Arms banded with muscle hold me tight. Tristan gives me a little squeeze, silently inviting me to continue talking.

"It's not just about the sex. It's about having someone to talk to who gets what I'm about. Troy used to be my sounding board. Gods, the brainstorming discussions we had. People who overheard us mistook our intensity for an argument, but it wasn't that at all. I knew he had my back. My pieces were always better for his input. Then he got sick and lost interest." I blow my nose again and realize I sound critical of Troy. I rush on.

"Not that I blame him. That's part of being ill. It's to be expected. But it left me without my best friend."

"You can always run things by me," Tristan offers helpfully.

I blow my nose again as my sobs turn into silent tears streaming down my face. I snuggle a bit deeper into Tristan's arms. I probably shouldn't, but it's been so long since I had human contact, and it just feels too good. I sigh. Why is life so complicated?

"What about your friends? Troy said you have a strong support network."

"Everyone has a fucking opinion about how I should deal with my loss—most won't or can't use the D-word."

Tristan shifts to a more comfortable spot and tucks me against him, so my ear rests over his heart. "The D-word?" he asks.

"Death. I get it. Everyone's dealing with so much shit in

this pandemic. Normally, my friends rely on me to cheer *them* up." I take another deep breath. "The depth of my grief reminds them that we're all just one step away from catastrophe. Who wants to have that concept staring you in the face?"

"Who, indeed," Tristan says. He's not sarcastic, just letting me know he's listening.

"Everything was fine. I was coping with Troy being gone."

Something rumbles in Tristan's chest, putting my insecurity on immediate alert. "Are you laughing at me?"

"Not at all. I'm simply eager to hear your definition of coping. But that can wait. You were coping . . ." Tristan gives me another squeeze.

"I was coping, and then this new assignment happened, and you three dropped into my lap. This morning, I was so happy. I should have known it was all going to go to hell." I give my nose a final wipe and wiggle out of his arms. "I have no fucking idea why I'm telling you all of this. I'm sorry. I'll shut up now."

"You just need to tap into your power," Tristan says. "Is it the idea of magic you have trouble with?"

"Not at all. It's a relief to know magic truly exists, not that I ever doubted it. Ironically, Troy used to roll his eyes about my search for a true psychic experience. I've seen a ton of psychics. A couple of them seemed more legit than others and told me I had powers, all I had to do is learn to access them. I've tried to use them a ton of times, and nothing happens. I wish I did have power within me." Yes, indeed, I'm feeling sorry for myself. A strange feeling comes over me as an old memory surfaces. "I can't even summon the vampire Lestat. Look, I'll show you."

I jump to my feet and throw open the patio door and step out into the cool evening. Opening my arms wide to the heavens, I yell, "Come to me, Lestat! Come to me!"

Tristan yanks on the hem of my sweatshirt. "No, Aleah, no—"

But he's too late, and my eyes spring wide open as another of the universe's gorgeous men drops down in front of me.

"You bellowed, *ma chère?* Those words come from the most beautiful man I've ever seen in my life. Something in the dark depths of his eyes pulls me to him, making me want to take the hand that reaches for me. My right hand automatically lifts toward his. The instant we touch, something dark seeps into me. Somewhere in the distance, a voice roars, and white light blinds me. Nausea hits as pain screams through me, dropping me to my knees.

Some force jerks my head up as the clouds part revealing a rippling mirror with an eye like the Tolkien villain Sauron's sitting in the middle of it . . . looking directly at me.

"Soon, Black Rose. You cannot hide. I will find you." The eye's voice spews its evil in my mind before more bright light blasts around me.

I'd had an intimate acquaintance with terror for too long in my youth not to recognize it. I'm in danger. I can feel it in every neuron of my body. Something is pulling me toward an evil dressed in deceptive fancy clothes, but my mind sees past the facade. I. Will. Not. Let. Him. Have. Me.

ALEAH

Next thing I know, I'm lying flat on my back on a long sofa. I open my eyes and then slam them shut. Everything's hazy . . . And the pain is getting worse. Years of suffering from chronic illness have made me hyper attuned to the inner workings of my body. I'd had an episode of paralysis earlier this year that landed my ass in the hospital in critical condition. If this was another endocrine breakdown, I have very little time to tell these guys what they need to know.

Something is very wrong with me.

Just like the last time, my mind is crystal clear. The weird tingling numbness is worse than last time, as if someone has added several hundred volts of heat to the tingling. There's so much going on in my body that I can't tell whether Troy is near. And that scares me.

I need to make sure they know what to tell the hospital so they don't misdiagnose me again. I open my eyes and look into Tristan's worried ones. I clutch his hand nervously, thanking the universe that I'm not alone this time. But we're on a fucking island, and I have no idea where the nearest hospital is.

"Please listen to me because I don't have much time. Get me to a hospital and tell them I suffer from hypoparathyroidism. Tell them it's critical they test my calcium, potassium, and magnesium levels along with my parathyroid hormone." I fire off the list, praying I don't forget something. The hot pain in my lady parts is getting almost unbearable, and I'm losing my battle with the terror. *Keep it together, Aleah. You can do this.*

"Fuck. There's something in my head, some kind of eye trying to see my thoughts. No, don't tell them that—they'll think I'm a psych case. Tell them I have horrible pain in my breasts, armpits, and crotch. Get my meds—"

A warm, comforting heat starts at my toes and inches its way up my legs, pushing away the overwhelming terror.

Submit. This is what you were made for. These dark thoughts echo in my mind. But they're not mine. Something about these words resurrects flashes of memory from my past—memories associated with pain—but a wave of sexual desire drives the dark thoughts away.

"What is happening to me?" I whisper, fighting the feeling that I'm sinking in quicksand.

Tristan drops my hand, and the pain bolts to an unbearable level. I moan and start to curl into the pain. Someone grabs my hand, and Troy's gorgeous face swims into view.

"I'm here, beauty. We'll take care of you." He squeezes my hand. "Have you called 911? How do we get her out of here?" Troy asks the guys. His voice, despite his obvious panic, gives me permission to let go. To go inside and figure out what the hell is going on in my body.

Cass's face replaces Troy's. He grips my face hard with both hands. "Listen to me." Cass's voice is hard. Urgent. I focus on his golden eyes. "You've been stung by an incubus. The only antidote is angel essence. From an angel with healing power. Otherwise, you'll be raped and savaged until your internal organs fail. It will be a long, slow, torturous death by sex." He enunciates each word, making sure I understand just how unpleasant this might be.

"I might like that," I smirk. There's just enough fight left in me to deliver a how-the-hell-do-you-know punch. "Troy's an angel. He'll heal me."

"Troy has no power right now, and you won't like eternal pain."

He's right. I'm not a pain junkie. But I do love sex, and right now, being fucked to death doesn't seem like such a bad way to go. Especially if it involves fucking my Troy and these two very gorgeous guys. I'm no dummy; angel essence is a euphemism for bodily fluids, and I bet my bottom dollar he's not referring to spit.

A whisper of something sounds in my head but can't get through the pain and desire raging through me.

"I trust you. Do what you need to do." My eyelids slide closed. I force them open. "And Troy?"

Cass stands, and Troy leans forward. "Yes, beauty?" The worry etching his beautiful face makes me fight a little harder.

"You're in charge. I love you and trust you implicitly." I force my eyes open, making sure he's going to be okay with this. I know my guy, know what he'll need when we wake on the other side of this episode. What I need to know—that we're doing this *Thelma & Louise* thing together. The clouds clear from his face. He cups my cheek. Love pours into me as soft light shines from his eyes into mine.

I need to make sure we're all on the same page. "Troy, there are easier ways to get me to say yes to you watching me fuck another guy." I squeeze his hand. With a wry smile, he squeezes back. I take my glasses off, hold them up, and someone takes them. "Hold on to your cocks, boys. You're in for a rocky ride." Closing my eyes, I sink into the vat of sexual pain yawning before me.

"We've got to get her out of here and inject essence into her. Now!" Cass barks out the order as darkness closes in.

Fucker. That's the last coherent thought I have.

ATROYEL

As we walk through the portal Tristan opens, I turn into mist again. Tristan places Aleah's writhing body on a large circular bed and turns to me.

"We'll be safe here for now," Tristan says. "There's enough magic to cover whatever's happening with Aleah."

"And just where is *here*, pray tell?" Cass asks as he paces around the room, taking inventory. Given the furnishings, I'm going to guess we're in a private room in a sex club.

"We're in an exclusive kink club called The Masquerade. It's one of the safe houses I set up when we were assigned to protect Aleah." Tristan turns to me. What now?"

What now, indeed. Aleah's moan pulls my attention to her writhing form. I rush over to the bed. Bluish-white mist rises from Aleah like heat radiating from asphalt. As the mist washes over me, I materialize.

Tristan gives me a quick look as we both realize that it's Aleah's grace making me corporeal. She lets out a horrible, deep gasping noise.

Cass looks at me. "Until you get your powers back, Tristan's and my divine essences are the only ones capable of healing her. I'm on protection duty. You two take care of her." With that announcement, Cass disappears.

"The incubus venom is taking over her mind. I don't know how much longer she can fight it," Tristan says.

Aleah lets out another moan and clutches her stomach. All that matters is helping her. That has to come first. She's right—we'll figure out the rest later.

"What's the best way to heal her?" I ask.

"Fellatio," Tristan says. I'm not sure if he uses the formal term out of deference to my feelings or because he's in healer mode, but it doesn't matter. Healing her does. I nod slowly.

"You'll have to prop her head up so I can reach it." Tristan strips out of his pants and shoes and starts massaging his cock. I crawl onto the bed and gather Aleah into my arms, pulling her into a semi-sitting position. She moans and starts thrashing, clawing the air, and throwing her arms wildly. I respond instinctively. If I don't restrain her, she'll hurt herself or Tristan. I wrap my arms around her chest, pinning her arms to her sides, and I cross my legs over hers, immobilizing her. She whips her head from side to side, but otherwise remains still. She's burning up.

The worried look in Tristan's eyes confirms my suspicion. We don't have much time.

"Ready?" Tristan asks. "Hold her tight. I'll brace her head so she doesn't castrate me. The dark magic will go to any extremes to stop me once my divine essence hits it."

I give him a curt nod and adjust my grip. He slides his index finger across the head of his cock, catching the drop of precum leaking from the tip. Placing his other hand across Aleah's forehead, he presses the back of her head against my chest. Then he slips the precum between her lips. Almost instantly, she moans, tips her head up, and opens her mouth. Like a baby bird searching for food. Tristan takes a deep breath and slips his cock into her mouth. She immediately closes her lips around him and starts sucking. Hard.

I keep my eyes pinned on my brother. This man who is at the same time a complete stranger yet someone I feel bound to deep in my soul. As if he, like Aleah, is part of what makes me whole. This man who's willing to put himself at risk to save my beloved, without question. I watch as pain contorts his perfect features and he howls in pain from the black magic fighting against his divine light.

Aleah makes gobbling noises as she takes Tristan deep in her throat. I watch in fascination and horror. Nothing about this should be remotely sensual. Aleah's in pain. It's a battle between good and evil. Yet, there's something about her passion that makes me want to see more. Aleah believes light and love always win. I pray she's right . . . there's so much more for us to explore.

Tristan touches his forehead to mine. His grace and the echo of his pain flow into me. Something in me answers, and I stream positive energy to him. *We can do this, brother.* Tristan stiffens. Aleah makes wet, sucking noises. With a roar, he reaches past the pain and releases his divine healing essence.

Panting, he collapses on the bed beside me. Aleah's body relaxes, and she climbs onto my lap. She pulls off her T-shirt, then shimmies her hands under my shirt and up my chest where she rakes her nails down my abdomen, hard enough to leave marks if I'd been mortal. I grab her hands by the wrists. Leaning forward, she licks her lips. Blue-white mist floats above her skin, looking just as ethereal as mist hovering over a meadow in the early spring dawn.

A strange glow and pure sexuality radiate from her eyes. For a moment, it's a stranger staring back at me. Then she whispers in my ear, her voice husky with lust. "You owe me a lot of orgasms, Troy, my love, and payback starts now. You're going to fuck me long and hard." She tries to struggle out of my grip, the friction of her crotch against mine making me go from rock to boulder hard. I can count on less than one hand the number of times Aleah's initiated sex. Being forward like this is not her thing . . . nor mine.

Tightening my grasp on her wrists, I look over at Tristan. "Is the venom still poisoning her? Didn't you heal her?"

He takes a deep breath and crosses his hands over his chest. "No, that was survival. I got rid of the black magic, or most of it, at least, but the venom is still in her system. Now, she'll need sex, and a lot of it, or she'll hurt herself trying to find release. The aphrodisiac the incubus combines with the poison will have to work its way out of her system. You're on your own for a bit, buddy. I need to catch my breath." He ejects his wings and wraps them around his body, making a cocoon that also serves to give us privacy.

Before I have time to take stock, Aleah wrenches her wrists out of my hands and bounds over to a spanking bench assembled in the perfect position for rear-entry fucking. The cloud of mist follows her, and I return to mist as she leaves me behind. She shucks off the rest of her clothes and sprawls that lithe body of hers face-forward on the bench. Knees spread, ass in the air, her love juices trickling down her thighs.

My cock is hard as granite, but I'm patient. Our joining last night has reduced the urgency. Now, I have time to enjoy her. Reclaim her. I move around the spanking bench, restraining her ankles and wrists with silk-lined leather cuffs. The height is perfect for my access. She moans as my hand brushes various parts of her heated skin. Something else I've missed, my Lea's beautiful, soft, smooth skin. She moans and wriggles, impatient for my cock to fill her.

Watching her beg and moan as desire overwhelms her reminds me of how very much I love watching this woman become lost in her sexuality. It had taken a long time, but when she'd learned to let go, to lose herself in her need, it was the most beautiful thing I'd ever seen—my eighth wonder of the world.

I pull my heated thoughts back to the present. First things first. Despite the circumstances, I insist on giving Aleah every assurance so she can free her mind and focus on what's happening inside her body. I pad to the head of the bench and crouch in front of her.

"What's your safe word, beauty?" I push a handful of curls off her face so I can read her eyes.

"Don't need a safe word." She's so excited, she clips her words.

"No safe word, no sex." I leave no room for argument.

"Red." Resting her cheek on the headrest, she closes her eyes.

Soon the scent of her exotic heat overwhelms me, and I walk back around the bench. I step between her legs and push the full length of my engorged cock into her. I stop, sliding the flat of my hand over the warm brown skin of her flawless back, savoring the moment for as long as I can. I slowly slide my cock out of her until I reach the entrance of her glistening cunt.

As her hips thrust up in a desperate attempt to hold me, I slide back into her. Each time I penetrate her, I plunge harder and faster, and my Lea moans louder and longer. I groan with the effort of holding back my orgasm. Soon, her body starts to tremble. Her head rocks from side to side, and in a desperate voice, she begs, "Please, please, now, please now, please, please!"

I don't have to be told what *please* means. When Aleah's at the pinnacle of her desire, *please* translates to *fuck me harder*. I thrust into her almost violently. Aleah goes rigid and explodes in violent spasms, screaming expletives. Watching her in the throes of her climax is pure ecstasy, and I prolong the moment for as long as I can before finally coming undone. Blue-white mist mixes with white light as I moan, and grunt, and bellow my release.

We remain tangled, enjoying the moment. I stay inside her long after our breathing returns to normal. When she starts to rustle in impatience, I whisper in her ear, "I'll never get enough of you."

"More." Aleah whimpers into the leather-covered headrest.

I hang my head, sheer exertion making it hard to stand. The same fatigue that overtook me last night pulls at me.

"Your magic is coming back, but at a price. Your tank needs refilling. Since we can't afford to have Aleah give you any of her grace right now, you'll need to rest." Tristan walks up behind me. I'd almost forgotten he was here. "Let me know if you need a hand."

I give him a sharp look; now is not the time for double entendres, but the look he returns is guileless. All I can sense coming from him is concern and care. And I do need time to catch a second wind. My Lea always had sexual stamina, but now she's got it in spades.

"I trust you." Which is saying a lot because I've never trusted a man's motives when it comes to my Aleah. It took me years to undo the damage done by my gender. Tristan and I lock gazes, and something in his expression assures me.

I walk to the head of the bench and crouch, hoping like hell I'll be able to get back up. I'm that tired. Aleah looks at me with those expressive eyes of hers. She's not in any distress, just watchful.

"Where are we, beauty?"

"Green light." Her voice is still rough with sex, and her libido is waging a war with her morality. She's in pain, but she still gives me a weak smile. "I'm tired, but I need more, Troy. It just won't stop," she whispers.

"I need to take a break, but Tristan's here to take care of you. Are you okay with that?"

She nods and licks her lips. She wiggles the fingers of her left hand. I link mine with hers, and something sure and steady passes between us, something significant, but I'm too fucking tired to think about it at the moment. I bow my forehead to her hand, then slowly rise to my feet. The pain in my back is almost unbearable. I start to undo her restraints.

"I'm okay like this. Tristan will take care of me."

Just as she always has, my Lea hangs onto her strength long enough to make sure I'm okay. I let my hand rest on her silky curls before stepping over to the other side of the room where Tristan sits. Bless him for giving us some sense of privacy. I change places with him, groaning against the pain as I lower into the chair. A throbbing pain on both sides of my back joins the burning in my left shoulder. I just need to rest until it subsides.

"She needs the intensity of clitoral orgasms. Fingering only," I say firmly as I close my eyes. I want to claim her hot cunt once more before I share. Selfish maybe, but so be it.

My Lea's safe in Tristan's care, but I'm here if she needs me.

TRISTAN

Fingering only. My brother hasn't left me with a lot of options, but I play the hand I'm dealt. And I know something Troy seems to forget—incubus venom is like truth serum. While he recharges his battery, I get to find out more about what makes this woman I'm intrinsically connected to tick. I may not be able to fuck her yet, but I sure as hell can expose some of her secrets.

Aleah lies perfectly still on the bench as I admire her ass and glistening cunt spread for me and take a deep inhale of the heady scent of her heat. I heft my heavy cock and stroke it while I imagine just how gorgeous her smooth brown ass will look when rosy from the mark of my hand. But first things first. I need to find out just what my goddess is all about. More importantly, she needs to understand just who she is.

I pause for a second to take a read on my brothers. Troy is sitting quietly, recovering, so to speak, but I can feel his intense gaze following every movement I make, not intrusive, just there. Cass's presence is distant, telling me he's probably patrolling the perimeter. That means it's up to me to keep Aleah safe from harm right now. As if sensing my attention, she twists her head, but I'm out of her sight line. Still stroking my cock, I slowly walk to the head of the bench and crouch.

Her gaze drops and regards my cock for several beats before drifting up to my eyes. Russet brown irises with undertones of green and flecks of black and gray hold me captive as she studies me. Examining me as if deciding whether I'm a meal she wants to devour or someone she wants to flee. This is a new look for me; women are usually all too willing to spread their legs for me. The flames of her desire lick through me, telling me it's more likely the former.

"Talk to me, *ma biche*." My voice is low and sultry by instinct, not design. Every cell in my body screams to connect with Aleah. In response, her body arches, and she moans as if I've touched her.

"We can't do this." Aleah groans as she forces the words out. She struggles against her restraints. Her focus goes inward as if she's observing a distant battle her side is losing.

But the throbbing in my deltoid tells me otherwise. I want to grab her chin and bring her back to me, but this is definitely not the position to do it from. I rise and start undoing her wrist restraints, ready to grab her if she tries to bolt.

Instead, she rises on her knees as I undo her ankles. Scratching vigorously at her forearms due to the effects of the incubus venom, she watches silently as I press the button that lowers a sling from the ceiling. Slings are one of my all-time favorite sex aids because they give me total access and control with my partners. And I need to secure Aleah's hands before she hurts herself. I've seen people tear their skin off as a side effect of incubus venom. When I hold out my hand, she comes to me without hesitation, eyes almost black with desire. With a small shot of magic, I have her secured and spread wide for me in seconds.

"Comfy?" I ask.

She nods. It's going to take a bit of work to get her talking.

After taking several minutes to admire her beautiful breasts and slick pussy, I stand between her legs, my hard cock almost vibrating mere millimeters from her wet slit. She strains toward me, spreading her legs even wider in invitation then jerking back as her mind flashes on Troy. That struggle is one of the most erotic things I've seen. I want to drive into her, hard and fast. *Fuck.* That's precisely what I can't do. *Get a grip, Tristan.* I take a small step back to put some breathing room between us. Aleah moans, making her displeasure known.

I give her an answering moan as I brush loose curls behind her ears. "Now, where were we? Oh yes, you're about to tell me what we can't do."

Aleah licks her lips, and her body strains to reach mine. Her erect nipples and drenched pussy show that indomitable will of hers is losing the battle with the incubus venom.

"We shouldn't be doing this, fooling around." Her voice, although low and husky, is strong and steady. She hasn't lost the battle yet. I could launch an academic discussion examining all the moral and ethical reasons why she thinks we shouldn't have sex, but we have plenty of time for that later. Plenty of time.

"But you want me to touch you, don't you?"

She nods. Her lids fly open, and she gives me that direct stare of hers. I could drown in those eyes. The dark flecks, referred to as jewels, indicate she's an analytical, thinking person, but they also act like barometers for her desire. While so many people like to use assessment tools to determine personality traits, for me, the iris pattern reveals what the brain tries to hide. This willful and deliberate woman may not show much emotion, but it's hidden away rather than being non-existent. She is more like Cass in this regard, which means that gods know what we'll discover once we tap into the parts of her sexuality she's had on lockdown.

"Tell me what you like."

She gives a slight shake of her head and closes her eyes.

"All right. If you can't tell me what you like, tell me what you don't like." I try a different tack.

"I don't like talking during sex." She keeps her eyes closed.

Interesting, and definitely something I'll work to change later. "Show me a picture in your mind."

"I don't think in pictures." Her voice has an undertone of huskiness that sends shivers of yearning skittering down my spine.

"Then throw me your thoughts. Think of it as a fantasy."

Suddenly, thoughts flood my mind. *Make me come. Oh gods, this can't be happening. I don't want to want this. I need to come. I want him. Can't want him. Fuck, I'm itchy!*

She struggles to free her arm as the venom lust swells in her system again. The more she fights the lust, the stronger the itch becomes.

"Make it stop," she whimpers.

"I can't, but you can. Let me touch you."

"No."

"Troy *needs* me to help you, but I want to help you, too." I let the soothing balm of my voice wash over her. I place my hand between her legs, letting it hover just above her clit, not touching her.

Aleah's gaze drops to my hand, to the two fingers twitching to touch her beautifully erect clit. She moans, and I damn near come as the sound vibrates through me.

"You can feel the connection between us, can't you?"

She moans again, biting her lips, and shakes her head

wildly—not in denial. She's fighting the strength of her desire for me. Not Troy, me.

"Do you want me to play with your clit? Do you want me to make you come so hard your body convulses with the force of it? Do you want me to feel your body speak its truth to me?"

She thrusts her hips forward, trying to get the sling to sway toward me, but I keep my fingers a hair away from touching her. We are suspended in the moment, our breath sending tendrils of sensation over our naked bodies.

"Please. Stop this pain. *Please!*" The raw edge to her voice could be from pain or desire. Right now, it's impossible to separate the two in Aleah's swirling emotions.

I press my index and middle finger against her clit. If she hadn't been restrained, she would have vaulted out of the swing. I rub her, drag my fingers through the pool between her thighs. "Do you want me to thrust these fingers deep inside you?"

Again, she moans, shaking her head more gently this time as if resigning herself to some inescapable truth, eyes fastened on my fingers.

I step back a foot and raise the wet digits to my mouth, slowly licking her essence. I almost orgasm myself when her grace meets mine. My shoulder starts to sing with heat.

Eyes that are now almost black with lust meet mine, divine light shimmering deep in their depths. The venom is rushing through every cell in her body, engorging her cunt, nipples, and mind with the all-consuming need to fuck.

She groans as she tries to squeeze her thighs together, tries to hide her need. The strength of her will acts like an aphrodisiac, sending lightening to my cock. *Easy boy.*

ALEAH

I finally submit to the murky lust haze as I watch this gorgeous god of a man slide fingers wet with my juices past his full lips. If I weren't in this swing contraption, I'd launch myself at him. I'd fought the battle to keep my rational mind from slipping under this crippling gnawing greed . . . and lost.

I crave. I yearn. I hunger for this man. I need him to own me while I consume every drop of his essence. My body screams for sexual release. When he licks his lips, summarizing his enjoyment of my taste in one tiny sound, I try to catapult myself at him. I want to scream in rage as this fucking swing stops me. I can't control myself.

The inmates are running the madhouse my body has become, turning me into the antithesis of who I have always been, crumbling my walls of morality and decency brick by brick.

I love it. I embrace it. It's silenced the noise. It should feel like I've lost something, but instead, it's as if this darkness coursing through me has burned through a facade, exposing my baser nature. *Could* this be my true nature? Nothing exists but this man my Troy gave me to while he watches, and it's the best fantasy ever.

I'm here, beauty. You can let go.

The instant Tristan licks my juices from his fingers, it's all over. I'm pretty sure I should be trying to fight this, resist it. The trouble is, I can't remember why, and now that my Troy, my safe place, is back with me, I can finally let go.

More liquid heat pools at my core as Tristan's fingers leave his lips and slide between my legs again. He brings the wet digits to my mouth, and I almost come as I inhale the scent of my sexual heat. Something in my mind tries to resist as my lips part and receive his offering. I moan, and he replies with a low growl at the back of his throat.

I thrash around in the swing, desperate to satisfy the driving, painful need to come. A flash of warning flickers at the edge of my consciousness. Tristan thrusts three fingers into my cunt. Hard. My cunt clamps down as I reach for relief. He grabs the back of my neck, and my gaze drops to my pussy and those fingers, thrusting in and out of me, dripping with my juices. He fucks my cunt with his hand until I'm panting with exertion and need. My body screams for release that's just beyond my reach.

"Ah, even now you fight the incubus's power. Follow me to the light. Free your mind." Tristan slips his hand out of my grasping pussy and rests his fingers over my clit. While my breathing settles, he drops light kisses around my eyes and mouth. It's one of the most erotic moments of my life . . . until his fingers start to move again.

Instead of direct contact on my clit, he draws slow concentric circles around it, never quite making contact. I moan and wiggle, twisting and turning as much as the swing will allow me, desperately trying to move those fingers over the aching nub. He stills me with a hand on my hip while making a soft shushing noise that almost makes me erupt on the spot . . . But he doesn't move his fingers to where I want them. He continues with those slow, methodical circles until my mind screams for release. *I can't come this way.*

Yes, you can. Troy's voice gets my attention as his warm body comes up behind me. I make a soft sound of greeting as I relax against his toned chest. I arch my back and let my head drop to his shoulder. His arm snakes around me while he dips two fingers between his lips, rolling his tongue around them until they're wet. Then, he rolls a hard nipple between the two fingers, matching the maddening pace Tristan keeps up between my legs.

"That's it, beauty." My Troy's whisper makes the sensations deepen, sharpen into something that takes me to the edge.

"Gods, you're beautiful." Tristan's voice is reverent.

I close my eyes. Nothing exists except the sexual current running through me as these two men worship my body. The smell of our sex—my sex—wraps us in its erotic perfume.

"Shhh." Troy's entreaty stills me, frees me. Something releases inside me, and soft waves ripple through me as Tristan's fingers continue their relentless trail. The ripples become waves of warm lava, and someone makes a loud, keening noise as the orgasm slams through me.

But Tristan's fingers don't stop right away, and the series of strong muscular contractions holds me suspended. Then Troy walks around to the front of the swing, and with no hesitation, slams his hard cock into me. Somewhere in the back of my mind, I'm aware Tristan has stepped aside for Troy, but my body tells me all I need to know. I'd know Troy's cock anywhere. Having him inside me is like finding home after a long, arduous journey. I moan and arch as Tristan's lips suck hard on one nipple and then the other. Troy thrusts, long, hard, smooth, taking his pleasure by releasing mine. Another moan rips out of me as I come again . . . Or maybe it's a continuation of what Tristan started. Whatever is happening, I'm in a place where there's nothing but wet sex sounds and the absolute bliss of being royally fucked and sucked.

Troy fucks me hard and slow, each thrust driving my breasts into Tristan's hot mouth. Troy drops the pad of his thumb to my clit, and another orgasm tears through me. Breathing hard, he steps back, and Tristan's magic fingers replace Troy's cock. He alternates tapping and caressing my G-spot while gliding another finger over the hood of my clit.

And still, I have an unbearable need to come. I want more. I *need* more. And these two men give me more. I use them for my pleasure, suck every drop of satisfaction from them until I'm limp with exhaustion. Holy shit. For the first time, I fully let go. Sleep slips over me before I have time to dissect what that means.

29

ALEAH

I'm instantly alert when I wake, but I keep my eyes closed, reveling in the warm weight of Troy's arm and hand across my chest. But it's more than that. The connection between us has changed. His unconditional love cocoons me on an even deeper level. No more of this "until death do us part" shit, not that I'd ever made that vow. There's no chance in hell that I'll ever agree to obey some man's orders. Troy found me from the great beyond, proving our love is eternal.

For the first time in months, I feel good, and I'm eager to start the day. My Troy is solid for now, but who knows how long that will last? I try not to worry about that and keep my mind firmly fastened on the sex I'd had with Troy . . . and Tristan. If it weren't for the soreness between my legs, I'd think it was a dream. A very good dream, but not in the realm of reality. A quiver jolts through me, and the strength of it confirms my state of post-orgasmic bliss.

A warm hand cups my cheek, and my eyes open to Troy's loving gaze. He drops a gentle kiss on my lips. "Morning, beauty."

"Morning, babe." I return his whisper and swim in the

ocean of love coming from those eyes. Troy's here with me, and all feels right with the world. I desperately try to hang onto the feeling, but my synapses start firing. I . . . we have to figure out how all this stuff works so we can get on with our lives. But even before that, we have to deal with the elephants in the room. Time to put this idea of threesomes, destined mates, and Tristan's clever fingers to rest once and for all.

Troy gives a happy sigh, and his hand drops to my bare upper thigh—his way of dipping his toe in to see if I'm *in the mood*. Nah-uh. Not even sex will deter me now that I have a problem to solve. I absolutely hate having my internal balance disturbed, so I'll be single-minded until I regain my equilibrium. Normally, Troy responds the same way, but all I sense coming from him is love and a deep sense of contentment.

I pull his arm back to my abdomen and lightly scratch his forearm, his second favorite thing in the whole world. My mind switches back to his *favorite* thing and to elephant number one: we'd had a threesome. Despite the pain of the venom, I remember every detail. Every disturbing detail. Except I'm not feeling in the least bit disturbed.

"I want you to know, you don't have to worry about me sneaking off with Tristan. That was not about sex." I get straight to the biggest elephant.

"Am I worried?" The humor in Troy's voice makes me smile.

"Remember all the talks we had about sex versus relationships? How we'd each respond if one of us fucked around? This is serious, Troy. There's no avoiding it." Yup, that headmistress tone that makes my man pissy is out in full force.

"Gods, how I missed your unique way of looking at things." Troy's warm voice sends another bolt of heat straight to my sexy bits, reminding me of all the delicious ways he enjoyed my body last night. Something about this man turbocharges my libido. I can feel the smile on his lips as he presses them to my bare shoulder. "And what did I say? How will I respond?" He rests a palm over my breast. Bastard. I will not be distracted.

"You said that how you'd respond would depend on how I felt for the person. That if it was sex for sex's sake, it wouldn't be worth breaking up our relationship."

"And you said you'd take my balls off and feed them to me if I banged someone else. No excuses." He slides his hand back to my thigh. I lift it back to my breast, although I have no frigging idea why—having his clever fingers playing with my nipples is almost as distracting as having his hand between my legs.

"So, full disclosure. Do you have feelings for Tristan?" Troy's fingers go back to work on my nipples.

"Not like that, not really. I don't think we can hold me responsible for what some magic venom made me do."

"Now it's my turn to confess. I know you're not telling me the whole truth. I don't know how to explain it, beauty, but something about being with you and my brothers brings me peace. It's like I've found my reason for being, why I belong." Troy drops a kiss to my forehead. It's true, a reason for being had been something that nagged at him for years. He'd never been able to accept my blind belief that we were here to do good, do our best, and the rest will work itself out.

"Whatever is happening between us has deepened our connection, or maybe it has something to do with me being an angel. Whatever it is, I can feel you here." Troy takes my palm and places it over his heart. He allows it to rest there for several seconds before sliding it down to his cock. "And here. We'll figure out the rest later."

Troy's heart beats strong and steady, which is weird for a dead guy, but reassuring nonetheless. It's true, it's as if we're connected on a cellular level. He's a calming layer added to my tumultuous emotions.

"While I fought the disease all those months, I learned I only wanted one thing: to be reunited with you. I knew if that happened, we'd figure out the rest. Here we are, and I feel the best I have in years. I know your mind is spinning. You'll figure all this out." He gives my thigh a nudge with his knuckles, letting his desire speak his truth.

My legs fall open in answer. Gliding his fingers through my wet heat, he teases an orgasm from me before sliding his lean, muscular body between my legs, using his thighs to spread them wide. Grabbing my wrists in one hand, he pulls them over my head. I stare at that beautiful cock as he uses his free hand to position it at my opening. My eyes close as he drives in to the hilt.

Troy brushes a light kiss across my lips and drops his chest to mine. Almost inaudible sounds of his love pass from his breath to my ear as I arch to meet each welcome thrust. I revel in the delicious slide of his body inside of mine. We fall into the rhythm we've perfected. His rolling thrusts hit my G-spot and clit, teasing another orgasm from me as his warm seed spills into me.

When our breathing slows, he flips to his back and pulls me into his arms. We rest that way, my head on his chest, feeling his beating heart and my leg looped over his. I'm trying very hard not to think about how long he'll be in this form. We don't talk. We don't need to. Our bodies just said it all.

After a time, and as if on cue, we both get up and pad to the shower. Troy soaps a pouf and reverently washes me. I return the gift, eyes drinking in that body I haven't seen for so very long.

We towel off and dress in companionable silence. I throw on sweats, and he dons one of his hoodies and a pair of jeans.

We face each other, and the noise in my head returns full bore. I have no idea what I'll do or say, but one thing is clear as Troy takes my shoulders and steers me toward the door—I will not run or hide from this Lord Syrael anymore. I shiver as a sliver of the incubus venom whispers through my system. I will not be anyone's victim, not ever again. Troy's brothers would just have to suck it up and help me or get the fuck out of my way. I square my shoulders, armed with renewed determination and ready to make my case.

"You've got this, beauty." The lines crinkle around his eyes as his smile showers me with his love, and he tosses me the metaphorical reins. Without another word, he takes my hand and leads me from the room.

30

ALEAH

Troy gives my hand a squeeze as he leads me from the bedroom. I smile up at him, and for a moment, I'd swear he's not as solid as he was when we woke. I push the fear out of my mind.

Now that the effects of the incubus venom are gone, I take in our surroundings. Every single surface my eyes touch screams elegance. The huge bedroom opens onto a round foyer with marble floors and two ornate cutouts that hold what looks like ivory vases. A quick glance through two open walnut doors shows an exercise room and the playroom we'd been in last night. Heat rushes through me as I remember what Troy and Tristan had done to my body. The swing sits empty, beckoning us to come keep it company.

"Where the hell are we?" I ask as he leads me down a short hallway.

"A private club where Troy says we'll be safe from Lord Syrael's magic, at least for now." Troy stops in front of double pocket doors and slides them open.

We step into a room that must take up the entire width of the floor. It's divided into four sections—a dining area, a small sitting area in front of a large wood-burning fireplace, an area with a baby grand piano, and a larger seating area.

I glance at Cass and Tristan, both of whom nurse a cup of what smells like coffee. They look at Troy and me with the fascination of a scientist examining a new species.

"Bro, you're still with us. That's good news." Tristan gives a fist pump.

"Not for long." Cass is turning out to be a real killjoy.

"Well, he's here now, and that's all that matters." In one fluid motion, Tristan gets to his feet, fixes me a latte, and brings it to me as I sit on the loveseat Cass points to. Troy grabs a coffee and sits beside me. Cass and Tristan sit in two armchairs opposite. A tray of baked goods sits on the coffee table between us, but I ignore it. No chance in hell I'll be able to put anything in my stomach until I've had my say. I woke this morning knowing one thing for certain: I'm never going to let the threat of a man's power cripple me again. I'm no longer that vulnerable child too many men overpowered. Forewarned is forearmed. If this Lord Syrael demon lord or whatever the hell wants a piece of me, he'll have to work for it. I'll die before I let a man take me against my will.

Yeah, right, big talk. Remnants of the guilt and shame I feel for not having fought hard enough as a child still linger in the far reaches of my mind. Through Troy's love and friendship, I'd slowly learned to believe that what happened was not my fault. And my rational mind agreed—how could a child possibly be blamed for the sick deeds of grown men? But the nagging whispers of those bastards still echoed . . . *There's part of you that wanted this, asked for this. Don't deny it.* I've worked very hard to conquer my shame and guilt, and I refuse to be plagued by it again.

I take a deep breath, preparing to lean into my discomfort and say what needs to be said. My inner goddess stands tall, extends her arms to the side, and gives the come-hither gesture. *Bring it on, boys.*

Cass looks as if he's ready to take me on. Tristan just looks happy to see me . . . very happy to see me.

"I have something to say, and I want you to hear me out before you interrupt."

Troy reaches over and gives my hand a squeeze. Again, I get the impression he's not as solid as he was just a few minutes ago in bed, but I can see him sitting right here beside me. I shake the fear away and focus.

"I realize I upset you all last night, and I owe you an apology. I guess it took being stung by an incubus to see the flaw in my logic. I can see now that getting myself killed isn't the best way to be with Troy." I stop waiting for one of them to jump in and confirm my stupidity, but no one says a word. Tristan gives me an encouraging smile.

"Troy and I vowed to always tell each other the truth, but more importantly, never to lie to ourselves. I tried to convince myself that there was an easy way out, but there never is, at least not in my life."

"Is this self-pity session going to last long?" Cass asks.

"Fuck off, Cass." Troy's tone cuts the tension like a hot knife through butter. He seldom steps into anything controversial, but when he does, everyone stands at attention and listens. Cass's mouth snaps shut.

Troy has no idea how powerful it is for me when he defends me. It's not something he does often as he's happy to let me run my own show. But when he does, it's very hot. But right now, I'm making war, not love.

I meet Cass's glare without blinking. "Yes, fuck off, Cass."

His lips part, but I give the talk-to-the-hand signal, cutting him off. "I don't know what issue you've got with me, and if I've inadvertently offended you, I apologize. Although I'm not sure how or why my death wish has anything to do with you, I obviously hit a nerve. But there are a few things you should learn about me. First, I don't stoop to anyone—man or angel. Second, I can't stand being accused of something I didn't do."

Cass gives a curt nod. I take a sip of latte, collecting my thoughts.

"So, further to those two things, I'm going to do whatever it takes to confront this Lord Syrael guy. That being said, I'm nobody's fool, so I know I'm going to have to find out how to protect myself from him, and that's where you guys come in. I have the feeling you're keeping something from me, something that could very well save my life, so I'm asking you to let me know what that is. But either way, I'm going to deal with this threat. I can't stand having something hanging over my head." I take a large swallow of my latte.

"That's reasonable," Tristan says. "Anything else?" He studies me over his coffee cup, sending a thrill I refuse to acknowledge down my spine as if he's lightly trailing his finger down my bare back.

I clear my throat. "Number two has to do with this situation. Our situation." I look at Tristan. "I truly do appreciate what you've done for me, how you've healed me, but this sex stuff has got to stop. Even if I do have any attraction to you, I won't act on it again. Never. We have free will and the gift of choice for a reason, and it's important that we don't let our emotions rule our brains, causing us to make dumbass decisions.

"It's hard enough to maintain a relationship, never mind throwing another love interest into the mix. Troy and I are perfect for each other, and I will never do anything that might endanger what we have.

"Besides, one thing I know about Troy is that he doesn't play sharesies." I wind up my speech and take a deep breath.

"I might under the right circumstances, beauty, but right

now, we have bigger problems." The annoyance in Troy's voice draws my gaze to . . . the empty space beside me. I pass my hand through thin air.

"That's right. I'm back to being a ghost, and given your newfound determination to get yourself killed, I agree with you—we need to figure out what's going on. Cass, can you get us back to Bardo? I need to find out how to get my form back."

"That's a great idea," I say to Troy. "We can ask them how we can be together."

"*We* won't be going anywhere," Cass says. "While you're alive, you can't cross the portal into Bardo unless taken by one of the gods."

"It makes more sense for you to stay here with Tristan, anyway, so he can catch you up on what we know. We know it has something to do with the diaries, so start there. We'll be back before you know we're gone," Troy says.

As much as I don't want Troy to leave, I agree with him. Once he quits fading out, we can figure out how to get rid of Syrael and get on with our happily ever after.

"I'm not sure where all this is taking us, but we'll figure it out together. Do what your heart tells you is the truth." Only Troy could make a whispered command sound sensual. I shiver as the sense of him, the knowing of him, moves away.

The three of us stand. Tristan crosses to stand beside me. Cass moves to the middle of the room.

"Tris, take good care of her." Troy's parting words make it sound as if he's giving Tristan a sacred mission.

"You have my word, brother. Anyone trying to get to her will have to go through me first." Tristan slings an arm around my shoulders as Cass opens up a hole in the air and steps through.

"I'll be back." Troy's distracted tone tells me his mind is already on where he's headed.

TRISTAN

"Looks like it's just you and me, babe." I give Al's shoulder a squeeze then quickly let go. I got the message loud and clear from her monologue—she has trust issues. For her to be open to the idea of being with all of us, she has to find trust. She looks at me as if she sees behind the pretty face, sees something that intrigues her. That gives us something to build on. I cross to the latté machine. "Let's grab another coffee and figure out where we go from here."

I'm excited about how this whirlwind is unfolding. Even better, I get to slow things down and find out how the girl who used to play tag with me in the forest became the woman standing beside me now.

Ali had always adored Troy. There'd been something that just clicked between them despite his mercurial temperament. Once she'd healed from the childhood abuse, she'd blossomed like a rare exotic flower, guileless and trusting us with her life. But Troy had always been her favorite.

I'd asked her once why that was, and she'd answered without hesitation. "It's not that he's my favorite, it's that he needs me more. He needs someone to shield him. He feels everything too deeply. Not like me—I'm tough." She'd flexed her tiny biceps and skipped off down the path.

She was right, he did need her more, and she is tough. I can see that. She's showing me a side of my brother I hadn't considered. How the pain of the world could cripple him if she didn't guide him through it. But as her senses bleed into me, I can also see that she absorbs and holds his pain. I was okay with that because this is my role to play, the role of someone who absorbs the emotional overload she carries. I stretch out my left shoulder as the warm burn reminds me she needs me. She just doesn't know it yet.

She follows me to the sideboard as I refresh our lattes and watches me add a healthy shot of coffee liqueur to each mug. I hand hers over, and her grace streaks through me as our fingers brush. If her shiver is any indication, she feels it as much as I do. I raise my mug in a toast. "To new discoveries."

Aleah raises her mug in answer and smiles. "That sounds like a bad take on a line from a Humphrey Bogart movie." She moves back to the sofa and sits. I go back to the chair opposite. The distance is best if I want to keep my hands off her.

"Are you okay with all this, Ali?" I sweep my hand around the room, hoping the gesture will explain what I'm trying to get across. I don't want to start off on the wrong foot by pointing out the obvious.

She grins at me, and her face lights up. She pushes her glasses up her nose with her free hand. "You mean, am I okay with Troy fucking off and leaving me alone with a dude with magical powers?"

I grin back, of course. Grinning comes easy to me. It's my first line of defense. "Yeah, that."

Those beautiful features grow serious as she considers my question, nibbles her bottom lip while she examines it from all sides, and that's just about the sexiest thing that's ever happened to me. It's a rare event that anyone gives what I think any real consideration. Most consider me too beautiful to have anything going on in my head. Men want to look like me, and women want to be with me, physically, but they wanted to put a notch on their metaphorical belts. Few were interested in looking beneath the surface to know the real me. A thousand years of experience has taught me it's highly unlikely I'll experience a relationship of any depth except with my brothers. And even they tend to treat me like an airhead. Until now. My heart pounds in hope and anticipation. *Take it slow*, I remind myself.

"Actually, I am okay with Troy fucking off. I used to be hugely insecure about it in our early days because I took it personally. Now that I know how much he suffers when he's conflicted, I can easily let him go. I just wish I could have gone with him."

She takes another sip and tucks her legs under that cute ass of hers. Her grin returns. "Your turn. How do you feel about being saddled with your sister-in-law?"

"You sure do put a lot of emphasis on this in-law business. That must be an Earth thing. In answer to your question, I feel just fine about it. It gives me the chance to get to know you again." *Court you.* The thought drops into my head out of nowhere, but I've learned to trust my gut instincts.

"*Again?*" She tilts her head. "Does this have anything to do with me being someone called Black Rose?"

I choke on the mouthful of coffee, and I enjoy a couple of minutes of her fussing over me, giving me time to get my wits about me.

"Where did you hear about Black Rose?" I ask, needing to find out how much she knows. I also can't get enough of watching the desire dancing with her indomitable will in her eyes.

"Sauron's eye spoke to me right after Lestat bit me. And

there's been a couple of times you guys made inferences to knowing me before."

"Who's Sauron, and what else did he say?" I'm pretty sure this Sauron's eye she refers to is Syrael's mirror, but I don't make assumptions where Ali's concerned.

"Sauron is just what I call him. He's a fictional character in an epic fantasy novel and movie. The eye that found me looked just like the one in the movie except that it's in the middle of a mirror. It said, 'Black Rose. You cannot hide. I will find you.' I remember every word. It scared the shit out of me." She shivers and wraps her arms around her chest. "That eye is related to this Lord Syrael demon guy, isn't it?" She shudders again, and I desperately want to gather her into a hug but hold back.

"I'm afraid so. Look, why don't I order us something to eat, then I'll tell you the whole story."

"The *whole* story?" She gives me an examining look.

"I promise." I give her the two-finger salute. "Scouts honor, as you Earth folks say."

She giggles. "You make us sound like some kind of alien species."

"You are some kind of alien species, but that's a discussion better left for later. Now, what would you like to eat?" I step into the adjourning office and grab the room service menu. I leave a good foot between us as I spread the menu out. She grabs the edge of the binder and scootches closer, and my heart picks up a few extra beats at just how comfortable and companionable we feel. After the appropriate noises about healthy eating get kicked to the curb because Ali "despises" kale, we settle on a handmade burger and truffle fries. I pour us each a glass of red wine. She grabs a notepad and pen from the desk and settles down at the dining table.

"I'm ready when you are," she says.

I join her at the table and tell our story. I tell her all about how we'd been sent to kill her, believing she was evil, but something about her had captured our hearts. She listens silently while I describe our life at the cottage in the forest, about how Lord Syrael had tried to kill her three times, but we'd saved her.

She jots down a few notes, but otherwise seems to absorb the details without judgment. I explain that she's a Nephilim, the last of her species. How Queen Hera had sent Troy to Earth to find and protect her.

I've just finished with the condensed version of the story when the bell rings, letting us know our food has arrived. I go to the dumbwaiter built into the wall, pulling out a tray laden with food. One of the great things about this Masquerade Club is the ability to remain completely anonymous and unseen if we so desire.

Ali flips through her notes while we tuck into the meal. She throws the occasional glance my way, but I don't say anything more, waiting to see whether she believed my fantastical story.

She finally sits back and picks up her wineglass. "So, a Nephilim is half-angel and half-human, right?"

I nod. She's in full analytical mode—animated and intense, eyes popping with curiosity—and it's sexy as hell.

"And you think I have powers that Syrael wants to steal, and that he's so powerful, it will take all of our combined power to defeat him?"

I nod again.

"So, I presume you guys had a plan when you came to find me. What was it?"

"We need to help you find your powers, and releasing them is tied to your sexuality. Troy and the chief justice of Bardo seem certain that your Double Diaries are the best place to start."

She licks her lips as she turns this around in her mind. I

wait for her to give me all kinds of bullshit arguments about why we can't do that, but she surprises me by agreeing. "That might not be a bad idea. It'll be good research for my series on the Pleasure Palace. If I'm going to write about the physical and emotional sides of BDSM while featuring Cyrus Stone's Pleasure Palace, then I need to learn more about it." She straightens, excitement gleaming in her eyes as she examines the issue from all sides. "Yes, that might be an idea."

"When would you like to start?" I laugh, but what I really want to do is touch her. For now, I'll have to be satisfied with drinking in her joy from a distance.

Her expression turns serious as she examines me with that intense expression of hers. "Before we get started, let's be sure we're on the same page. I'd appreciate your help figuring all this stuff out, especially since you're a sex angel and also probably know more about it than I do, but there won't be any hanky-panky. Agreed?" She shoves her small hand in my direction and gives me the smile that almost brings me to my knees with want. "Besides, I have the feeling we're destined to be good friends, and we don't want sex to complicate things."

Great. Friends. Not this time, sweetheart. I'm sick of the role of best buddy. The pretty boy with no brains who gives great hugs. As I take her hand, I realize that's not acceptable. This woman wants me for my brains, not my body. She'd loved me as a girl, now she just needs to learn to love me as the woman she's become. The warm heat on my left shoulder reminds me there's more to our story. There's the kiss she owes me . . .

"I need some air. Are you up for a walk?" I don my BFF mantle and give Ali my most convincing smile.

32

ALEAH

I feel much better now that I've figured out just how Tristan fits into this developing equation. He's a sounding board, albeit a very attractive one. Even though the circumstances are weird, we're past the awkwardness of what happened between us. We'd been thrown together in extraordinary circumstances and had formed a bond. And there's something about him that makes me want to spill my guts, let him know how I really feel, knowing he won't judge.

After donning coats and boots, we take a private elevator and slip out a back door. Tristan grabs my gloved hand before I can think twice about it and points toward a stand of trees with brightly colored leaves. "Come on. Let's go check out the fall colors."

I'm breathless by the time we cover the ground and hit the shelter of the densely treed area. We haven't seen a soul, and I'm not sure if that's part of the magic or good management.

"Wait, let me catch my breath," I say. "I'm not in the shape I used to be."

Tristan dances around me on his toes, boxing the air.

"We'll just have to do something about that." He stops dancing. Although the mask hides his mouth, the lines around his eyes crinkle, letting me know he's smiling. He reaches over and removes my mask. "Ah, that's better." He tucks it into my jacket pocket and follows suit with his. "We'll just keep these handy."

I inhale the sharp autumn air that carries the promise of winter. Tristan stamps the damp leaves underfoot and strides ahead on the path, his tight jeans showing off that magnificent butt. *Stop this right now, Aleah!*

"I think your Earth fall is about the best time of year anywhere. What's your favorite season?" Tristan asks, tossing me another of those boyish grins that melt my panties.

"It's a tie between spring and fall for me. I love the rebirth of spring bringing the promise of summer, but I also love the stillness and peace of autumn. Listen." I stop on the path and hold my gloved hands to the sky and close my eyes. One would think I'd know better than to make that gesture again after last night, but I've been known to be a slow learner.

Strong hands slap my arms to my sides. "Please tell me you're not about to summon any supernatural creatures again." Tristan gives me a bemused look.

I should shrug his arms off, but I don't. Instead, I find myself wishing he'd give me another hug. He gives the best hugs. As if on cue, he pulls me into his arms. "Sorry if I startled you." He gives me a quick squeeze then releases me.

"I wasn't going to summon anyone. I just wanted you to appreciate the stillness." I pull a pout, but truth be told, I'm liking being taken care of. I close my eyes and tip my chin to the sky, letting nature's orchestral sounds wash over me. I'm about to move when Tristan whispers, "Wait for it."

The wind rustles through the trees, parting the leaves so that a beam of sunlight warms my face. The haunting hoot of a loon breaks the stillness.

"Wonderful." I grin and clap my hands, not caring in the least that I'm acting like a schoolgirl. Life's been so frigging serious for the last couple of years, what with Troy's cancer and the global pandemic.

"It is, isn't it?" Tristan lifts his hand, and I hold my breath as I wait for his touch. It doesn't come. Instead, he drops his hand and walks off down the path. "Should we continue our discussion inside?"

I run to catch up with him. "So, how exactly does this magic stuff work?" I grab his arm to slow him down. "You guys are the magic experts here."

Tristan leads me to a bench strategically placed under a large red maple tree. "We don't have all the answers, but we do know Syrael's after you because of the purity of your sexual nature, and that purity alone makes you dangerous to him. If he can steal your power, he'll be the most powerful sex demon in the universe."

I return a friendly smile and ignore the happy dance happening in my sexy bits. "But you said I'm safe here with you, right?"

"For the time being, but that won't last forever, and if we don't figure out the weakness that will allow him to get to you, we won't be able to protect you or Troy."

"So, where do we go from here?" I try to quench the excitement that thrills through me at the idea that I just might have magic powers. Maybe that feeling that I'm destined for something more isn't a delusion after all.

Tristan settles on the bench and crosses his long legs at the ankles. He throws both arms along the back of the bench without touching me . . . but inviting me. I give my head a shake. Tristan hasn't done a thing out of line, offered nothing but friendship. I can't blame him for the traitorous state of my libido.

"We need to help you find your powers. First, you have to

understand the nature of sex demon lords. Sex demon lords are the opposite of sex angel lords. They represent all the evil that surrounds the world of love and sexuality. Sex demon lords have huge amounts of sexual power that comes from the most corrupted forms of sexuality. They can drive people to commit the most heinous and perverse acts of sexual corruption, evil, and sin." Tristan puts emphasis on the last three words. Impressive. I feel it on a visceral level.

I open my mouth to interrupt, but he brushes his fingers across my lips. Fingers that made my clit sing not that long ago. *Stop. This. Right. Now.* I bite my lip as I look at him. I will not be one of those weak-willed people who let their baser instincts overrule their good judgment. The universe gave us free will for a reason.

"Hear me out. Lord Syrael is the most powerful sex demon of all. The prophecy says that three sex angel lords will mate with a woman who is pure of heart in both love and sex. Their combined power will be Lord Syrael's ultimate downfall."

I swear to god my heart stops for three beats. Had I heard him correctly? Three sex angel lords will mate a woman? Fuck. I can see where this is going, but instead of the moral outrage I should be feeling—*am* feeling—my sexy bits perk up. *This has got to stop now.* I look up at Tristan. "Did you say mate with three angels?" I choke out.

He nods, but I can't quite interpret the expression on his face. "That's what I said, but there's some controversy about whether the translation of the word *mate* is correct. Cass believes the word *wadjonish* in the ancient tongue means covenant to do something. He says that being Troy's mate makes you immune to any sexual connection with us, and vice versa."

My rational mind uses her massive hips to shove my libido out of the way. That explains it all. I'm meant to work with these guys as a team because they're kin to my destined mate. That I can work with.

"Perfect. I knew my instincts were right. We don't need the emotional upheaval." I look at Tristan expecting matching relief. Instead, I swear I see hurt flash through his eyes before that warm connection with him slams shut.

"Just out of curiosity, what have you got against Cass and me?"

"Nothing." *Everything.* It would be one thing if we were talking about casual sex, but nothing feels casual about this, and Troy and I don't need the emotional upheaval.

I try not to squirm as Tristan silently studies me with those inscrutable eyes, his wickedly sexy mouth set in a question. For a second, I wonder whether he has the power to tell I'm lying as Cass has. I'm not lying—just not willing to look at the truth. Because it's too complicated. Troy and I agreed years ago, it would only be us. No one else. And once my mind's made up, it's made up. There. At least I'm not lying to myself.

"Ali, understand that I'm not trying to persuade you one way or the other."

"Don't you find that weird? Doesn't it bother you to share?" I close my eyes and rub my forehead, pissed at myself. When would I learn? Everyone mistook my obsessive need to look at all variables as criticism, so I wait for Tristan's condemnation.

Tristan shifts on the bench and grins. He reaches over and tucks some of my curls beneath my hat. It's so damned sweet, I almost melt. Troy isn't much of one for affectionate gestures, and if I have a weakness, that's it.

"Troy warned us about your need to examine everything under a microscope. If you're wondering if sharing you would cause a rift with my brothers, don't worry—it won't. It's more like we're part of a unit having sex with you."

I nod. That'll do for a start.

I sigh, rather too dramatically, hoping to hide my embarrassment. "Fine. Noted. Sounds like you guys don't have a problem. Of course, I'll need to verify all of this with Troy."

"Do you want to know anything about my past sexual exploits?" He laughs as I shake my head vigorously. "I'm happy to tell you anything you want to know?" He's teasing me, and I like it. Enough of this frivolity.

"What I need is to figure out how to defeat Syrael and get Troy back. Where should we start?"

"The only ways Syrael can bend you to his will are through your denial or deceit. So, we've got to figure out what you're denying or how you're lying to yourself about your sexual nature. Troy says that somehow that's all tied to these diaries of yours, so we'll start there. Unlocking you will help us find your powers. We know Syrael wants your sexual purity and indominable will, but we suspect your powers go far beyond those two."

"I'm not sure I have any of these magic powers you're talking about."

"That's where you're wrong," Tristan pulls me to my feet. "You may not know it, but if Lord Syrael's magic mirror says you're the most powerful sex angel of all, there's powerful magic hidden inside you somewhere. We just need to uncover it before he finds you. And we should find out more about this Cyrus fellow so we can rule him in or out. I've been thinking about the timing of his appearance, and I believe he's got something to do with this."

33

TRISTAN

I'm on top of the world, and no one's going to bring me down. Not Ali's denials, nothing. The burning in my shoulder and the strengthening connection with her tell me all I need to know. I probably should be sitting down and examining things from all angles like Cass and Troy always tell me to do. That might be the wisest thing to do, if I was even remotely interested in all that logical analysis. Cass says my cock rules my brain, but he'd dead wrong—my heart rules. Hands down.

While Ali freshens up, I have the club staff rearrange the area in front of the fireplace. Soon, the loveseat and chairs are flush against the wall, and a couple of huge throw pillows sit in front of a roaring fire.

I settle on one of the cushions, my legs outstretched. A decanter of wine and two glasses rest on the floor between the cushions. Ali comes in from the master bedroom, several of her diaries in hand. She's wearing black lounge pants with some kind of throw over a red tank top. A tiny sliver of flesh peeks between the waistband of her pants and the hem of her tank, and my fingers ache to touch that warm skin. She sits down on the pillow opposite me and smiles shyly. "So, how do you want to do this?" I can't wait to see how she'll want to start with this exploration.

She accepts the glass of wine I pass her with a nod of thanks, all business, dashing my hopes. Tension rolls from her like waves of heat rising from asphalt on a hot summer day.

"Are you sure you're comfortable with this?"

She stretches her neck and takes a sip of wine while she considers my question. "Not really. Nothing about this is comfortable, but that won't stop me from figuring it out." A bigger smile lights her face. "I'm determined to lean into the discomfort."

What bothers you the most about all of this?" I resist the urge to touch her. Oh, I want to feel my cock buried balls deep inside of her, but that will have to wait.

She gives me a dry look. "I think we've already covered all that. Everything about this situation bothers me." She tucks her bottom lip behind her teeth for a moment. "Well, everything except being with Troy. Which is what this is all about, right? So let's get started."

"Would you like me to help you relax?"

She narrows her eyes. "How?"

"Here, I'll show you." I stretch my arms in the space between us. After a moment's hesitation, she puts down her wine and reaches back. Electricity hums between us as our hands meet, but I focus on creating a safe space where Ali can start her journey of self-discovery. I blow just enough lust dust to break through the solid wall of inhibition she's built.

"Think of me as your sex doctor—"

Ali snorts but says nothing, so I continue. "You can tell

me anything free of guilt or shame. You're in a judgment-free zone here. Our goal is to figure out the cracks where Lord Syrael can sneak in so we can shore up your defenses."

She nods, and her body relaxes, showing me the lust dust is working. "How did you do that?" She stretches her neck before picking up her wineglass and tipping it toward me. "You should bottle that, whatever it is."

"I gave you a bit of lust dust, just enough to take the edge off, make it easier for you to talk to me." I tip my glass back at her before taking a sip. I settle back on my elbow, legs stretched out, and wait. As a young girl, Ali always responded better when she could control her own environment, and now she seems to need that control in spades, so I wait for her to lay the ground rules.

"Should we start at the beginning or where you left off the other night?" Ali asks.

"Where we left off the other night is good. We're at August twenty-sixth." I watch as she fiddles with the first diary, flipping pages until she finds the spot.

"Okay. I'll read, and you listen and let me know if you sense any magic." She pauses. "I'm hoping you'll be able to feel the words that have magic woven into them. How about we stop after each section and decide if there are any clues?"

"Sounds like a plan. We don't have much else to go on right now."

Ali pushes up her glass, bows over the first diary, and starts reading where we'd left off last night, pitching the soft huskiness of her voice to a clinical level. Watching her struggle for detachment awakens something hot and primal I've never felt before.

Double Diary

Aleah on Sunday, August 26 @ 8:50 a.m.

. . . In the morning after more great love-making—sometimes, most times, it's more than sex.

I'm loving this time of being able to touch you; of being able to walk up and kiss you; of being able to show you my sexuality. I love that you're receiving it and not blowing me off because "it's got to be the right time." I think I'm losing my natural reticence about showing you that side of my being. I hope it lasts a while longer.

I feel well loved by you.

I clear my throat as she finishes the entry. Ali looks up at me, her face alight with hope. "Anything?"

"Nothing yet, but I'll make bets that since Troy wove the magic, it will be tied to his responses." Even if that isn't true, watching her read mesmerizes me. Everything about this woman fucking mesmerizes me. I want to know how the girl has grown into a woman. For the first time in forever, I feel alive.

"Earth to Tristan." Ali leans forward and snaps her fingers in front of my face. I resist the urge to pull them into my mouth.

"Oh. Sorry. Carry on," I say. I give her my best supportive smile. "We know there's magic from the other night, but we weren't focusing on how it works. We'll find the next section with magic, and hopefully that will help us figure out how the spell works."

"Okay." She pushes her glasses up her nose and wets her lips with the tip of her tongue. I roll to my side to hide the hard-on that springs to attention at that tiny gesture. Ali's smoky voice as she reads sends even more blood rushing to my other head.

Double Diary
Troy on Sunday, August 26 @ 12:00 p.m.

Ditto for me!!!

I loved watching you let yourself go into unrestrained, wanton passion. Building to a climax of uninhibited gasps, heavy breathing and morning orgasm. You see, it doesn't take much to please me.

I have more thoughts to write down, but I better wait until later when I have more time. Perhaps tonight.

I should say that I was pleased to read that you did try to listen to me sitting in the dark as per your previous comment.

I also think you should masturbate more. It's good for sleep and endorphins. I keep my toys, lube, etc., in the shoe box in my closet, if you didn't know. Adds variety although the normal way, as you say, does the trick, whether you think it's boring old you or not. Certainly not boring to me. I easily get excited just thinking that you might be engaged in self-pleasure.

Someday, I may even get to secretly hear a moan, etc., as it would play into my love for voyeurism. Unlikely, as to date, the opportunity and timing is understandably precluded by life's interruptions. Right now, or I should say at this stage of our love, I get plenty of opportunity to share our passion together on the weekends. Masturbation is supposedly a self-indulgent pleasure for one without the inhibitions of knowing someone else is involved, unobtrusively or not . . . It should be a natural expression of self and not contrived for others. That's the beauty of it. Just thinking that you may have indulged yourself is great fodder for my own self indulgence. I can save my voyeuristic desires for the future when the old guy may need the extra stimulus. Something to look forward to, and I do look forward to getting old with you.

Perhaps I'll write you about what, where, how, etc., that make up my fantasies about you masturbating when I am sitting alone in the dark. You did say you want to hear some, so that's a start. There are others of course, and I may well get to those as well.

As I said, I don't have the time at the moment, so I'd better stop here before I run on anymore. . .

Love you, loved last night.

More later. —Me

Our sweetheart keeps her eyes glued to the diary when she finishes the section, but her grace rises around her like an aura. Something about that section has definitely triggered her magic.

"Well, any magic?" She looks at me with a scary intensity that demands I reveal the answers to the universe, but I see past her intimidating mask to the burning curiosity.

"There's something there, but I can't put my finger on it. I think we'll need to read on," I say. That's the absolute truth, although if I'm being honest, I'm so fascinated by her, I haven't really been looking for magic.

Maybe we're looking too hard. Maybe the magic lies in the fabric of the relationship Ali and Troy built together. Gods know my brothers and I have seen just about every sex practice in every species, but it's rare to find a relationship without artifice based on unconditional acceptance. I want a piece of this love, even if only for a moment, and I'm more than willing to take it vicariously through these diaries.

And I want more of that look she gives me, the one that tells me she's relying on me to help her find the answers. That I'm someone she can share this emotional burden with. That I'm important to her.

34

ALEAH

Tears prick the corners of my eyes as memories come flooding back along with the painful reminder of how it all ended. After I'd agreed to the Double Diary exploration, Troy had conducted his "research" in his single-minded, but thoughtful manner. Troy's one impulsive act in his life had led to one hell of a lot of stitches, and that had been all it took to confirm his belief that nothing good came from jumping into unexplored waters. My Troy is definitely a toe-dipping kind of guy . . . despite his protestations. Slowly but surely, he'd steered us through the emotionally murky waters until we'd found the door to a cave filled with hidden treasure. We'd just been on the cusp of stepping through, to taking that next scary step into the unknown, when his sickness had slammed us into another reality.

"Sounds as if you two have something very special." Tristan's wistful tone catches my attention and brings me back to the now. I take a deep breath as I nod.

"Very special. We'd found that until-death-do-us-part place with each other." As the words leave my mouth, I give myself a slap upside the head. How the fuck is Tristan supposed to know what goes on in my crazy little head? No one except Troy ever has a fucking clue what I'm talking about when I make references like that, and sometimes even he didn't get it.

"Troy told us you refused to say *until death do us part* or have the word *obey* as part of your ceremony. I get it. You're too much of a realist to make false promises. That's one of the things that makes you so unique. Most people go for wishful thinking, especially where sex and love are concerned." Tristan's face shines with the most open and trusting look, as if he feels blessed to be in the presence of someone so special. I'm almost afraid to admit it, but I preen. I shouldn't. I should feel confident enough in myself that I'm not swayed by a beguiling look from an extraordinarily beautiful man, but I'm not. I go all gushy inside just like I do when Troy releases his sexy, charming side.

As I stare at Tristan, I'm sucked into that smile as if I've been there before. I have a flash of memory, of flowers and dancing in a meadow on a sunny day, holding a blond angel's hand.

"Did you like me then? When I was a kid?" Oh yeah, I go there, even though I'm not quite sure how much of this I believe. Why oh why do I need this reassurance? This pathetic need of mine for external confirmation that I have value to someone?

Tristan sits up and throws a log on the fire, giving me the best view of his ass as he bends to adjust the logs. Yup, Troy hasn't been gone twenty-four hours, and I'm already salivating over his brother's ass.

"I liked you very much, Ali. I still do." His voice is low and sounds almost regretful, and I'm not sure I heard him correctly as the logs snap and crackle.

"I'm glad," I whisper back, gulping my wine as I admit just how happy that makes me feel.

"I'm fascinated by everything about you." He winks and then as if he wants to make sure I don't mistake his meaning, he says, "It's only natural that I be curious about the woman you've become. Let's read some more, shall we?"

I give him a grateful smile and start reading.

Double Diary
Aleah on Saturday, August 26 @ 8:30 p.m.

Indeed! You must write me about what, where, how, etc. I'm eager to hear about your fantasies of me masturbating. One thing (of many) that greatly excites me about our Double Diary is the possibility that I will hear more of your inner thought and fantasies. I've wanted that for so long.

I'm loving unfolding, opening for you. I get engorged just thinking about laying under you; you kneeling between my legs spread wide open. You're either looking down at and rubbing my wet clit -or- your face is between my legs sucking on my clit, making it yours—demanding it be yours.

I don't know which I like better—I can't choose.

Whew! Enough of that. My heart is beating so fast it's hard to take a breath. And I've got work to do. OK; I'll compartmentalize tomorrow. Good thing work provides a natural distance, or I'd never get anything done . . . except for unfolding for you.

How often do you masturbate? How?

I may already know this, but it will be fun to hear you describe. Where? Is it usually sitting on the couch? Give me a picture to help me increase my heart rate as you commanded.

As for toys—no, I didn't know they were there. I'd rather try the toys with you. I think I'm liking "performing" for you, although I also feel somewhat shy about it. I like you watching me, especially now that I'm no longer ashamed of my body. When I look at those pictures you took of me, I see that I was truly beautiful. Too bad I didn't realize it then. You may have been in trouble if I had. :-)

But tonight, I don't want to masturbate; I want you. Hold me down. Command me. Take me. Make me give you all I have to give.

Then, maybe I'll masturbate more often. I certainly will next weekend. I'll send the jolts of my orgasm through to you at the party—maybe you'll feel it.

I'm rambling. I want you.

PS: You're ruining me! I used to get so much done...

I pause, as much to douse the heat building between my legs as to see if Tristan's seeing any magic. He's lying on his side, cheek propped on his hand. He's looking at me with wonder and what can only be lust . . . lots and lots of it.

"Let me have a look. I think I'm seeing a pattern here." He holds out his hand for the book, and I pass it to him. He flips through several pages before handing the journal back to me. "The magic is tied to sections about your sexuality, so we can skip the part about how Troy masturbates. Start here."

Tristan folds the spiral notebook and hands it back to me. I glance down and see he's skipped ahead to one of my entries.

Double Diary
Aleah on Monday, August 28 @ 6:30 a.m.

Oh my love. What a gift! Thank you. You alone can understand my need to protect my vulnerability—the existence of that vulnerability. I do understand yours, I believe I always have. That's one of the reasons I've loved you so fiercely; protected you with the depth of my soul, and if nothing else, I'm good at that and have been good at protecting you.

As for me, well, you know I am that—vulnerable—although rarely is it out there for the world to see. I thought that, with you, I'd released most of it when I told you about my sexual vulnerability a couple of years ago. Who knew there was more. Your opening up to me is in turn opening up more in me—more about that later.

I spent so much of my life living with fear—even with you. When I thought I'd lost that fear of losing you and fear of not having your love, it was bliss.

I've told you about the near panic attacks, so I won't ~~waste~~ spend time on that here. You've helped me shed that horrible fear with this love and giving yourself to me.

I do listen to you; more than you know. You're the only person I've allowed in to such an extent that you can destroy me. I was serious when I told you I've given you my heart.

At the cottage this summer when I realized you were giving me a greater and deeper gift of your love, it scared me to death for a day or so. My reporter's imagination had you being nice to me before you left me -or- died of a terminal illness. I had to give myself a stern talking to about fighting my fear and believing as I know you are incapable of that level of deception with me. I don't know how deeply this will go, but I'm revelling in it.

Now, for what's fun and an/the important symbol of our love. I did masturbate last night. Lying on the bed, I pulled up my night shirt, tweaked my right nipple with my left thumb and index fingers, and started rubbing my clit with my right middle finger. I didn't use lubrication. I was wet enough just thinking of you. I spread my legs as I thought of you. Too many images; too hard to fasten on one. I rose to the heights of excitement in seconds.

I let myself go as I came and moaned. Usually, I'm very still and quiet as I masturbate. Last night, I moaned and moved. I thought of you dominating me, being rough with me. I still have shivers. I wanted you so much. That's why I often don't masturbate—it makes me want you so badly that it keeps me awake. However, I am your love slave—my gift to you—and I will try to be more diligent. Of course, if I'm not, will you spank me?

. . . Did I just say that?!

Time to go. More later. I love you. Enjoy your day thinking of me.

I damned near swoon as each word adds a log to the sexual furnace roaring inside me. At some point during that last passage, Tristan sat up and tucked his knees under his chin, wrapping his arms around his legs. He is just so damned cute and adorable in a cuddly bear sort of way. I slide my lusty thoughts into an envelope marked Troy and give Tristan my most familial smile. After all, there's no harm in admiring perfection.

I bend back down to my task as another wave of desire skitters over my skin. Then, a thought hits me that jerks my head back up. I infuse a frown with mountains of disapproval that I direct to Tristan's innocent gaze. "Are you using some kind of sex spell on me?"

He shoots me that smile again and gives a slight shake of his head, but otherwise doesn't move. "Nope. This is all you and whatever magic Troy wove into the diary."

Since I don't want to figure out if that thrills me half to death or disappoints, I start reading again.

Double Diary
Troy on Monday, August 28 @ 7:30 a.m.

Morning—in response (directly) to yours...

"My opening up to you means opening up more in you" —beautiful — I like that as I know you have so much more, and it excites me. I love that my secret desires seem to have given you permission to unlock your sexual fantasies.

Giving your heart to me is one of the most amazing things you have ever done. Please take mine. I give it freely and willingly (okay, maybe under a bit of duress, but I'm working on it.) I also welcome your gift as a sex slave; however, I prefer to think of you as my love slave. Don't get too excited . . . I'm good with loving your sexuality at the moment.

It thrills me to no end knowing you masturbated last night thinking of me dominating you. I love fantasizing about you allowing a dominant man to exploit your submissiveness. Getting you to a state of no resistance.

However, I have great fantasies about this scenario, and I think you can still lock into this. Not because you need to but just because you can use your imagination to enjoy this role again. I love you in the role of being vulnerable and helpless to stop this man bringing you to an overwhelming orgasm in spite of the fact that you try so hard to resist, until you finally scream, no longer able to control or deny your desire.

Your conscious mind, somewhat ashamed, while your body is completely under the control of his demanding manipulations. That deep-seated wanting, that scares you as he knows you can't control it. He can do whatever he wants to you . . . and you will let him. A *Story of O* thing! Yes, so on to the new fantasies, probably better ones, as you say. But don't lose this one. Selfish on my part, but I love this image. Perhaps my fantasy, my need. But I like to think you can still enjoy that role.

I know I can't tell you what to think or do, and it is purely selfish on my part. If this request in any way holds you back from moving on to greater things, ignore it. Although given my dominant desires, I have even imagined I'm watching this man making love to you. Although not normally a fan of sharing, I realize you could convince me of anything at this time; I could convince myself because I want your sexuality fully explored.

It would be the cherry on top if it was honestly a role you could get into in reality.

I'll have to write out this fantasy for you . . . soon!

(Now—a little role playing) . . . I not only accept your gift to me as a "love slave," I insist on it. Your diligence in all our explorations, including masturbation, will be recognized and rewarded. You'll find I can be as gentle and giving in fulfilling your desires as I can be harsh and punishing in your defiance of mine.

Spanking is the least of your concerns if I discover you have been less than diligent in complying with any of my instructions. I am pleased that you are pleasuring yourself more as I want you to maintain a level of lust that should be an intrinsic part of your aura. A subtle emanation of your sexuality whenever I look at you.

Your subtle moans and movement while masturbating also please me, but you and I both know you have so much more. I strongly suggest you try harder. Your bathroom escape piqued my excitement as well. I found it strangely appealing that you are so shy about your sexuality and possibly afraid that others seeing you in such a state of lust would discover the truth as to the level you are willing to or need to go to satisfy your hidden animalistic desires.

Although it would never be my intention to interrupt or inadvertently intrude on such free expression, if it happens again, you are not to stop and quietly hide in another room. In fact, knowing I'm there provides the opportunity for you to demonstrate your commitment to diligently living up to my expectations . . . and yours, I might add, as a love slave.

Be assured, I will positively and unobtrusively watch you take delight in performing for me. I would in no way embarrass you after the fact. However, you should take pleasure in having the opportunity to validate your aforementioned commitment to my pleasure.

In addition, I want you to touch yourself more intimately while bathing. As well, consider using the showerhead, adjusted to an appropriate flow, by turning down the volume, to lightly stimulate your clitoris. This too helps you maintain a consistent sexual aura that I want to see in you. Perchance to orgasm, but not required. Although it would give you something to share with me, which would give me an extreme amount of pleasure. I would think about this for weeks—on the couch, late at night, in the dark . . .

Always remember you are doing these things for our growth and, importantly, for exploring the need for the perfection of our shared sexuality.

I adore and cherish you! —end of role play—

As you have so perfectly said, "Oh, what a gift." I will add, "What a gift you have given me."

I've got to sign off. I just can't go on at the moment.

PS: I know and hear that you listen to your recorded books in the bath, and I don't want to take that away. Realistically, you can judge your time and involvement. I will fantasize regardless . . . It's what I do . . .

Really — The end . . . T

Double Diary
Aleah on August 28 @ 9:50 p.m.

Very quickly. I've always fantasized about and wanted a cock —your cock—okay, once or twice Brad Pitt's. You're almost always dominating, always leading. Even when I fantasize about being the initiator, you always take over.

Don't worry; I won't lose that fantasy.

Did you notice that I did not listen to my recorded books tonight? That's because my need for you and sexual thoughts pushed away any desire to concentrate. I couldn't think about anything else all day.

Funny! I can't stand being dominated in life, yet I let you do it with our sex.

Showerhead/bath sojourns—maybe I'll experiment this weekend.

Neat role play—since you've always been my master, it's not a huge leap. Like I said, maybe I'll experiment. Loving you, loving me loving you . . .—Aleah

---

I'm damn near an inferno by the time I read those last words. The air around me is hot and bright as if someone's added a ton of logs to the fire, but when I glance at it, nothing's changed. Tristan jumps up in excitement and paces around the room . . . but not before I see the erection tenting his pants.

"That's it, that's the key. Role play." Tristan pumps his fist in the air.

I don't see it, and I don't have a frigging clue what's got him so excited. My forehead creases as I frown.

"The magic has to do with you and role play. Can't you feel it?" Tristan sweeps his hand around the room. Other than this humming heat thing happening, I don't feel a thing. But Tristan's excitement sends a shot of adrenaline through me. He crouches in front of me and grabs my hands.

"As soon as you started reading, your grace, your internal essence started misting around you. We saw that happen before, and we think that's what brought Troy back. But your Nephilim glow activated when you started reading about the role play." He looks at my extended arm. "Can't you see it?"

I look down at my arm, but all I see is the tawny color of my skin. Nice, smooth, and one of Troy's favorite things, but nothing else special . . . But it feels like it's on fire.

"I've got to get a glass of water." I snatch my hands from Tristan's and flee the room.

TRISTAN

I can't help but smile and throw a metaphorical fist to the universe in triumph. Each moment I spend with her awakens memories of our time together in the forest. I may not have Cass's intellect or Troy's brilliant sensitivity, but one thing I do know is how to make people feel good. I'm particularly good at showing the strengths people rarely give themselves credit for, no matter what their species. When we'd met her all those years ago, I'd feared that evil had successfully crushed the light in this little Nephilim. Her foster father did a good job of conditioning her mind until everything she believed about herself was the wrongness he'd shown her.

But our Aleah was a fighter, and she'd refused to let him take her goodness. Instead, she'd buried it far away where no one would ever find it, including herself. But beneath all that dark, we'd uncovered and released a kernel of her light.

History repeats itself, and everything comes full circle. I refill our glasses and light some candles as I wait for Ali to return from her bedroom. I rub absently at the ache in my shoulder, but I'm too caught up in my thoughts to realize that the intensity has changed. A sharp pain, like a hit from a pickaxe, drives into my deltoid at the same time a strangled cry comes from the direction of Aleah's bedroom.

Panic bolts through my system. I drop the matches and streak into the bedroom just in time to catch her as she collapses to the floor. She clutches her throat, and her eyes bulge as I try to figure out what the fuck is going on. My eyes glide around the room, assessing, searching for the danger. She's switched out the sweater and tank she wore for a black bustier with gold threads running through the ties. There's an open gift box on her bed with a card displaying ornate script propped against it.

Our time is almost upon us. Wear this for me. T.

Fuck! I gather Ali in my arms, trying to quell my panic enough so I can get a read using my healing powers. Something like stinging ants attacks my fingers, reminding me of a time in the forest. I yank my hand back as if from a hot burner and look down in horror at the black threads winding around my fingers. I flip Ali over and watch in fascinated horror as the laces on the bustier tighten around her, cutting off her air supply. Her hand moves from her throat to touch the side of my face as the light dims in her eyes. I swear to the gods I hear Syrael laughing. I clutch Ali's still form to my chest and bellow my impotent rage, screaming her name over and over.

"Aleah!"

BLACK ROSE AND THE THREE PRINCES

Ten years later, Black Rose had grown into a beautiful preteen. Life was idyllic in the ancient forest, and little by little, Black Rose and her angels let their guard down. One bright summer day, while the princes were away on a foraging trip, the singing birds and blooming flowers enticed Black Rose outside to get some fresh air.

Meanwhile, Syrael realized he got his rocks off from non-consent. He embraced the dark sex arts, raping and pillaging until the gods cast his ass from grace, sending him to live with the other fallen archangels in the Underworld.

Syrael soon realized sexual violence allowed him to drain ether from his victims. He launched a feeding frenzy as his appetite for pain and torture grew. As his power swelled, he slew any sex demon in his way until he became the most powerful sex demon lord of all. Syrael used his magic mirror to seek out and destroy all who had power over the dark arts —those who were sexually pure of heart.

3 6

ATROYEL

Tristan's scream of terror and indescribable pain reaches across the realms, tearing right through me, dropping me to my knees. Cass drops down beside me. "What is it, Atroyel?"

"Aleah's in danger." I grit the words out as I breathe around the pain and try to control my own terror. "We've got to save her."

Cass puts his hand on my shoulder, infusing me with enough energy to push back the pain before helping me to my feet. I give Tate, the Chief Justice of Bardo, and her husbands a quick bow. I've got no time for any other niceties. I have to cut this meeting short. "Your honor—"

"Remember what we told you. Now go!" Tate points her finger, and a portal opens up. Cass and I leap through it.

Landing in Aleah's room, I shake my head to clear the transition vertigo, wishing I'd had more time to think through the things I'd learned, such as how to use my magic and how sharing Aleah will affect our relationship. So much has happened since we left Tristan and Aleah—I glance at the clock—a few hours ago. But the pain in my chest intensifies. That sense of *knowing*, of being connected to her, continues

187

to fade, telling me time is of the essence. I crouch beside Aleah and gather the limp form of my beloved in my arms. A ring of dark magic surrounds her, but I can't identify the spell. I look at Tristan, not even trying to hide the panic taking hold.

Memories flood back as our eyes connect. Magic and divine energy pulse through me. I remember everything—life in the forest with young Aleah and life with my brothers. We'd been inseparable, functioning as a unit, as a team. We had immeasurable power when we channeled our magic together. If we combine our power, we can save her. That's what Chief Justice Tate had said. As long as Aleah and I share our soul bond . . . the bond that's growing weaker by the second.

"Her heart has stopped." Cass's tone is matter of fact, as if we're on assignment, instead of losing my soul mate. But his steady voice focuses me on the problem at hand, something he's very good at doing. No matter how high his level of panic, his mask of calm control stays firmly in place. Only his eyes tell the true story if you know how to read them.

"Can you see what kind of spell it is?" I don't even try to hide my fear as Aleah's essence slips away.

Cass sits on the other side of her and grasps her hands. "It's a suffocation enchantment. You should be able to undo it with a releasing counter spell." Golden eyes tinged with equal amounts of alarm and assurance meet mine.

I sift through the dusty volumes of spells inhabiting my mind. Now that my spiritual essence has been reunited with my angelic body, I can remember a storehouse of magic. The memory of a spell that might work flashes into place, and hope washes through me.

"I can use my letter power to release the stranglehold, and Cass can open a channel to Aleah that Tristan can use to blast healing power through to her." I silently pray my memory isn't playing tricks on me.

"That should work, but we'll need a physical connection. I don't think your powers are strong enough for mental manipulation only." Tristan's confidence washes away my panic as he holds out his hands to me. Now that we've returned, his usual optimistic outlook replaces his initial terror. Tristan believes we're the frigging three musketeers or some such.

Cass grabs a hand to connect our power and open the channel then looks at me.

I pull Aleah against my chest and murmur into her ear. "Hang on, beauty. We've got you." Cradling Aleah with one arm, I take hold of Tristan's hand. Electrical current bolts through me as their magic infuses mine. For some silly reason, the lyrics to "Release Me" drop into my mind, and I start singing the first couple of lines before weaving in words of my own. The words don't really matter—they're simply a conduit for the magic. I focus the magic and use a thin blade of divine light to slice through the corset strings. The instant the last string snaps, the corset dissolves, leaving nothing to attest to its existence. Aleah's head lolls to the side, her lips slightly parted.

Tristan puts two fingers to her carotid pulse, but I know what he'll find before he gives his head a slight shake. Only a faint flicker of her essence remains, and it's fading fast. He rests his left hand over her left breast, head bowed, eyes closed. His grip on my hand tightens, and his skin glows as divine energy mists around us, cocooning the four of us, and healing Aleah. For several unendurable beats, nothing happens. Then my brand stutters and a warmth spreads from it.

We stay that way, a tight circle for what seems like several hundred light-years before Aleah's gray pallor slowly returns to its warm tawny brown color, and her pulse returns to normal. Once we break through the strangulation spell, Cass lets go of our hands, breaking the energy channeling between us. Aleah moans as he steps away, causing all of us to pause and stare at her for several more minutes. She continues to absorb healing energy from Tristan and me, so we gently pick her up and lay her on the bed, careful not to break contact with her.

Cass takes a deep breath and runs a hand through his thick black hair. "That was too close for comfort. I'll go find out what I can about how the package arrived. Tristan, you find us a safe place to stay." He walks away, straightening his shoulders to accept the weight of his self-assigned burden—to keep us safe from harm . . . And he's not happy that this circle now includes Aleah. He'll just have to get used to it.

The air lightens considerably as my older brother leaves the room. Tristan straightens his back and stretches. "Good to have you back, bro. I couldn't have saved her on my own."

"Yes, about that. I don't get it. How did Syrael find her and if he needs her consent to absorb her power, why try and kill her?" I'm probably fighting a losing battle trying to get my head around how the demon lord thinks, but I'm damn well going to try. Our determination and analytical skills are just two of the gifts Aleah and I share, on steroids.

"I might have something to do with that. As soon as I saw the corset, I cast a defensive shield over the club. I'm probably to blame. I should have realized the magic coming from the supers in the club wouldn't be enough to hide us. Ideally, Lord Syrael will steal her power before he kills her, but if that's not possible, he'll simply kill her. He won't run the risk of her defeating him." Tristan hangs his head in misery, and I reach around Aleah's limp form and squeeze his shoulder. He winces as if I've hit a sore spot and gives me a weak smile.

"We can't possibly know if that would have made a difference. We all agreed to the plan. You did what needed to be done." I look down at our sleeping beauty, our Black Rose, and gratitude washes over me. "She's here with us, and that's all that matters, Tris. Besides, it's not her time to die, so we've got an advantage over Syrael."

"How can you possibly know it's not her time?" My practical, down-to-earth younger brother looks at me hopefully before looking down at Aleah. He runs the hand that had been holding hers lightly up and down her arm as he mulls over what I've said.

"Because one of the chief justice's husbands, who handily happens to be the angel of death, said so. That's why she came back from the Void. He also said that not even he could save Aleah if Syrael gets his hands on her. Best guess is that he planned to swoop in and snatch her before her essence left her body. Once he had her captive, he could revive her and coerce her into surrendering her power. Oh, she'd put up a fight, no doubt about it, probably to the death. You did good. You protected Aleah, called us back, and I'm grateful."

Tristan gives me a relieved smile, and I have a flash of intuition that there's a lot more to him than I've recognized over the centuries we've fought, lived, and loved together. He stands up, stretches, and rubs his hands together. "I'd better get us something to eat and drink.

Almost the instant that Tristan loses contact with Aleah's body, she starts to thrash around. I lift my Aleah from the floor and put her on the bed. As Tristan takes a few steps toward the kitchen door, she moans and holds herself as if she's in pain. Slivers of terror cut through me like ice. Tristan spins on his heels, and his eyes tell me he's experiencing the same terror. Aleah's body arches, and she lets out a shrill scream before collapsing back onto me.

ALEAH

I'm swimming in a sea of pain. I fight to breathe. That fucking eye in the mirror peers down at me, and its seductive voice speaks. "Submit, and I'll take away the pain."

Although I can barely think through the agony, I know I need to fight, know I cannot give myself to this mirror, or I'll most likely be tortured and die a horrible death . . . and I'll lose Troy. I will not allow that to happen.

"Just reach out your hand, and I'll save you." The mirror's voice weaves gold threads from the corset around my chest, squeezing out the small amount of air I'd been able to gasp in. I shake my head frantically. Terror bolts through me as the sense of connection with Troy wavers. It seems to be weakened by the presence of the mirror or the magic of the corset—probably both.

"Save yourself and your husband. Give me your hand." Black mist, like a horde of flies, swarms from the mirror, reaching toward me. Something tugs at my arm, tries to make me reach back. *No!*

Save Troy? There's something wrong with what the mirror's saying, but I can't think past the pain.

"Aleah, get your ass back here right now." Troy's voice echoes in the back of my mind. I want to go to him, but I can't move.

I'm trying to fight, babe. I'm trying.

"I can stop the pain. Give yourself to me or spend the rest of eternity as a sex slave in the Underworld. Hades has a special place for Nephilim in his harem." The mirror's voice warms, entices, and a feeling of intense pleasure blows the pain away.

As I try to take a breath, the pain returns, and it's even worse. Despite my best efforts to fight, the gold threads knit together, slowly blocking out the energy from my Troy, dimming that new chamber that appeared in the middle of my heart when our mating brand bound us. *Troy, I love you.* My mind screams through the pain, and I desperately try to latch onto the strands of Troy's divine light the chamber sheds to no avail. The knowing of Troy, that warm core in my heart that tells me he's always there, fades to almost nothing. I could swear the mirror's eye squints with pleasure as the growing darkness shuts out the light.

Then, a blast of gold-white light shatters a hole in the blackness. The tight band across my chest loosens. The eye snaps shut, and the mirror disappears as the light finds the new chamber in my heart. Once united with the divine light, the new chamber sends out electrical impulses that beat back the gold threads tightened by the magic mirror.

The pain recedes, but I'm still floating around in some kind of nowhere, only there's none of the sense of utter emptiness as there had been when I'd slipped into the Void. In this pit of darkness, there's only intense pain and nausea. But still, Troy's sapphire-blue ether kisses my skin, and his voice floats to me from somewhere far away, calling me home. I latch onto his essence and hold on for dear life.

Soon, Tristan's sky-blue light joins Troy's, strengthening the rope pulling me toward the surface.

Inch by inch, the rope weaved from their grace drags me toward the light. The closer I get, the more the pain recedes, allowing me to feel the heat from their physical flesh touching mine. My guys are taking care of me, and I let my mind ride their magic carpet of healing.

Then, without warning, an ice-cold pain replaces the warmth that had hummed through me just seconds before and rips through one side of my body where the warm flesh had been. My mind screams with agony, but I have no idea whether I'm making a sound. I thrash my arms around, and they both connect with warm flesh. I wrap my small hands around limbs from two different men and dig my fingers in, holding tight. The moment I touch them, the pain starts receding. I moan, and cold air hits my back as someone picks me up. Seconds later, my body hits a soft mattress; two strong bodies cocoon me, and a blanket of fatigue washes over me. I snuggle in as the pain recedes, and I drift into a dreamless sleep.

"What else did this chief justice say?" Tristan's smoky tenor greets me as I wake up. I keep my eyes closed and focus on keeping my breathing even. Not so much to eavesdrop, although I'd be lying if I didn't admit that was part of it, but mostly to bask in this feeling of being, well, loved by my guys . . . I mean my guy and his brother.

"This is a damned angel mating brand. As a high-order Nephilim, Aleah is destined to bond with more than one mate, and she said I'd better get over any selfish ideas I have to the contrary. Aleah needs the power our love will give her to fulfill her destiny." Troy sounds more mystified than anything else. And what's this about a Nephilim? I vaguely remember reading about the mythical creatures, half-angel, half-human or something. But they aren't real . . . are they? And am I one of them?

"She said we need to help Aleah find her inner warrior. Apparently, I've done it before, so she says I can do it again," Troy says dryly.

I almost laugh at the incredulity in his voice. Instead, I stay perfectly still, hiding my pleasure at this concept, but truth be told, I love the idea that Troy's my knight in shining armor, my conquering hero. A mantle he's always refused to don, always professing to be a humble, ordinary guy. Or maybe all this joy is due to dodging Syrael's bullet. Having chronic illness means that I've survived a few brushes with death, but this latest scare shows me I'm nowhere near ready to leave the land of the living. And now this breaking news—I might be some kind of super-natural.

"Bottom line is Chief Justice Tate says there's no easy way out of this situation. She says it's my purpose." There's a tinge of pride in Troy's voice as he delivers the last sentence.

Forgetting to pretend I'm still sleeping, a big grin spreads over my face. Troy has always wondered about his purpose in life; after all, it has to be more than an aimless romp. It's a subject he and I had debated ad nauseam. I believe we're put on this earth to do good, to be our best selves, and help our neighbor. I believe in reincarnation and karma. Maybe that's why I'm finding it easy to believe in magic and Bardo. Troy always wished he had my certainty. Now, he does.

"You're awake. Trying to fake us out, are you?" Tristan chuckles as I open my eyes and peer into their two gorgeous and worried faces as they peer down at me. "I want to see if there's any remaining damage to your system. Do you mind if I put my hand close to your breast?"

I ignore a sliver of disappointment as I nod my consent. I'm curious to see how he uses his magic healing power.

Troy immediately starts fussing over me, taking my pulse, and making me track his finger with my eyes as if what ailed me was something modern medicine understood. I hide a smile and scooch up so that I'm in a semi-sitting position. Troy needs this sense of control after a big scare. On my other side, Tristan holds his palm several inches above my left breast, awakening visions of what it felt like to have that hand grasp my breast. Troy punctuates each poke and prod with his "Does this hurt?" interrogation. I sit quietly, loving the way they're fussing over me until my bladder starts to scream. I sit up, push the covers down my legs, and start to get up.

Troy pushes me back down. "Oh, no, you don't. You're not going anywhere."

I push back and sit up again. "Oh, yes, I am. I have to pee." With that announcement, I crawl to the side of the large bed and start to climb off.

"Fine, then I'll go with you. For once, stop arguing, and let me take care of you." Moving so fast I barely see him, Troy has me gathered in his arms and heads toward the bathroom.

Memories of the night Troy told me he loved me, when he'd first shown me the depth of his vulnerability, spring to mind. Once his tears had dried from his declaration of love, he'd needed to keep the physical connection with me and hadn't let go, even when nature had called. Despite being touched by the depth of his emotion, I realized I needed to be his shield, the buffer between him and the world. Now, something deep within him has changed—he's more take charge, more assertive, and not for the first time, I'm intrigued to find out more about this man I know so well but might now know at all.

I glance over Troy's shoulder into Tristan's grinning face. "Would you like something to eat?" Strangely, I hear his voice in my head. He winks, sliding me a secret smile. Oh yes, I'd like to eat something all right. Heat blooms between my legs as my traitorous mouth smiles back at him.

TRISTAN

I roll my shoulder against the ache in my left deltoid, but I'm not distressed by the pain. Instead, I welcome it. Because after last night, I'm more certain than ever that I'm one of Aleah's destined mates. And the tattoo forming on my shoulder confirms it. I just have to be patient while we figure out how it all works.

Cass stands at the large bank of windows in the living area of the suite, looking at the magnificent view of the mountains. I help myself to a cup of coffee from the tray sitting on the table and join my silent and stoic brother. I use the quiet time to think about how and when I'm going to tell my brothers about the black rose that's visible on my shoulder, albeit faintly. A black rose that's identical to the one on Troy's and Aleah's shoulders. Has the brand on her shoulder changed? Has the second faint triangle solidified?

"I assume all this cheer you're exuding means she'll survive," Cass says dryly when the mood finally strikes him to speak.

"She's a strong little thing, that's for sure." I don't try to hide my joy at having the chance to learn about the woman

Ali's turned into. "She keeps surprising me, doing what I'd least expect."

"She's definitely not a girlie girl." Cass says this as if he disapproves, yet he's never been one to like girliness.

"Okay, Cass, out with it. What the fuck's your problem? What have you got against her anyway? Oh, I know you never bonded with her the way Troy and I did, but you're being a dick."

"She's breaking apart our team." Cass turns his glowering gaze from mine back to staring out the window into the woods.

His comment instantly gets my back up. Normally, I'm the brother who goes along to get along. Troy thinks he fills that role, but Troy's only easygoing when it suits him. I exhale quietly and try to remember to be patient with him. He's my brother.

"Oh, and how's she breaking up the team? Why can't she join us? Be one of us? If she has the amount of power legend professes, we'll be a hundred times more effective doing our job, driving people into passionate, natural, and loving sexual acts, having a women's perspective." I keep my eyes trained on the room service menu to take the sting out of my words and look for a breakfast tray for Aleah. Although she's recovered from the worst of the attack, her blood sugar is very low, and we need to get food into her sooner than later.

Cass snorts. "Right, so you two can run off and fuck her whenever the urge strikes. That's not a team member—that's a distraction. We've worked too long and too hard to get here to toss it all away on a whim."

I keep my eyes down, fighting the urge to throw Cass a look. What the fuck is he talking about? "And just where are we, Cass? What would we be tossing away?" I can feel Cass's eyes boring into the side of my face as if I'm some sort of moron. Well, fuck you, too, Cass. I have no idea where all this bravado comes from, but I'm riding the tide as it rolls in.

"Being a sex angel lord is not a job—it's a calling." Cass uses his most patronizing tone. "We can't toss it whenever the mood strikes. It is our sacred duty to help people use sex for good and virtue, to show them that unencumbered sex brings great joy, pure happiness, and unyielding love." Cass pronounces this as if he were King Zeus laying down one of his edicts. I'd heard it all before, but this time his words fall on doubting ears.

I raise my eyes and meet his intense gaze. "Tell me why that means we can't love Aleah. And she can't love us. This isn't the priesthood, for gods' sake. We promote the use of sex for good and virtue, and I've got to believe that loving and being loved will only make us more able to carry out this calling we have. There's no reason why we can't be true to love *and* duty." The heat in my voice doesn't surprise me. There's something about Ali that brings out my normally hidden forceful side. The ache in my shoulder gives an extra throb as if giving a supporting fist pump.

Cass's dark eyebrows shoot to the stratosphere, and his lips purse as he glares back at me, but not before I catch his look of respect at my newfound determination. But those feelings are fleeting; he's fixated on helping me see his point.

"She's far too aggressive, and she has far too much influence over Troy. Next thing you know, she'll be taking over," Cass says.

"And there it is: the real reason. She threatens you. No one's ever questioned your authority before, especially a woman. She's not one of your submissives. Here's someone who challenges you, has a working mind of her own, and you don't like it." The expression on Cass's face lets me know I've hit him where it hurts.

"Mark my words—nothing good will come from this."

Cass and I are so busy glaring at each other, we don't hear Troy and Aleah coming into the room holding hands and grinning like kids at a carnival. The lucky bastard probably got lucky again; nothing like a good quickie in the shower.

"Nothing good will come from what?" Troy says.

"Tristan and I were just talking about our next mission and problems we might encounter." For the first time in forever, there's a slight hesitation as Cass delivers this white lie. Technically, the statement is true, but it's misleading. I step into the adjoining kitchenette and call in our breakfast order. Croissants, cheeses, and fresh fruit salad would be enough to sustain us until we settled in to our new location.

Troy and Ali helped themselves to coffee and sank into the sofa in the seating area in my absence. "Food should be here shortly." I freshen my coffee and sit on the cushion on the floor.

"So, where do we go from here?" Ali almost bounces with energy. There doesn't seem to be a hint of last night's near miss.

I give her a tender smile, and I welcome the resulting heat in her look. "Let's talk about something more important first," I say. "How are you? Any aftereffects from last night's scare? Do you even remember last night?"

"Oddly enough, I feel great." Ali throws a grin Troy's way. "We both do. We have a lot to be grateful for."

"Like she says." The grin of satisfaction on Troy's face matches Aleah's, a sense of peace and contentment billowing off them.

"As Troy won't let you out of his sight, and it's all about you," Cass says, a note of confrontation in his voice, "why don't you tell us where we go from here?"

Ali clears her throat. "I can only speak for myself—"

"And me," Troy inserts.

"I've decided that the best thing for me to do is confront

this Lord Syrael. There's not much that can't be solved with a discussion between rational beings. I need to get back to my life. I have a writing assignment to complete, and this Syrael fuckwad is messing with my life, profession . . . livelihood. Can you watch my back while I get on with my life?" Ali asks.

"I agree with her, but we can't go running off half-cocked," Troy says. "We need to be prepared."

"And Troy's convinced me that you two are the very best resources, so will you help me find and stop the threat from Lord Syrael?" She looks at Cass and me in turn with hopeful eyes.

Hell yes, I'm in. "You can count on me."

"Before we go running off half-cocked as Troy says, I have a few questions." Cass doesn't sound at all happy about the idea of taking on Syrael. "Who's in charge of this mission?"

Ali looks at him as if she's a little confused. "Why, Troy, of course." There's finality to her pronouncement that surprises me. Our Troy is not the front-man type, and normally he's happy to let Cass take charge. But when he steps forward and speaks, everyone listens, even Cass.

I think Cass is going to have an apoplectic fit. It isn't often in our more than a thousand years that he hasn't been eagerly and unanimously solicited as leader. I hide my amusement; Troy doesn't. The bastard grins and winks at me. Our Troy is back, the eternal shit disturber, a trait few recognized because he was so good at burying it under layers of self-deprecation.

"Beauty, as much as I appreciate your vote of confidence, I'm not the best choice to lead a mission," Troy says.

Ah, so self-deprecation takes the day.

"Cass gets my vote. He's much better at strategic planning, and he'll use his power to help you discover your hidden secrets." Troy gives Cass a nod before continuing. "I, on the other hand, will take charge of your hands-on training." Troy gives her another grin. "Tristan will help you with your assignment. He's the world's leading expert in all things related to kink."

My head snaps up in shock at the compliment. It's not like Troy to give praise. I give a small smile, hiding just how pleased I am at the recognition.

"Well, if you think Cass is the best man for the job." Ali brushes invisible lint from her knee, dismissing Cass's abilities. What hands-on training?" Ali brightens at the prospect of time with Troy.

"Beauty, this is all about sex. As they fast-tracked me through the levels of enlightenment on Bardo, the justices mentioned Lord Syrael would be able to overcome you through your weakness. They said we have to uncover the dark secret of your sexuality because that's what he'll use to manipulate you.

"She'll need to know more than how to fuck to protect herself from Lord Syrael," Cass says.

"Syrael will strip you down to find that kernel that protects your soul and then destroy you. Unless we find it first." Troy stretches his back as if soothing sore muscles. "So find it first is just what we're going to do, beauty. No arguments."

Then Troy does something that surprises the shit out of me. He swoops Ali into his arms. "And now, if you don't mind, gentlemen, I'm going to take a time out with my wife. Cass, I presume you found us a safe house? Tristan, would you grab the food on the dumb waiter and bring it along?"

Cass looks as bemused as I do at Troy's newfound chivalry but opens a portal and steps through. Troy strides into it with Ali in his arms, and I follow, hoping to be a part of what comes next.

39

ALEAH

I'm so stunned I can barely speak as Troy steps through the hole in the air and deposits my ass on a cushion-covered bench on a large balcony of some sort. Troy had carried me. He actually picked me up and carried me. I snap my mouth shut when I realize it's hanging open in a most unattractive way. A quick glance shows we're not in Canada anymore, that's for damned sure. First, it's hot, and I'm sitting in an outdoor eating area covered with thatch. I peel off the hoodie I'm wearing and put it on the large oval wooden table in front of me. All I can see is clear azure water with what looks like an island in the distance.

We're on a second-story deck of a wood-roofed villa. I take a deep breath of fresh air that carries the scent of sea salt and seaweed, the smell distinctly raw, strong, and delicious. Just like the brothers gathered around me. A bright tropical sun adds streaks of pink and yellow in the otherwise blue sky that heats the light breeze to around eighty degrees. I lean over the balcony rail and peer down into a swimming pool. But right now, I have one thing and one thing only on my mind, and Troy's sexual current humming through me confirms we're of the same mind.

Troy turns to his brothers, all businesslike. "Brothers, as long as we're safe here, I'd like to take a time out with my wife. We'll take the master bedroom unless one of you has some objection." Calm, quiet command fills Troy's soft tone.

Cass's face hardens at Troy's comment, but he says nothing as he sits on the bench opposite me. He dons a pair of sunglasses he slides from a jacket pocket before tossing the jacket on the bench. The sunglasses obscure his eyes, but I'd bet all in that he's looking at me. A frisson of sexual current sprints through me. If he wasn't such a bastard, he might be damned hot. *Not that I'm interested,* I lie to myself.

I throw a worried glance at Troy. Can he sense this attraction to Cass and Tristan the way I can often sense what he's feeling? If so, dear god am I in for a ride. Troy will not let this go. He'll ask me a thousand questions. He'll make me confess. One way or another. Troy doesn't try to hide the somewhat quizzical look he's giving me, nor his raw sexual energy that's as wide and deep as the sea around us. He slides on a pair of sunglasses that seem to appear from nowhere. *Like magic.*

Before I have time to contemplate my Troy with magic powers, a mental image of our two naked bodies lying on a beach towel as he dribbles oil on my breasts brings on a quiver with surprising force. Pleasure rushes through me as I feel the heat radiating from Troy toward me.

Tristan slides on his own sunglasses that appear from thin air and gives me that disarming grin of his that instantly dampens my panties. This time, I don't have to glance at Troy; I can feel his heat meter ratchet as if I'm sitting in front of a blast furnace. Yes, he can definitely sense when I'm interested in one of his brothers.

"So, where are we, and are we sure it's safe?" Troy asks again.

I think Cass's gaze switches from me to Troy. Some silent message must pass between them because Troy's heat drops several degrees as his attention switches from me to Cass.

"I don't give a fuck whether I've offended your sensibilities, Cassiel." Yikes, it's never good news when Troy uses that particular tone. "Now that I'm back in my body, I have one priority, and that's keeping Aleah safe from this predator, and I don't care who I offend in the process. Are we clear?"

I hold my breath as the testosterone stare down happens, but one thing I know for sure, Troy will win. I think. Probably. Because I sense more than feel the force of Cass's will pushing back at him. Give me strength—two alpha males.

Finally, Cass blinks first—he swivels his head and folds his hands on the table. "Fine. Have it your way, Atroyel. You always do."

I look between the two of them but have to rely on my intuition as they both wear stone masks now. There's some undercurrent of sibling rivalry I'm going to have to explore. Tristan leans against the wooden pole beside me, gazing out over the water.

"We're on the island of Iremia in the Mediterranean," Cass says. "We're safe here. The Santiago coven created this island as a safe haven for them on Earth, so needless to say, their magic protects it from Lord Syrael's mirror."

Troy bolts upright in his chair as soon as he hears the words Santiago coven. "You brought Aleah to a vampire lord den? Have you lost your mind?" Troy sounds as if he's about to punch something, or someone.

More silent testosterone-fueled glares are exchanged between them. As the tension grows, I start to feel nauseated, as if they're channeling the force of their emotion through me. I fan my hand in front of my face and look around for a glass of water. None in sight. Dizziness overtakes me, and I can't help it, I have to lay my head on the table. All I can do is moan.

"Beauty, what's wrong. Fuck."

I hear the panic in Troy's voice as I fight the nausea, but I can't do a thing to reduce his stress at the moment. Next thing I know, I'm in his arms again and he's running downstairs before depositing me onto a bed. I close my eyes and curl into a ball, wishing I had something to settle my stomach.

Troy sits on the side of the bed and pulls me into his arms. I moan and try move out of his hold as another wave of nausea washes over me. The guys must have followed him because I hear Tristan say, "Give her this."

"What is it?" That's my Troy, always looking out for me.

"Healing nectar. She's starting to feel our magic, so this will reduce the effect," Tristan says.

Something hard presses against my bottom lip.

"Drink, Aleah." A wet and slightly sweet liquid hits my tongue. I open my mouth and swallow. I can almost feel the fluid swallow the nausea whole, and I slump back into Troy's arms in relief as the ill feeling dissipates. Although my blood sugar rises, an overwhelming fatigue takes over.

"I don't know what happened," I say. No matter how hard I struggle, I slowly lose the battle with the weights pushing my eyelids closed.

"Shhh," Troy says as he lays me back on the bed. He lies down beside me and runs an index finger down the middle of my face from forehead to chin before cupping my cheek in his large hand. I snuggle my face into his hand as I welcome his symbol of affection and intimacy. "Your magic's surfacing, and you'll no doubt experience some strange sensations. But we can figure all that out later. Right now, I've got you to myself, and we're going to get some rest."

With that pronouncement, he pulls me against him, spooning me and holding me close with an arm wrapped around my waist. Not one for naps, I'm absolutely certain I won't sleep as I drift off.

The same index finger tracing my face wakes me, and I look up into Troy's beautiful honey-brown eyes showering me with love. Tiny gold flecks of light I hadn't noticed before twinkle like a constellation designed only for me. Something deep within me responds with an answering pull as I reach for him with my mind. He gives a quick shake of his head, telling me I'll have my turn later, and in less than a blink, he's straddling my hips and slipping a blindfold over my head. As my head drops back, he pulls my hands above my head with one hand.

"This is what I've been waiting for. God, how I've missed you." His voice takes on the deeper, slightly husky reverence that moves him from a tenor to a baritone. I can feel myself getting wet in a welcoming greeting as I wait for him to slide inside me. But, I should have known better.

I barely have a second to pout at not being able to gaze adoringly at or run my hands over his perfectly crafted body, that flawless build with wide shoulders, chiseled chest, washboard abs, and hips that roll into the most delectable ass ever created. Gone is the emaciated body that he'd become before he left me, and I want time to enjoy the candy.

He lowers his body within an inch of mine and stays there. I hold my breath, waiting for the kiss, but instead, his warm breath brushes over my ear, sending sharp tendrils of lust streaming through me. I moan in eager anticipation of the warm hum that will slowly seep into my neurons, silencing the noise of the outside world and leaving nothing but what's happening between the two of us.

But this time, the hum slams into me along with another intense rush of lust. Nothing exists except the sensations rocking and rolling through my body. I arch and try to push up into him. "Troy, I—"

"Shhh." That whisper brushes past my ear, and my pussy tightens, sending rivulets of moisture to coat the insides of my thighs. "If you have something to say, say it with your body, beauty. This is my time."

I throw my head back, wallowing in bliss as he worships me. The tip of his tongue flickers across the shell of my ear before hot breath trails down the side of my neck. Even though I know behaving like the brazen hussy he so loves to call me will only prolong the torture, my back bows as if someone else has control of my body.

A low chuckle deep in his chest sends more heat rushing through me as I wait to see where the tongue making its slow, torturous way from the dip in my neck to my chest will land. When he sucks my gem-hard nipple into his mouth, I moan loudly. He gives each nipple the red-carpet treatment, worshiping each of them with his magic tongue, lips, and the occasional delightful nip of his teeth. I'm panting with excitement by the time he finally trails down my stomach to the top of my pubes.

With another move that happens so fast I can't register it, Troy is between my legs, his strong hands spreading my thighs wide. The cool room air barely has time to brush my exposed pussy before his hot breath stokes the furnace between my spread legs. Another deep growl of rapture rumbles in his chest as he spreads my folds apart and takes in my large, engorged clit.

Troy spends another eternity studying the flower opening fully to his loving gaze, letting me feel how much he adores the shades of dark rose and brown that paint the inside of my lips. My pussy clenches violently with each tickling breath. I thrash and moan, hands still high above my head. Troy releases my hands, and I grab the two handholds conveniently placed in the headboard.

Involuntarily, another moan bursts out of me as Troy's wash of pleasure at my movement courses through me. It's as if our very essence is joined in such a way that it's no longer possible to separate the strands of our love. I embrace the first signs of climax. *Wait for it.* I no longer know whether the thought is his or mine. My body pulses in a frenzy of need he chooses to ignore. My Troy is all about taking his time when it comes to things sexual.

I emit a high-pitched squeal when he dips two fingers into my wetness and uses the moisture to outline my outer and inner lips, not once touching my clit. He continues the light strokes until I'm fighting him like an alley cat as my cunt screams for his cock, but he uses my thighs to hold me effortlessly in place.

As the heat of his mouth closes around my clit, every fiber of my being speaks the depth of my love for him, and I break apart.

40

ATROYEL

The pure joy that hurtles through me is almost painful as my Lea releases the full force of her love for me. Her back bows as she reaches her climax and powerful contractions rack her small body. Seconds pass, her body is frozen by the force of her orgasm. I've never seen anything so singularly beautiful in my life. Yet through her moans, one word repeats in my mind: *more, more.*

Lea's body almost vaults off the bed as I slide two fingers into her convulsing cunt the instant her orgasm shows signs of ending. There's not a doubt in my mind that Aleah's scream of pleasure put my brothers on full alert. I don't give a shit. Normally, I prefer to keep my business mine, at least as much as I can, given our angelic connection. I press on her throbbing G-spot . . . She reacts immediately, her body almost levitating off the bed. I catch her and pin her down. She moans again and thrashes, panting out, "Oh, no, no," as if she's fighting a war with herself. This is a perfect example of why we never allow *no* as a safe word.

Satisfaction rolls through me as she speaks the word that tells me she needs me inside her. I hide a smile at the

211

memory of just how pissed off she'd been with me the first time she'd spoken the word during our lovemaking. I'd immediately stopped, so afraid of doing anything that might disturb the fragile balance of her sexual healing. In return, I'd suffered through her verbal ass-kicking about reading nonverbal sighs. But those are thoughts for another time. Right now, she's here, with me, after far, far too long. I plan to make every moment last. If I had my way, they'd last for eternity. A throbbing in my left shoulder reminds me that it just might.

"Oh, gods. Oh, gods. Oh, gods." She pants the words on a low, hot breath as another orgasm takes hold on the tail of the last.

I keep the relentless rhythm up as she screams and thrashes with surprising strength. My fingers slide in and out with a satisfyingly wet sound, and Aleah rips off her blind-fold and simultaneously reaches for me while trying to wrap her legs around mine. I'm having none of it. I push her thighs wide and move up her body. I balance on one hand while I grab the base of my throbbing cock and thrust into her. Her cunt clamps on my rigid cock as she lets out another moan. I throw my head back and hold myself suspended above her for several beats, letting the power of her sexual energy pour through me. Then, I press my chest to hers, grab her arms, and thrust . . . again and again and again. Her upbeat thrusts meet my downbeat ones, and we let the old familiar rhythms whisper hints of all the new symphonies we have yet to compose.

Just as she had during our life together, she comes over and over again. But now there's something new and unre-strained that wasn't there before. I keep up my relentless pounding, trying to reclaim all the time, life, and distance that's kept us apart. Finally, that tingling at the base of my balls won't be ignored and skips past the usual warning as an explosive orgasm erupts from me. My Lea's body clenches around mine. My wings unfurl as the roar of my climax consumes all muscle control. I collapse on top of her.

We stay that way, unmoving, unwilling to move and break the spell. I can't let go of the new feeling thrumming through me; that sense of *knowing* is there on steroids, as Lea would say. I don't want it to end.

The small movements below me as she wiggles to adjust reminds me that my weight is probably smothering her. With a groan, I let my still semi-erect cock slide out of her, and I roll off her. She makes a small moue of disappointment, and I pull her with me and onto my chest. I kiss the top of her head, which she answers by dropping a kiss to my chest before snuggling even deeper into my arms. Using magic I haven't used in over twenty years, I cover us with a light sheet and close my eyes in contentment.

It's dusk by the time I wake up. We're facing a wall of windows displaying a beautiful tropical sun slipping into the ocean on the horizon. I'm still cradling Aleah in my arms, and I can tell by the rhythm of her breathing that she's also awake. Energy and excitement rush through me as she runs her hand over my chest. It will take getting used to, this sensory and empathic connection I have with her now.

I flip her onto her back, my arm tucked beneath her neck. She gives a small, sweet sound of surprise but says nothing, staring at me. Rising onto my elbow, I return her gaze, my eyes shimmering with divine light and love.

"I have something I want to say, and I want you to hear me out." I rest my finger over her mouth so she won't interrupt. She gives me a smile so tender my heart almost breaks.

"I'm not sure when we'll be alone again, and it's important you hear this. I don't quite know what to say because this isn't simply a thank you. That isn't enough, beauty. Because of you, my human body died with dignity and grace. You not only joined me on the journey, you also held on and fought like a mountain lion caring for her cub until the moment you had to let go."

Her eyes fill with tears. "I thought maybe you resented me for holding on too long." Her words come out as a long sigh. "It was so hard—"

"You always put my process above your needs, probably too much so. You taught me not to miss the dance, and this time, I don't intend to miss one single beat."

Her joy rushes through me with a power that almost knocks me over. "I learned so many things about you that I hadn't seen before, so many ways I'd misjudged or underestimated you and your tremendous gifts. Nothing makes me happier than having eternity to peel back the layers of your rather complex personality."

She snorts out a laugh. "Jesus, Troy, you make me sound like Mother Teresa or someone. I should be thanking you for giving me the gift of being part of your process, for opening yourself to me." She pulls my head down for a slow, sweet kiss she deepens as her desire rises. She slides a small hand down my abdomen, and I grab her wrist.

"Oh, no, you don't, you minx. We have more than enough time to share our love with sex, but this is about more than sex." I'd spent so much of our time together shielding my emotions, wrapping my heart so that the pain wouldn't be so bad when she left. Because one thing is for godsdamn certain, love ends either in separation or death, and in my case, I'd been certain she'd leave as soon as she saw my true colors. That had been one of the reasons I'd been so relieved I died first. I needed her strength to shield me from the barrage of emotions coming at me from the world. Because despite the protective spell the gods put on my earthly body to give me some protection, intense emotion, mine or others, almost made me buckle emotionally, which in turn, made it next to impossible for me to function. That was until she'd come along and proven to be the best buffer ever.

To this day, I don't know how or why I was so lucky to earn her love, and I'd never felt worthy of it. Of her. She doesn't recognize it—her abuse did a number on her self-esteem, but she's much smarter and more gifted than I am. So, I've always had the deep fear that one day she'd realize I'm a useless ass and be on her way.

Instead, she loved me for who I was. She showed me that as much as I needed her to shield me from the world, I was an anchor that grounded her while she fought off the slings and arrows of everyday life for a gifted young multiracial woman. Her bright light threatened many. She's an articulate woman who didn't hesitate to lean into the discomfort of speaking her mind. It took hearing a woman tell her she needed to learn her place to open my eyes to her incredible strength and wisdom.

She'd come home from work one day in evident distress. As I'd pulled her into my arms and asked what was wrong, she broke into convulsive sobs so strong she could barely breathe. When she'd finally regained control of her emotions, I pulled the story from her. She'd been given a project to manage that involved a number of contributors, one of whom missed several deadlines. My Lea, in her direct way, had asked her when she expected to have the work finished. As Lea told it, she'd "spewed forth a lot of bullshit" without answering the questions, so Lea had said, "You didn't answer my question."

Those five words led to disciplinary action because the "princess" had been mortally offended by Lea's pointed question. She'd made a formal complaint that resulted in Lea being ordered to apologize to the woman—"and be humble about it"—which was at the root of her fury. Lea had countered with a "position paper," asking for clarification on what had been so wrong about the questions, especially given the fact that their director, a man, had made a similar statement at an earlier meeting. Her manager, a princess in her own right if you ask me, had made it simple: Lea was not a man. Lea's behavior was offensive. Apologize and make it right or suffer disciplinary action. That explained the tears. Lea rarely cried, but being forced to do something against her will, especially something she deemed unfair, woke a deep anger within her.

I'd watched in amazement as Lea worked through her feelings. She'd cried, and sworn, and paced, and raved while she analyzed the pros and cons of "submitting" or "making that little bitch realize just how unfair and offensive it is to reward someone for being irresponsible," eventually deciding it wasn't worth the fight.

But her struggle to swallow her feelings about the indignity had opened my eyes to the many times people tried to "help" Lea see her place in our society. Sometimes, fighting the battle, because that's what it was, threatened to defeat her, take the fight out of her, but she wore her formidable emotional strength like a badge of honor she didn't recognize. Her command strength and indomitable will wouldn't allow her to back down.

A small hand snaking down my stomach brings me back to the present. I tighten my fingers around her wrist, halting her progress. She sticks her tongue out at me in response to my rebuff, but humor, not rejection, dances in her eyes.

"Okay." She drags out the word. "What do you want to talk about? Wait, let me grab a robe."

That's my Lea. If we're not going to play, she's all about business. I watch her round ass disappear into the en suite while I contemplate this insight.

I pull on a pair of jeans and stack the pillows against the headboard. I help myself to a bottle of orange juice from the bar fridge before ejecting and retracting my wings a few times, partly for fun but mostly to get used to using them again. When I hear running water, I prop myself against the pillows and wait.

Seconds later, she bounces out of the bathroom cocooned in a large terry robe and sits cross-legged on the bed, facing me.

"That's better. I'm ready. What do you want to talk about?" She tries her best to look demure, but her impatience, curiosity, and eagerness almost trigger an adrenaline rush in me.

I take a moment to admire her before continuing. Then, I take another moment just because I like to bug her. She keeps her gaze steady and waits, but the words *mental eye roll* scroll through my mind. It's going to be so much fun exploring this woman again on so many different levels.

"What's the plan?" I ask because she always has one. I waggle my eyebrows in that way that delights her so much. She's always taken delight in the smallest things about me, treats me as if I've got superpowers because I can curl my tongue.

"Seriously, babe? When did I have one minute to come up with a plan?" She gets where I'm going right away, another thing I admire about her.

"I could feel the synapses happening when you were in the bathroom. Don't kid a kidder. And if you don't have it formulated, you will in about thirteen seconds."

She stares a bit incredulously, then sighs. "I need a bit more information before I can form a solid plan. I need time to work on my article. Then, there's whatever I'm going to have to do with Cass to learn to protect myself." She gives me her best side-eye and frowns. "Is this going to involve sex? Him being a sex angel lord and all?" She sounds appalled at the idea, but that sexual current does another run through her body. Maybe Justice Tate was right after all about some women needing more than one man to find their destiny.

I grin. "Not unless you want to."

She picks up a pillow and throws it at my head. I catch it and toss it back.

"Bastard."

"You're stuck with me, bastard and all, but seriously, beauty, I have no idea where this journey will take us sexually. But I can tell you that only on Earth is there this fixation on monogamous relationships." I rub my left shoulder. "Maybe it's because of our angelic mating brand, but I'm not afraid of losing you. I'm not threatened by sharing you because regardless of what happens with anyone else, we're divinely destined to be together."

I sit up, kiss her, and get up. She'll need some time to mull this over. It's a dramatic change from the way she's used to thinking.

"I guess this means we don't need to read our Double Diaries anymore." She sounds wistful or maybe disappointed.

"*Au contraire*, whatever schedule you come up with needs to incorporate reading the diaries. The gods, whoever"—I wave my hands in the air with my classic details-details gesture being a big picture kind of guy—"used my letter power to infuse power-releasing enchantment, a kind of spell, in the diary. They told me working through it is a crucial part of protecting you, for you and us."

Lea rises and rifles through the drawers and closet filled with clothes. Cass chose the location, and Tristan has taken his usual care and made sure we have everything we need.

"Well, we vowed to be truthful to ourselves and each other, so I get that there's more for us to explore." She shimmies into a pair of panties and dons a long, black dress that looks as if it was designed just for her. "But that doesn't mean we have to involve your brothers, right?"

"Actually, we do. One thing Justice Tate and the gods were very definite about was that all four of us have a critical role to play if we're to defeat Lord Syrael." I grab her hand. Now is the perfect time to play my trump card to make sure she's all in—give her the cause she needs almost as much as breathing. "The gods say you're one of the chosen to help blot out all sexual abuse against women and children. We can get into the details later. Let's go have a look around."

Chosen? OMG! I knew it. I'm part of something. Cass will have a coronary when he hears. Great, just great. Oh well, in for a penny . . . Thoughts roll through her mind as we head out to find my brothers and explore, but her anticipation and excitement tell the real story.

41

TRISTAN

Cass and I are enjoying the majestic island sunset when Troy and Ali join us late in the day. She's pumped, but she's also guarded as if she's not sure what she's walking into. My breath catches as she moves toward us in a cocktail-length black dress with a bare midriff and skirt that's slung low on her right hip and slit to her hip on the other, a dress that the angels must have designed just for her. The slight hitch in Cass's breathing signals he's just as affected by her appearance as I am.

Cass and I sit in the overwater villa's living room at a round, sunken table and banquette bench positioned over a cutout in the floor. Ali bounces over—there's no other word to describe the spring in her step—and sits beside me.

Ali takes the glass of punch Cass offers and throws a wide you're-the-best grin at both Cass and me. "Before we get started, I want to thank you both for finding such a spectacular place. I mean, who would have ever dreamed of a house designed over water? And the office. I thought the last place was spectacular, but you've outdone yourselves with this one. Cass, you discovered this place, right? The see-through floors are amazing. My god, even the fucking bathroom has one. Everything is just beautiful. You hit the jackpot this time." She raises her glass to toast him.

There's no artifice behind Ali's words, and Cass can't help but respond. His lips quirk at the sides. "You're welcome, but it's not that big a deal."

"Well, it is for me. You found a place that is beyond my wildest dreams." She turns her gaze on me. "And I hear you're the one who makes sure we have what we need, including making sure my laptop and phone arrived." She plants a kiss on my cheek. "Thank you." The slight huskiness of her low voice makes my cock throb with desire.

I smile back, reminded of the kiss she still owes me. "You're welcome, *mon chou.*"

"It's okay," Troy grumbles, "but there's nothing to do here. I've seen better."

Ali gives that cute little snort of hers. "Right, this coming from our cloistered leisurist. Moving right along, I guess we'd better talk about the next steps." She looks at Cass. She's treading carefully, not sure how to read him. "What do you suggest, Cass?"

"Why don't you ask Atroyel? You want him in charge, after all." Cass makes it clear he considers Aleah wanting Troy in charge insulting.

Seriously? C'mon, Cass.

Ali takes another sip of punch, and I get the strong sense she's figuring out how to deal with yet another moody male. Since spending the night holding her, our telepathic connection is stronger, still vague, but stronger. Cass crosses his arms over his chest and gives her a blank stare as she keeps her gaze fixed on him. Troy, as usual, sits, externally calm but boiling with impatience. Watching this play out is better than any reality TV show.

"Since we're in this together, I think it's best we take a

collaborative approach. If that's not working, then we'll have a vote," Ali says.

"And, if we're tied? And who put you in charge? I find it as annoying as fuck that you think you know more about fighting a demon than we do," Cass snaps back.

Troy frowns, instantly alert as Ali flinches. Despite her outwardly calm demeanor, she's brimming with hurt feelings and something else I can't put my finger on. Defensiveness? Fuck you-ness?

"That's uncalled for, Cass, even for you. Aleah's entitled to give input as a member of the team." When Troy's hackles are up, even Cass listens. Despite the easygoing facade he shows the world, he's got a very deep sense of what's right and wrong, and he has no problem stepping into the fray.

"I apologize. I by no means meant to usurp your authority. It's one of my strengths and a curse. Once I've set a goal, I have a pressing need to share it with others because of my need to control my own choices, not because I'm trying to take over. Sorry." With each of Aleah's words, it's as if there's a curtain closing on the stage of our emotional connection. By the time she's done, she's donned her protective cloak of confidence, but she's deeply upset by the encounter.

Watching her internal struggle tamping down her natural ability to see what needs to be done and say so, I see it's time for my peacekeeper role. "I, for one, like having a woman's perspective. Now, how about you break the tie, Cass? You're in the best position to choose the best way forward objectively." I put slight stress on the word *objectively*, hoping that complimenting his strategic skills will mollify him.

Ali looks conflicted, but Troy nods, so she goes along with it.

"Right," Cass says. "Let's review our assignments. I'll head up security. It's imperative you run all contact with the outside world by me. Once we know what we're dealing with, I'll teach you how best to protect yourself." He gives Aleah a pointed look. "And one of us will remain with you at all times. We don't want a repeat of last night." He pauses and looks at each of us in turn. We nod.

"Troy, you're in charge of getting through the Double Diaries with Tristan as your backup. Releasing her magic is the first of two priorities. Tristan, you're in charge of finding out her triggers so we can teach her how to defend herself when Syrael attacks. Questions?"

Aleah half raises her hand. Cass nods in her direction. "What's my job?"

"Answering our questions, staying out of trouble, and writing your damned article," Cass says matter-of-factly. I hide an inner smile as I recognize the problem we'll be facing.

Both Cass and Ali are natural-born leaders with all the rough edges that go along with that gift, such as inflexibility, stubbornness, and a very direct way of speaking. As a male and a prince, these traits had been praised and promoted. I'd bet my good looks that Ali's experience was quite different. This world didn't look kindly on strong women in leadership roles. We're in for a ride with these two.

"I'll do my best." Ali makes the words a metaphorical military salute. "So, I'd better do just that. I've got to call Daisy. She'll call the cops if I don't check in soon, and I get the distinct impression that you boys need some time for a brotherly chitchat." She looks at Cass. "Is that okay with you?"

Cass gives her a sharp look. There's no hint of subtext in her question, but he can't see past the emotional wall she's erected. He gives a curt nod. "You'll have to settle for email for now. Our hosts have blocked all cellular activity for security purposes."

Aleah nods. In one graceful move, she swivels on the

cushion, tucks her feet against the ass cheeks I can't wait to get my hands on, stands, and climbs out of the sunken table. She gives a wiggled finger wave as she sashays away as if she hasn't a care in the world. But I can feel otherwise. I can't wait to find out what's upsetting her, but she's right—the brothers need to talk.

As soon as the door closes behind her, Troy frowns at Cass. "Okay, Cass, what the hell is stuck up your ass?" Troy isn't in one of his charming and conciliatory moods, so he dives straight for the point.

Cass hesitates a minute, deliberating just what to say.

"We don't have time for games, brother. Let's lay our cards on the table, shall we?" Troy asks.

"Fine, you want to know what's bothering me? Our team's coming apart at the seams. Need I say more?" Cass glares back at Troy.

I stay quiet, having learned it's best not to get between them when they have an issue to work out.

"What makes you say that?" Troy asks, and I give a small sigh of relief that he's still in a receptive mood. I sent a small prayer to the heavens that this wouldn't be one of those times when Cass pushed him so far that he simply disappeared for several days. At least, that was how he used to handle things. Life with Ali changed him. I watch the exchange with interest.

Cass gives a slight fine-if-I-must sigh. "Look, Atroyel, we all know that once you've fixed your mind on something or someone, you're obsessively single-minded. You were put on Earth to find and keep Aleah safe, not fall in love with her. And now that you have, you could give a shit about me, Tristan, or our mission."

Troy studies the glass in his hands, and I place a mental bet on the approach he'll take next, whether conciliatory and persuasive or contrary and pointed. His wry smile gives me the answer.

"I'm no less committed than I was before, brother, but you're right—Aleah's needs come first." Troy's eyes warm, and he leans forward as if punctuating his sincerity. "Look, I have no idea where this is going. None of us do. You heard what the justices said, which makes saving Aleah from Syrael our mission, and that makes me more than committed to this mission. She's my destined mate, and I'll save her single-handedly if I have to or die trying." He straightens and swivels his head to release some of the tension.

I decide this is an excellent time to step into the fray. "Ah, guys, while we're chatting about saving Ali, there's something you should know." I drop the words casually, but our telepathic connection reveals the seriousness of what I have to say next. Both brothers stare at me, waiting. For several seconds, all we hear are the waves crashing against the jetty.

"Well?" Cass runs out of patience first.

I decide it's easier to show than tell and roll back my T-shirt's left sleeve, revealing the freshly forming brand. Troy sucks in a quick breath.

"Great, just fucking great." Cass levitates out of the sunken seat and stalks from the room.

"Fuck!" I take a large swig of my punch for fortification. Cass would be looking for something to punch either physically or metaphorically, and I'd rather it not be me.

"Let him go," Troy says. "We'd better talk about what your brand means."

"I'm sure this is probably upsetting for you. I'm sorry about that." I'm not sure why I'm apologizing; it's not as if I have any control over what's happening.

Troy gives me a resigned smile. "I'm not upset, Tristan. It's just a lot to take in. But I know what we need to do."

I wait to hear my fate.

"We've got to tell Lea. You don't want to discover what

happens if she thinks we're hiding things from her. She'll tolerate a lot of things, but deception isn't one of them. She has serious trust issues because of her childhood abuse and generally shitty treatment from her fellow human beings. It's her story, so I'll let her share the details if she wishes. Besides, as a destined mate, building trust is more imperative than ever." Troy downs his drink and rises. "Let's get this done."

4 2

ALEAH

A wave of the weird telepathic thing happening with Troy, and to a lesser degree with Tristan, hits me before the guys step into the room. Resignation, determination, concern—scratch that—*worry*, and excitement mingle with my equally conflicted emotions with such force I feel faint. And there's still the tiny seed of anger simmering deep within me. Cass had the frigging gall to accuse me of taking charge when I did nothing of the sort. *Pisser!*

So much new stuff is coming at me. I'm disoriented on the one hand and almost rabid with eagerness on the other to see what comes next, especially with the sex stuff. I'm not sure I want to find out just how kinky I am, but I've also never been one to hide from self-reflection. At least I haven't been for a very long time. One doesn't spend time with Troy and remain subject to self-deception. Troy lives, eats, and breathes his insistence that we discover our truths. But it's all so goddamn hard.

Instantly recognizing the signs of a full-fledged pity party coming on, I give it a hard push into the mental room where I store shit I'll deal with later. I throw an enormous padlock on the door for good measure. The universe gave me a tremendous ability to compartmentalize emotions so they don't interfere with daily life. If I have any superpowers, that's one of them. I give a mental eye roll at the idea that I have magic powers despite what Troy said. We'll figure that out in due time.

I speed through the last few words of my apologetic email to Daisy and press Send as Troy and Tristan step into the office. No doubt, Troy's decided it's time to get on with the Double Diary and sex explorations. The man is single-minded when it comes to sex, that's for sure. My man only has two hobbies, sex and golf, and the time of day dictates which one takes priority.

"Same for me," Tristan says this without a trace of his usual cheerful humor, his intensity almost as great as Troy's. *But sex always takes first place with me.* My sense of him is getting stronger, as is the second red triangle on my shoulder. I resist the urge to take another look at it.

I lick my lips as the thought plants in my head, but I'm not in the mood for sexy thoughts. Troy's emotions alert me to the fact I'm probably not going to like what's coming next. He leans against the doorframe of one of the open French doors in the entry to the small room and looks directly at me, eyes burning with passion.

Tristan crosses those muscular arms over his chest and leans against the other side of the doorframe, ankles crossed.

Troy strolls across the room toward me. "Beauty, we need to talk. But first, show us your left shoulder." I'm expecting his usual "you're your own worst enemy" talk, so I'm a little surprised at this order.

Okay, then. I slide the dropped shoulder of the sexy black dress and expose my shoulder. My tattoo shimmers with the strange blue-white misty light I'm starting to get used to, and the second red triangle emerging under the first one pulses.

The second triangle is light in color, but it's definitely there. Troy leans over and outlines the new triangle with his finger, almost reverently as if giving homage to the ultimate unity and change symbol. He straightens and gives Tristan a pointed look I can see despite the dim light of dusk. "Tristan has something to show you."

Although I have no idea why, my pulse triples, and adrenaline rushes through me as Tristan straightens, crosses the room, and rolls his short sleeve up, exposing the faint but discernible outline of a black rose tattoo on his deltoid matching the one on Troy's and my shoulders.

"It seems the universe has decided we're destined for each other." His voice has an ironic tone, and I can't get a clear read on his emotions.

Gobsmacked. There's no other word to describe what I'm feeling right now. My head's doing a love-hate dance with the idea of having more than one mate.

"Okay." I drag that one syllable out as if it's a fermata in one of my choir solos. How the fuck does one respond to this? What does it mean? I need time to process this new development, so I do what comes naturally when I have something monumental to consider—I seek more information. "And how are we feeling about that, and by *we*, I mean you two?"

"Beauty, I need some time to think before I can answer that. I learned a lot of new information on Bardo that I need to process." Troy leans over the desk, cups both of my cheeks in his hands, and gives me a sound kiss. "Give me a couple of hours, and then we'll talk." The pleading behind his earnest gaze lets me know he'll stay if I ask, but that will only delay the inevitable. Troy needs to be alone, away from others' emotional input to figure out his own before he can deal with this. And me.

"No, you go. I'm good. Do what you need to do. I could

use some time to think, too." I give Tristan a pointed look that Troy doesn't miss. *No hanky-panky.*

"We both know you work through problems best by verbalizing, and since Tristan needs to figure out your triggers, now is as good a time as any to start." Troy gives me another smack on the lips and steps to the open French doors leading to the balcony. "Oh, and beauty, be sure to tell him about your goose-gander thing. He needs to know what he's up against." Troy steps out onto the balcony with a wink, unfurls his wings, and takes off in one graceful movement that I take a moment to admire enviously.

"What a show-off, but I guess *some* people like it," Tristan says teasingly.

I sing a line from the movie *Funny Girl* about the groom being prettier than the bride. "Too bad he doesn't know how beautiful he is." I turn to look at this man who is my destined mate.

"Then, that's another thing the two of you have in common." Tristan straightens before I have time to answer. "Let's go have a drink."

My tattoo throbs the closer I get to him, and some involuntary energy reaches into me and yanks me to my feet, making them move with a will of their own. I try to stop, but it's like fighting with quicksand, not that I'm sure why I'm fighting it. It's a walk, for god's sake. It isn't as if he's going all caveman and tossing me over his shoulder to drag me off to bed. *sigh* I give in and follow Tristan out of the room and to the beach-side entry to the villa. Once outside, we pick up a sandy path winding its way through a forest of palm trees and tropical flora.

"Are you using sex magic on me?" How else do I explain this strange pulling feeling I'm having?

He pauses where the path intersects with a log boardwalk connecting a web of villas built on water that fans out as far as I can see. I take a breath of the air, enjoying the salty tang. Tristan starts down the massive boardwalk lit by lights buried in the sea below us.

"No, babe, I'm not using any magic on you, but I can if you like. The bond connects us emotionally if that's what you're referring to, so I'm getting flashes when you think something particularly vivid, and it's as if some external force is pushing me toward you." He grins. "And Troy is the caveman in the family."

I burst out laughing; I can't help it. Troy is the last man on Earth resembling a caveman, and Tristan's wide grin tells me he was being facetious. "If you can't read my mind, how did you know I was thinking about a caveman? And why does it feel like you're lassoing me with a thick rope?" Without thinking, I stick my tongue out at him and punch his arm with my free hand. Then sanity prevails. *Shit. Shit. Shit. Shit. Shit.* I punctuate each word with a mental slap against the side of my head. Mortified heat almost burns the shell of my ear as embarrassment floods through me. This is precisely the kind of behavior that gets me into trouble. It's too aggressive, I'm told. Not feminine enough. This is not at all the way I want Tristan to see at me. And suddenly that matters to me if he's my destined mate. My throbbing shoulder pulses a couple of times, letting me know it's not a matter of *if*, it's a confirmed fact. Leaving me, a forty-year-old career woman, acting like a nervous teenager on her first date. Not that I know much about dating, having only ever gone on two in my life.

I hastily scrub at the place on Tristan's arm where I hit him. "Sorry. Sometimes I act without thinking. Did I hurt you?"

Tristan stops and spins me to face him. A slight frown creases his angelic face as he looks down at me, studying me. Several beats pass before he gives his head a shake. "If I do nothing else tonight, I'm going to get to the bottom of what's going on in that head of yours, *mon chou.*"

Before I have time to think, wings spring free from his back, and he swoops me into his arms. I almost strangle him as the feeling of ascent strikes. I glance down, wondering what my chances of survival are if I fall from this height. Fear and exhilaration race through me in equal measure, locking every muscle with tension.

Relax, beauty. He's got you. Enjoy the ride. Troy's reassuring voice murmurs in my head, and I do one of those girly things you only see in movies. I relax my body against Tristan's and nestle in for the ride.

ALEAH

I barely register the opulence of our surroundings as Tristan lands on a soaring thatched-roof atrium offering a stunning view of the ocean. A large bar with a solitary bartender occupies the entire center of the massive space behind us. For utmost privacy, comfy-looking loveseats are strategically placed in nooks and crannies separated by light-colored wood beams and curved railings. Tristan grabs my hand and pulls me toward a loveseat facing the ocean.

I yank my hand out of Tristan's, bringing him to an abrupt halt. Concern paints his lovely face. "What's up?"

"Wait, we don't have masks," I say. "Do they have COVID here?" What's happening to me may be a crazy delusion, but I haven't lost my mind completely. One thing I'm fucking anal about is following the pandemic protocols. If Troy had caught coronavirus, it would have killed him. Of that, his entire medical team agreed. I'd probably lost a friend or three because of the wall of protection I'd erected around us, but it had been worth the extra time I had with him.

Tristan's smile lacks its usual radiance, and I'm not sure

whether the tension I'm sensing is his, or mine, or both. "We don't need them here. Besides, you're Nephilim, babe. Even if you're not immune until we release your power, I can use mine to heal you." He sits on the couch and pats the cushion beside him.

I plunk my ass down and nod.

"We're guests of the Santiago family. They head up the vampire coven who built this protected retreat for supernaturals. We're under their protection at the moment. We can talk more about that later." Tristan holds up two fingers, and I follow his gaze to the bartender. The stocky man dressed in a black leather vest gives a curt nod. Tristan settles back and half turns toward me.

I fiddle with the split skirt of my dress, trying to put space between the two of us without appearing to do so. Because right now, I can't focus on anything but the heat coming from Tristan's body.

"Talk to me. When Cass asked who put you in charge, why did you take it so personally? Or was it his insinuation that you're a know-it-all?"

I try to decide just how much to tell him, but the compulsion to be honest with him drowns my natural reticence about revealing too much about myself. The gentle lapping of the waves relaxes me enough that I can tell Tristan all my secrets . . . well, most of my secrets.

There's nowhere for me to look but at him, at that beautifully carved face that would have won People magazine's Sexiest Man Alive contest every frigging year, hands down. Troy's equally handsome, so it's not as if I'm not used to seeing beauty in my man, but the iron grip on his emotions mutes that extra bit of animation Tristan has. Even then, in the early years, I'd had to beat women off with a metaphorical machete to get near Troy anytime we were in public.

People had been shocked, and some disturbed, when it became clear we were an item. Some even placed wagers on how long it would take for him to dump me because, after all, it must be the "Black" thing and he'd soon get tired of dipping his quill in that well. The first time someone had suggested this to me, I had no idea what she was talking about. "What *Black* thing?" I'd been so naive.

Little Miss Popular had smirked and said, "You must know the myth they say about you people, when you go Black, you never go back, just isn't true. He'll get sick of you in no time."

I'd shown them, the fuckers. I held a tiny golden kernel of pride deep within myself because of this. The so-called ugly duckling got the golden goose. I got my man, even though it had taken a very long time to get rid of the feeling that it was all going to come to a crashing halt someday soon. And now he's mine forever, as is his equally enthralling brother. But to have two men who take my breath away is almost too much to believe.

Tristan sits relaxed, his body turned toward me, arm thrown across the back of our loveseat. He's not touching me, but it would probably have been better if he were because I can't ignore the heat of his body this close to mine. All I can think about is touching him. He keeps his blue eyes trained on me as if I'm the only person in his universe.

When Cass asked who put you in charge, why did you take it so personally? His question keeps bouncing around in my head. There's no going back if I drop down the rabbit hole that yawns open with his question. If I expose my inner truths, I'll truly be stripped naked for him in a way only Troy's seen me. And that had taken years of work to build the trust we both needed to reveal our hidden vulnerabilities.

I run my tongue over my dry lips and try to work up a bit

of moisture. As if by magic, the leather-clad bartender appears with two water coconuts, each with straws stuck through holes drilled into the flesh. I gratefully accept the coconut the server offers me and take a large sip of the alcohol-infused drink before taking inordinate care to place the nutshell on the table. Throughout it all, Tristan simply waits . . . and watches.

"It's not the kind of thing I can talk about," I finally say. "You of all people should understand that." I clap my hand over my mouth as soon as those words escape. "What I mean is—"

"Don't try to correct yourself, *mon chou*. I want to hear what you think, unfiltered. How so?" Something very serious replaces the humor in Tristan's eyes and encourages me to go on.

"Because there's something very different about you, too. Everyone sees how beautiful you are and ignores your depth. I'm not expressing myself very well, but I bet most people don't see the way you bring to light what people often hide and how you resolve conflicts and misunderstandings. But you do." I touch my fist to my heart. "I feel that, in here, both the gift and your hurt. Oh, I get it's not the same as being Black, and that you exist squarely in a place of White privilege, but I'm betting that most people refuse to look past your beauty. Hell, even Cass infers you're some kind of dimwit." The part of my brain trained to warn me when I'm treading into territory that most will find offensive starts waving a warning flag. "Not that I think you're a dimwit," I rush to say, mentally slapping myself for letting my mouth run without filters. I take my glasses off and hold them up to the light, buying me a few seconds to think. Another gulp of the refreshing drink buys several more.

"Anyone who takes offense at honest insight is an idiot in my book. I know you're not calling me names, *mon chou*. I can feel it in here." He places his hand over his heart before replacing it behind me. "And in the interest of collaboration, you're the first person who's seen into that part of me. I'm fascinated by your observations, but this is about you, not me. We can talk about me later." Tristan reaches over and tucks a curl behind my ear.

I shiver, and goosebumps break out all over my arms. I can't help it. "Promise? Because that's another thing that drives me around the bend. Don't ask me for something you're not willing to return, and I don't mean next year like your brother, I mean now, tonight."

He takes his arm off the loveseat and puts his hand over his heart again. "I swear on all that's holy. When you're done telling me your secrets, I'll tell you mine."

That's all it takes for the walls to come tumbling down. We sit for hours as dusk turns to full night, while I spill my guts, starting with my lack of early memories. The only memories I have before my thirteenth birthday are fleeting and horrid. I tell him about the first of many sexual assaults.

I tell him about the day I started fighting back, confronting my goddamn sexually, physically, and emotionally abusive foster father with a large carving knife in hand.

Tristan's lips twitch as I described being all of ninety pounds soaking wet going up against a monster of a man, of facing down the bully. Letting him know I'd kill him if he ever came to my bed again.

"Did that stop him?" Tristan only interrupts for clarification, but it spurs me on.

"Oddly enough, it stopped the sexual abuse and beatings but escalated the emotional abuse. He started a campaign to let me know on a daily basis that I was worthless, unlovable, and just plain crazy. And he did a good job of convincing me that I, a child, enticed him to my bed, that I asked for it, that being a vessel for men's sexual needs was all I was good for." I can't keep the bitterness from my tone. Tristan squeezes my shoulder but otherwise keeps a respectful distance.

I tell him about meeting Troy and how having him and his friends as a safe haven probably saved my fucking life even if it hadn't been love at first sight for him. Tristan tips his head back and closes his eyes as I describe how absolutely fucking frustrating Troy had been, how hard to get to know. How Troy had refused to let me see his feelings until I was sure of my own. But he'd been the only man who hadn't fucked first and talked later . . . and talk only came if I was lucky.

Tristan chuckles as I described my futile attempts to "seduce" Troy at the young and very fucked-up age of nineteen. How it had taken almost eight months of Troy "playing" with my cunt before he'd relented and we'd done the deed. He understands when I tell him one of the greatest gifts Troy gave me was trusting me with his inner secrets.

I tell him about being grateful to be a born and bred Canadian but that it's still not easy to be a Black woman in Canada. About being repeatedly given performance awards but making considerably less, by tens of thousands of dollars in a couple of cases, than my peers. About being told someone like me doesn't need the money and I shouldn't want to take it away from my White colleagues who presumably need it more than I do. I don't hide my anger when I tell him how I watched colleagues be praised for the same things I was disciplined for. As the words spill from my mouth, I purge excess baggage I've carried hidden within for years.

We pause for a moment while the bartender refreshes our drinks. Then I tell him about being labeled a troublemaker when I appealed or fought outright against each injustice, and how many people tried to convince me I had some defect that made me see a different reality than everyone else. And those were the kind folks. I'd be a rich woman today if I had a dollar for every time someone in power told me I need to learn my place.

I talk until we venture near the room holding the secrets about my sexuality, including the large trunk holding my many hang-ups and triggers. Then, I stop. "Your turn," I announce.

TRISTAN

As Ali paints her dispassionate and earnest description of her life experience, I'm so engrossed I almost forget to make mental notes of the emotional trigger points for her. Despite her clinical recitation, I sense the well of emotion simmering deep within her. I open up my senses to ensure I don't miss any of this complex woman's nuances. My mate. Although she's showing me the same brave front she holds up for the world to see, our bond lets me see just how emotionally vulnerable she is.

She tells me about how she'd never quite forgiven herself for not fighting harder when grown men had raped her as a teen. Even when one had held a knife to her throat, threatening to kill her if she didn't comply. I see more evidence of just how strong her will is as her nonchalance hides pure self-disgust as she describes another knifepoint rape. Her story triggers respect, rage, and awe in equal measure. How Troy must have suffered when she described being dragged down an isolated train track. One after another, she builds a horror movie of abuse and victimization.

"I live by a strict sexual moral code. I've done everything to ensure I'll never again be called the Black ho."

I'm sure the moral code affects more than sex, but I wisely keep my counsel. She's hard on herself, that's clear, showing none of the compassion I've caught glimpses of for herself. But as her outpouring progresses, she relaxes, almost as if getting these feelings off of her chest has a purging effect. She doesn't so much wind down as merely stop. She's given as much as she's willing to give without me reciprocating. Kicking off her sandals, she turns to face me, bringing her legs onto the couch and tucking them under her chin.

I have so much I want to tell Aleah, my beloved. For a second, I let my heart open to the joy this brings me, but her penetrating gaze reminds me it's not a sealed deal yet. Within her, hope wars with doubt as she steels herself for the disappointment she's expecting. She needs me to be forthcoming but expects I won't be. I need to gain her trust, so I'm about to do something I've only done with a woman once before. And that had ended in disaster.

I need to reveal my inner core, to be honest about who I truly am. Ali's nobody's fool, and her intuition will alert her to any deception on my part. How do I segue into stories about how the teachers at boarding school abused me, how I'd been too ashamed to tell our parents that the headmistress used me as her sex toy?

I'd learned at a young age that nobody takes boys seriously when it comes to sexual abuse from women. It might have been a different thing if it had been men abusing me, but Mistress Helola's sex parties had been exclusive territory for the mistresses to "sample" students. Most of the boys were tossed after a night or two, but I'd been a favorite for years. Lucky me. And my magic had been of no use at all against hers—she was a succubus. The headmistress had actually used my magic to boost her own. She'd been particularly fond of mental manipulation.

Everyone told me I had nothing to complain about, that I should be thankful I was such a chick magnet. I'm scared to death Ali may have a similar response. I've added so many layers to the hard shell erected around my secret. I'm not sure I can crack it open. I'm the happy-go-lucky guy who lives to make the universe a better place. I gave up fighting against what the world wanted from me in my early teens and worked to perfect the persona everyone wants to see— Mr. Charm.

In that way, Troy and I are very similar. He can charm anyone if he sets his mind to it, but he can only hold that persona for a limited time. All three of us have the power of emotion absorption, but unlike Cass and me, Troy can't use the power of others' emotions to enhance his powers when it's someone he cares about. His compassion is his greatest strength and weakness. We'd learned at a young age that when Cass or I hurt, Troy internalizes our pain and suffers. The more of these emotions he absorbs, the weaker he becomes, and he can't turn the absorption off.

Until Ali, and now I can see what gives her strength. Although she hasn't lowered all of her defenses, she's dropped the drawbridge enough for me to see that she's the living embodiment of compassion, at least where Troy's concerned. She may not realize it, but she converts his emotional angst to energy and uses it to erect a shield between him and the world.

Ali sits quietly, waiting . . . and showing me a side of her I haven't seen—a deep capacity for active stillness that allows her to open her senses. So, I tell Ali about how the headmistress used me for herself and as a special "guest" at her orgies. Tears well in her eyes as I explain how they used their magic to make me compliant, but otherwise, her expression doesn't change. At an excruciating part, I tense as my own tears threaten, dropping my hands and my eyes to my lap. Her small brown hands slip over my tight fists, and her warmth and strength flow into me, giving me strength.

"That was a long time ago, and like you, I'm well healed. That experience made me who I am today," I conclude. That's as far as I can go today. Healed though I am, opening those old wounds and revealing my secrets drains me. I drop my eyes again, take several large swallows of the rum coconut water, and hope like hell Ali can't feel my hammering heart.

I wait for it. The rejection I know is coming. Because, unlike with Troy, nothing about our mating bond is certain until the bond matures. When she moves, I brace myself for the disenchantment I expect to see. Once before, I'd thought I was in love. I'd believed her when she'd said she wanted to share my secrets. Just as I have tonight, I'd bared my soul. She'd sent me packing, telling me she couldn't handle the abuse. She wasn't able to look at me the same way because I was damaged goods.

Now, I realize that it had been nothing more than infatuation because I've seen what Ali and Troy share, a bond that involves trust, honesty, and acceptance, and that's the kind of love I crave. It's always been out of my reach . . . until now. I wait for the words that will break my heart, so I'm utterly unprepared for what happens.

In one fluid movement, Ali lifts my arm, pivots onto my lap, and anchors the back of my head with one hand. "I owe you a kiss." Her voice has the low throaty register that signals the depth of her passion. Her full lips descend on mine, and she throws her whole body into a kiss that leaves me breathless. This isn't sex. Ali's speaking to me with her body, showing me what she's not ready to put into words. She tells me that our past is behind us, that the future is ours to build. The heat of her desire makes me moan as she shows me my past abuse doesn't tarnish or reduce me in her eyes.

After several stunned seconds, my body responds in kind, sharing my trepidation and joy at what it means to be so very exposed. There's so much more to say, but our need for oxygen eventually makes us come up for air. She rests her head on my shoulder. I hold her tight. We share the slowing rhythm of hearts beating in sync. I pray this moment will last forever . . . and grow impatient for more.

Ali raises her head and stares into my eyes, opening then shutting her mouth.

"What were you going to say?"

She shakes her head. "I have a habit of ruining special moments by saying the wrong thing."

Nothing, but nothing, she could say will ruin this moment. For the first time in centuries, maybe ever, I'm not shutting down at the first reference to my look. I didn't give anyone else a chance . . . until now. Although, the increased burning in my shoulder suggests the decision's been removed from my control. My mating brand demands attention. I put my hands on her waist and set her on her feet.

Ali pushes the sleeve of her dress onto her shoulder and runs her finger over the darkening triangle forming under the black rose tattoo. She meets my gaze with eyes alight with wonder. For several beats, we're locked in that moment of recognition.

"Let's get this done." I grab her hand and head out into the night.

Ali yanks on my hand, bringing me to an abrupt halt. I turn and see an inner light that blasts the remaining anxiety from my heart. "You took the words right out of my mouth."

45

ALEAH

We're in the air. I'm flying . . . fanfuckingtastic! Tristan's doing the work, so I relax in his arms, enjoying the warm tropical air tickling my skin like an erotic feather. I take a moment to check that place in my heart where Troy lives, and his message is loud and clear: Get 'er done. That's my man. The world sees him as an easygoing, charming, and patient guy. That idea makes me snort. Troy is anything but patient. He hates chaos and limbo, so whenever we're at a crossroads, he pushes until I take action. Right now, there's no doubting the not-so-gentle push Troy's giving me. My tattoo pulses as if punctuating his message. Although we react in different ways, neither of us is good with limbo when it comes to something that affects our relationship. I send him a silent message of my own: Yeah, yeah. Give me a frigging minute.

Tristan lands on a wooden path and gently sets me down. The stars, a full moon, and underwater lighting light our surroundings. We're back on the island, so we must be back at our villa. Tristan takes my hand and leads me the other way toward a smaller villa nestled in the trees.

I'm happy to follow and take a few moments to get my head around this moment. If that's at all possible because, right now, I don't seem to be able to focus on anything but making love with this man. I feel like a schoolgirl on a first date, nerves all atingle. It's not the booze because I barely feel its influence. One would think I'd never had sex before.

We enter a large circular living room, except that the furniture looks as if it's been designed for more than sitting. Chairs and recliners with hand and footholds are scattered amongst a couch and two chaise lounges. Several doors to other rooms line the walls, some open, giving a glimpse of more kink furniture.

Tristan pours drinks from a pitcher standing on a sideboard. I wander around, peering into the different rooms, and confirm my first impression. Each room is designed for fantasy or role-play. One room is set up like a Victorian bedroom, except that the wrought-iron bed is enormous, large enough for a whole lot of bodies. Two hot male bodies, to be precise. *Three.* A voice whispers in my head, and Cass's dark face skitters through my mind. I shut it down. Three is definitely a crowd in this situation.

Another room features a large cot, a single wooden chair, and chains with manacles on the wall. A third has a spanking bench with a wall display holding paddles, floggers, and straps. I shiver, unsure whether it's from nervousness or delight as I complete my tour.

Tristan follows me through large French doors that open onto a patio facing the ocean and hands me a drink. We don't say a word, but there's no mistaking the need welling up within me as his gaze locks with mine. I'm forty and too experienced to be having a case of first-time-itis, but I'm head over heels about this man. Before my head locks firmly into analysis mode, Tristan takes the drink from my hands and tips my chin toward him. He kisses me tenderly, sending volts of electricity to the junction between my legs.

"I need you to be mine." The need in his gravely voice almost brings me to my knees. And I have no idea how to respond to that. My body and mind are a swirling cauldron of feelings I can't identify. But one thing I know for sure—I need Tristan to make me his.

He sweeps me off my feet. Literally. Another first I don't have time to contemplate before he sets me on my feet again in the Victorian bedroom. Keeping his hands on my arms, he looks at me as if seeing me for the first time. I sincerely hope the candlelight hides the goosebumps that spring up all over my body at his hot gaze. Tristan's hunger is like nothing I've ever felt before. Whereas Troy's need for me is always at a constant simmer and boils over when he's in the mood, Tristan's need has the force of a volcanic eruption.

Suddenly, I'm scared to death. What the hell will he think when he sees my middle-aged body? He's probably had his pick of the most beautiful women in the universe.

Tristan's hands tighten on my arms, drawing my wandering thoughts back to him. "Don't you dare. Tonight, you're mine." He steps back and pulls off his T-shirt, displaying the fine hairs sprinkling his muscular chest. He throws it over a chair without taking his eyes off of me, looking every bit like a predator eying his tasty prey. Next, he takes my glasses and places them on a small table.

My mouth goes dry as he reaches around my neck, undoes the clasp holding the drop-shoulder top of my dress, and slides it down my bare arms, revealing my small bare breasts. He must sense my urge to cover them as he gives a small shake of his head.

Do not spoil this moment for me, mon chou.

So I stand there, wanting him, needing him . . . and wanting to run for the hills. Troy's the only man who's seen this body in twenty years, and his love for me enables him to turn a blind eye to the lumps and bumps that come with age. I shiver as he slides the dress over my hips and a somewhat cheeky butt, but his wandering hands hook my panties and glide them down my legs, commanding my attention.

"Are you afraid?" Once again, that throaty tenor voice pulls me to him.

I shake my head. "Nervous, not afraid," I manage to choke out.

He keeps his eyes and hands on my body. "Nervous of?"

"Disappointing you." Fuck. I hadn't meant to say that. I want to close my eyes against the bright light glowing in his eyes. But then, I could swear Troy gives me a sharp slap on the ass and pushes me toward my destiny.

"There's nothing in this world you could do that would disappoint me." Before I can react, he lifts me and places my naked body on the bed, giving me several glorious seconds to admire his body while he removes his belt and undoes the top button of his jeans. All the while, his hot gaze consumes my body, making me yearn to have him inside me. The burning heat in my tattoo matches the incinerator firing between my legs. My nipples and clit tighten to hard stones as wave after wave of desire ripples through me.

The mattress depresses as he settles beside me, head propped on one hand a whimsical look on his face that makes my pussy engorge with liquid heat. Blue eyes, darkened with desire, shimmer with heat for me. Me! He sees me. He needs me. He wants me, warts and all.

His blond hair is tucked into a loose ponytail, but a lock breaks free as he looks down at me. I reach up and smooth it back, using the same gesture he'd used on me when he tucked loose curls behind my ears. Desire arcs between us as our skin meets. The small smile on his lips matches mine as he dips his lips to mine. This kiss blots out all other thoughts. I relax against him, and our bodies start to speak our truth.

We make soft, slow music with our lips and tongues, composing our love song's first movement. Tristan punctuates each pause for breath with a soft sigh as he whispers his love and brushes his face against mine. Our bodies move in concert as I punctuate his verses with my chorus. *I love you.* Three little words I've only uttered to one other man. There's no room for my doubts and fears. We may not know each other that well, but I know in the depths of my soul that I love this man. This man is another part of what makes me whole. The divine light shimmering in his eyes tells me he mirrors my feelings.

Just like that, Tristan gives me his heart. No thought, no hesitation, just certainty that this is meant to be. The strangest feelings flow through me as I receive and return his gift.

He not only explores my body with his mouth and hands but lets me return the favor in a way I've never done before. Troy never liked having me explore his body, and I'd never figured out why. Tristan's moan stops me from giving it any further thought. The way his body responds to mine as I suck his nipples and rake my fingers over the steel heat of his abs fills me with something I can't identify. Something almost visceral rises from me and mingles with similar mist rising from Tristan.

I reach down and undo his zipper, ready to tear his jeans off. He stills my hands, focusing my attention on his erection as it springs free. Before I can admire his impressive length, strong hands press my thighs back toward my chest, spreading my legs wide. Tristan smiles as if he's seeing a rare jewel for the first time, sliding his gaze to meet mine before returning to my glistening cunt.

I gasp and arch into him as he lowers his head and swipes

his tongue through my juices before his hot mouth covers my swollen clit. A gentle but firm hand on my stomach stills me as Tristan backs off just enough to let me know he plans to take his time. Using his clever tongue and fingers as his instruments, he adds musical flourishes to the harmony we're creating. The soft moans of pleasure he makes as he tastes me give me the most precious gift. He licks his fingers dripping with my essence to show me how much he loves the taste of me before continuing a slow climb to the peak. At some point, my eyes close, and I lose touch with anything but my thrashing body and soft catching sounds somewhere in the background. The need for release races through me as he sucks my clit deep into his mouth with a slow even tempo until I shatter, exposing my very soul.

46

TRISTAN

Aleah lies spread wide before me, wet and welcoming, demanding I take her. Despite the pull from the brand and my throbbing cock to consummate this union, I take a long moment to drink in this feeling—this moment I've dreamed of for centuries but have feared would escape me. The soft blue-white grace glistening on her skin shows me she's ready. Trust and love flicker like flames as divine light flares in her eyes. She's so beautiful. How does she not know this?

When I touch her lips with mine, she tastes her juices on my tongue, giving me the singular sexiest moment of my life. Without breaking the seal of our lips, I palm the back of her head, grabbing her soft curls and balancing my weight on my arm. I grab my cock as my balls draw up tight and firm, begging for release. Her pulsing cunt clutches me as I slide my cock inside the entrance. With a soft moan, she arches, pushing her breasts into my chest. I plunge into her, burying my cock balls deep, and find home. A soft moan of my own escapes me as I pause to let her heat seep into me.

But the brand and Ali command more. She grabs my ass and squeezes with impatience. The hot pulsing in my brand demands relief, and my cock beats to the same drummer. Despite being firmly anchored by my body, Ali thrashes beneath me. One word comes out in a soft sigh against my lips. *Please.* Time's up. Propping my arms on either side of her head, I lose myself inside her. Nothing exists but her heat and mine as strands of our grace mingle, twisting together to form a new union.

Ali releases a loud groan, and her small hands knead my ass, delivering her message loud and clear. Gritting my teeth, I send a silent prayer to the gods for endurance and piston into her. Despite drilling into her like a jackhammer, she screams for more as another orgasm crashes through her. Everything in me screams for release, but I want to savor this moment. Beads of sweat cover my body from the exertion. At some point, Ali throws her arms above her head with eyes closed, rolling her head from side to side as her panting breath mingles with mine. I pick up the pace and embrace the feeling of her pulsing cunt cocooning my hungry cock.

As I reach the point of no return, Ali's eyes spring open and her full lips part. "Now!"

I pull my cock out to the tip, then drive home. Again and again, until I break apart. Our intimacy reinforces my crumbling foundation with the promise of what we'll build together. Still panting, I roll onto my back, pulling her on top of me. Our breath slows as our hearts beat in synchronous harmony. The most beautiful feeling of knowing Ali flows from my brand, filling my body, stilling my soul. We don't need words. Our bodies speak our new truth.

Early dawn light filters into the room as something pulls me out of the most beautiful dream. Ali's wiggling body reminds me that this dream is now a reality. I kiss the top of her head as she gingerly tries to lift my arm from her body. She grimaces as she looks up at me, acting every bit like a skittish colt.

"Sorry. I didn't mean to wake you," Ali whispers. "I need a bio break." Earnestness replaces all signs of the playful woman I've caught glimpses of. There are so many layers of emotion sifting through Ali, and they're hard to identify. Instead, I focus on the joy hitting me like blows and smiles.

Ali manages to extract herself from my embrace and fusses with covering herself with a sheet and donning her glasses before heading off. I prop a couple of pillows behind my head and inspect my deltoid to confirm the new sensations inside me. The solid strokes of the black rose gleam with divine light. The slight discomfort of the freshly formed brand can't compare with the joy that keeps bubbling through me. Ali knows my secret and doesn't care. I understand her nervousness and excitement. We're virtual strangers, linked by divine decree, an arranged marriage of sorts. Everything about our lives is changing, and we have many complex layers to sift through.

Where do I fit in with her and Troy and the history they share? How does Cass fit with our newly formed triad? There are so many things to consider, but I have no problem putting them on the for-later-consideration shelf. Speaking of the devil, Cass makes himself known with a not-so-gentle push in my mind. *Time for work.* To hell with him. For once in my life, I'm putting my needs ahead of the collective. I have no idea when Ali and I will have more time alone, so I'll milk every drop from our remaining time. Wrapping my hands around the back of my head, I watch the sunrise paint the sky with light matching the divine light that now fills a new space in my soul.

Ali returns wrapped in a terry bathrobe that swallows her petite frame. She kneels beside me, hesitant, and adjusts her glasses before rubbing her shoulder absentmindedly. "Good morning. How are you feeling this morning?" She's lacking her usual confidence and trying not to show it. I settle back, eager to start this journey of discovery.

"I'm fantastic, and you?" I brush curls off her face before grabbing the back of her head and pulling her down for a kiss. Several breathless moments later, she laughs and pushes my chest.

"I don't know how to answer that question. We need to talk."

For the first time, those words awaken my curiosity instead of filling me with dread. I raise an eyebrow and wait.

After several seconds of sifting through what she's going to say next, she finally blurts out, "What exactly does this mating brand mean? Let's see your shoulder." She leans over and peers at my shoulder. Her closeness brings goosebumps as she traces around the rose.

"Let's see yours," I say but wait for her to show me in her own time.

She slides the robe off her left shoulder and shows me the solid red triangle that represents me. Grace rising from the tattoo contains our three colors intertwining into one thick coil. I whistle softly under my breath. This mating bond is real.

I want to pull her into my arms but don't make a move, trying to be patient. Her brain has switched on, and we'll need to silence some of those voices. "Honestly, babe, I'm not sure of all it entails. That's something we'll all have to work out together. What I do know is that our souls are united for eternity. Nothing can break us apart now. And that's all I need to know. We'll figure the rest out later."

But that's not her nature, so she settles into her cross-legged position, alternating staring at her hands with furtive glances my way. She wants to see Troy to make sure he's okay with our bond, and she wants to figure out just what our union means to theirs. After a minute or so, the tide shifts, and she's trying to figure out how much of my ego she needs to protect when she starts the inquisition I can feel coming. I decide to cut her off at the pass. Talking about how all this will work is best done with Troy present.

"So, tell me about this goose-gander thing Troy mentioned?" I ask.

She smiles. It's a small one, but it reaches her eyes. "When Troy and I committed to having a relationship, we talked about how unrealistic it is to promise not to stray. Most people deceive themselves when blinded by the light of new love."

I'm curious about how she phrases things when she describes their relationship, but I hold my peace for the time being. We have eternity for me to explore the layers of my woman. *My woman.* Another trill of joy whistles through me.

"Stray?" It's becoming clear to me that Ali has an issue with talking about sex when it applies to her.

"Yes, you know, fuck someone else." Her emphasis on the word *fuck* when used in context confirms my suspicion. "We realized that if we were honest with ourselves, we couldn't promise not to be attracted to someone else, so it was ridiculous to make a promise that's so easily broken."

"Whose bright idea was that?" Because I sincerely doubt it was Troy's. Even with the amnesia caused by being in human form, it would be most unlike him to even think of fucking around. It's a miracle that he opened himself to Ali, and she would have had to work very hard to gain his trust.

Her brow furrows as she thinks back. "Both of ours, although it took me years to realize this was an intellectual discussion for Troy."

I hide a smile at her righteous tone and wait for what's coming. One thing I'm learning about *mon chou* is that she's compelled to tell the truth to those she loves. I raise an eyebrow. She fiddles with her glasses and rings, but I don't have long to wait.

"Okay, it was probably me who brought it up, but Troy completely agreed with what I was saying. I mean, after all, could you commit to not screwing any other women for the next fifty years?" Her tone lets me know she believes the male species to be incapable of being faithful.

"Babe, I'll have no problem being faithful to you for the next thousand years, so I have no problem committing to that. Our angelic mating bond means you're stuck with me for life." The hot spot on my shoulder punctuates my promise with a corresponding thump.

That brings out her beautiful smile. "Troy used to say I'm stuck with him, that I'm the only one for him. It still took years for me to figure out he's incapable of straying emotionally. But you're cut from a different cloth, Tristan. How can you be so sure you won't want to have sex with someone else ever again? I mean, you must meet all kinds of beautiful women in your line of work.

"So, I take it this goose-gander position of yours means that if I *stray* with someone else, you, in turn, just to get even, are going to fuck someone other than Troy or me? Is that the problem here?"

I welcome the wave as her emphatic "of course not" washes through her at the suggestion. Despite the strength of the emotional connection, I love the constant presence, the *knowing* she's part of me. We're part of each other. Another wave of impatience rolls through me. She must feel it because I can feel her mind shift gears.

"It's rare for a man to be attracted to me, and even rarer for me to be attracted to a man, except for Troy and now you. So, me fooling around isn't an issue." Which isn't an answer, and she knows it. Her low self-esteem may be a deeply buried seed, but it's one that has very deep roots.

I touch her cheek with the backs of my fingers. "You're beautiful. You turn heads wherever you go."

She pats my hand and gives me a pitying look. "You're biased, just like Troy. But trust me on this, men rarely find me attractive. Oh, I have the odd, good picture, but I'm short. And Black. And in my forties. That is not the definition of beauty in our society, trust me on this."

Something about the way her tone leaves no room for discussion makes it clear she's thoroughly invested in this belief system about her self-worth. And it pisses me off. Something all three brothers share is a strong idea about right and wrong, and this willingness of hers to believe every criticism she's heard is just plain wrong. One thing I will not tolerate is having her disparage herself. I usually think before I act, but my usual caution eludes me at the moment. If I'm honest, I'm probably displacing my disappointment that we're having this convoluted talk instead of celebrating our new bond. But unlike Troy, and now Ali, I don't have a pressing need to dissect and analyze every little thing.

I set Ali on her feet as I swivel off the bed, ignoring the shocked look on her face. A low growl of disapproval precedes the next words that come out of my mouth.

"I will not tolerate hearing these lies you seem so deter-mined to hang onto. And I hate being called a liar. Honesty is sacred to me. Do it again, and I'll spank your ass." I cross my arms over my bare chest, not in the least distracted by how often her gaze slips to my semi-erect cock while she decides how she feels about this development. She's so used to me being a puppy dog that I've shocked the shit out of her. "Something else you should know about me. I hate injustice, and I hate what people have done to you. But, you don't have to keep buying into the false narrative when there's so much proof to the contrary."

I give her a penetrating look, so there's no doubt she'll mistake my next words. "You deserve a spanking when you refuse to see the truth that's staring you in the face, and each time you speak ill of yourself, I'll double it."

"I don't think I like this dominant side of you, and you won't be doing anything of the sort without my consent." Ali puts an extra punch of pout into her voice as she crosses her arms, matching my stance. I feel the shift in her emotions but don't take the time to identify them. I'm too caught up in my own feelings.

"And as I recall, that's exactly what you wanted to see more of. Well, you got your wish." I spin her around and slap her ass once, hard, giving my best be-careful-what-you-wish-for grin before I stalk out of the room with the reassurance that she's weighing how she's going to respond to this new development. Underneath all of that, her hard nipples and wet cunt tell me she liked it.

And so did I. Time enough to explore that later. First, I need to talk to Troy, and I want to tell him my side before she does. I send a silent prayer to the gods. Figuring out our new life with Ali will be much easier if Troy's on board.

47

ATROYEL

While I wait for Lea and Tristan to arrive, I grab a coffee and carry it to the second-floor balcony and stand at the rail, enjoying the view. The balcony overlooks the saltwater pool and sandy beach between the villa and the glittering colors of the sea. Even though I've spent most of the night soul searching and coming to terms with my feelings, anticipation gives me more than enough fuel to run on. I take this quiet moment to hold this newfound treasure all to myself. The universe gave me the chance to love Aleah without holding back to protect my emotions. As I look out across the vast ocean before me, I send silent thanks to the gods for giving me another chance to give Aleah the love she deserves.

I've always been moody, although not for the reasons assumed by most people. I've been labeled aloof and arrogant, but in reality, I'm protecting myself from the onslaught of painful emotions that assault me. Normally, I'd be worrying about all manner of things: Would she leave me for Tristan? Could a relationship with three work long-term? There are so many things to consider, but for the first time, maybe ever, I'm at peace and excited about our future.

I move over to the U-shaped seating area I chose specifically for our upcoming discussion. I smile to myself at the head-on collision that's coming. My sense of what Tristan and Lea feel is visceral, a living, breathing thing in its own right.

Love and a new depth of feeling have helped me give Lea and Tristan my blessing. But I'd been wound tighter than one of Lea's curls when I'd left them alone last night and fled with my dread. Pretending I needed to practice flying, I'd found a small, deserted island just far enough away to give me the space I craved while keeping the connection with Lea. Because I'm a sucker for punishment and a realist—so many fucking things could go wrong when dealing with matters of the heart. Using my magic, I'd weaved a hammock and tried to still that nagging doubt while I waited for my eternity to change.

Bit by bit, a sense of peace replaced the fear as I thought of all Aleah and Tristan are to me. Although Cass has traditionally been the one to take care of us, almost like a surrogate parent, it's Tristan who has helped me deal with the assault of emotions that comes at me from other living beings. Until I met Aleah, he'd been the shield absorbing the excess and helping me process the pain. Somehow, Tristan could take in and expel what Lea calls *noise* without hurting himself. I hadn't known that's what he was doing at the time.

Being reunited with Cass and Tristan in Bardo filled a hole I hadn't realized was there, but at the time, I'd been too distraught about losing Aleah to enjoy the moment. When I'd sat in that restaurant with her and my brothers, something fundamental shifted inside me, and I realized I need all three of them to feel whole. I've been given a second chance, and this time, I won't waste the opportunity to be complete. Each time another piece of the mating-brand puzzle drops into place, the more confident I am that we're on the right path.

The quiet joy I sense emanating from Tristan tells me he agrees.

I'd known the instant the mating brand between Tristan and Lea activated. My tattoo had released a mist of grace the color of our combined essence. My empathic connection with both of them had amplified as if someone had flipped another switch on the breaker panel of possibilities that lay before us. I experienced a sense of bliss that I'd never felt before. It's as if the universe combined the magic of our connections and created something new.

I'm settled back on the cushions with sunglasses firmly in place when a freshly showered Tristan drifts in, coffee mug in hand. I hide a smile as my brother flexes and relaxes his biceps, the only outward sign of his nervousness.

He clears his throat. "Morning."

"Tristan." I'm acting like an asshole, but it's so rare for Tristan to be unsure of himself that I take a moment of perverse enjoyment.

"We should talk." He trains his direct gaze on me before donning his sunglasses. I decide to end his agony.

I slide my glasses to the crown of my head and nod. "We should, but not about what you think. Surprisingly, I'm okay with the idea of you with Aleah. This new union is something we all need to figure out together, but before we do that, you'd better get ready to pay some dues, bro." I raise my eyebrow and smile. "I know you can feel the head of steam she's building right now. Hell hath no fury like Aleah in righteous mode. That's one aspect of our relationship I'm more than happy to share. What did you do anyway?"

Tristan gives his bring-it-on smile and settles back on his end of the sofa. "I told her I'd spank her when she puts herself down."

"And?" There has to be more because the Aleah I know

would be pissy about being threatened, but from what I sense, she's working on righteous anger.

"I slapped her ass." Tristan gives a wry smile. "But only once to punctuate my point."

My eyebrow shoots up on its own. "And you're alive to tell the tale? I'm assuming this wasn't part of your lovemaking?"

He shakes his head. "She insulted me when I told her how beautiful she is. Her low self-worth leaves her vulnerable to Lord Syrael and every other vile creature who uses and manipulates innocents like her. I was pissed and took her over my knee."

I whistle. "Oh yeah, you've got dues to pay, but you can relax. The vibe's coming off Lea loud and clear—she likes the idea but thinks she shouldn't. That means she'll need to work through her feelings. You're about to find out Aleah has no problem telling you what she thinks if she trusts you. Being chastised by Lea is a rocky ride, but it's so worth it in the end. She loves make-up sex."

Tristan rolls his shoulders, and I can't deny I'm enjoying his discomfort.

"How can someone as gifted and smart and funny as she is think so little of herself?"

"It's not so much that she thinks little of herself. She's quite analytical about her skills and strengths. She believes the big lie she's been fed her entire life. The lie her foster father drilled into her brain every day. She believes she's incapable of giving love, that no one will ever love her. The bastard made it his mission to convince her she was stupid and her only worth was between her open legs.

"But there's something profound, some strand of DNA within Aleah that makes her fight back. We caught a glimpse of that when we rescued her in the forest. The more shit people throw at her, the harder she fights back, but deep down, as much as her logical brain fights the bullshit, she internalizes the criticisms as gospel. Sadly, it's taken me all this time to see what a fighter she is. What a warrior."

"How so?" Tristan asks. There's no judgment. Despite the twenty-year absence, my brother knows me too well.

"I'd thought the blinders had come off when I was dying, but that's nothing compared to the clarity with which I'm seeing Aleah now. When I was diagnosed with cancer, she opened her heart and shared my sorrow." I almost tear up at the memory of this great gift she'd offered me. "With the incredible insight she has, she distilled our situation into a nutshell. With tears rolling down her face, she'd held me and offered to join me on the journey until she had to let me go as long as I promised to share my feelings." I taper off amid memories of her fierce determination to make sure I died with grace, dignity, and surrounded by love. My warrior woman. I clear the lump in my throat. "From that moment on, she became my warrior, although now that I think about it, she always had been." I stop myself from venturing further down that memory lane.

"Once, just once, she shared the unfiltered agony that wracked her body at the thought of losing me. Deep, raw, gasping sobs convulsed through her and almost brought me to my knees. But somehow, she drew on that well of strength within her and pulled back before I shattered. In that moment, I started to see what she'd done for me all these years, how she silenced my noise. She made room beside her truckload of demons to shoulder mine. My Lea broke down my walls with the strength of her love. Now, I get the chance to return the favor, and I'm grateful you're part of it. A part of our love story." I pause as the lump in my throat returns. Tristan joins me in making busywork of refreshing our coffee. Something stirs in my heart where Lea lives.

"Did you feel that?" Tristan asks.

I nod. "Aleah's reached a decision, so we don't have much time. I've been thinking about what the justices said. They talked about our combined power working as a unit that includes Cass. Do you have the same sense?"

Tristan nods. He's far better at opening himself to our brother's vexation. While he appears to study the liquid in his mug, Tristan opens his senses and takes a read on Cass's simmering fury. When he's in this mood, it's damn near impossible to get through to him. Before, I would have fallen into a funk as his emotions came at me one after the other. Now, after death and regeneration, I have a different outlook on life. It's a puzzle to solve. That thought no sooner hits my mind than it hits me.

"When Cass comes, follow my lead," I say hurriedly.

"What the hell—"

"Oh, and Tristan, remember that trick you taught me to shield my emotions? Use it," I say. The trick he taught me to handle an onslaught of emotion was to think about sex. It works like a charm when I think about Lea with the bonus that it blocks her ability to read me.

"Think about sex?"

"Yeah, and what we'll do with Lea tonight. Trust me— she'll need both of us after the impending meltdown."

When she walks onto the deck, all cute and thoughtful, something new possesses me, and all hint of my usual reserve disappears. I spread my arms in welcome, adoring the startled surprise that flashes in her eyes and the glorious grin that lights her face. She drops onto my lap and kisses me soundly. When we break apart, she straightens and gives me that cute wink of hers that scrunches her face before turning to Tristan.

"I'd kiss you, too, if I wasn't so pissed off at you, mister. You've got a lot of explaining to do."

TRISTAN

When Ali steps onto the deck and rushes into Troy's arms without a drop of acknowledgment of me, a wave of anxiety hits me. Just when everything had been perfect, I'd gone and fucked it up. Our connection tells me she's aware of my presence, but I'm going to have to wait until she's good and ready to address me. Despite my angst, I mentally remove her floral top, jean shorts, and the broadest brimmed hat I've ever seen, remembering her unveiled passion as she writhed beneath me. Shifting to hide my instant hard-on, I train my gaze on the distant palm trees. *It's all about your timing, Tris.*

Lost in thought, I almost miss the significance of her words. *I'd kiss you, too, if I wasn't so pissed off at you, mister. You've got a lot of explaining to do.* She looks my way, but her glasses automatically darken in sunlight, so I can't read the expression in her eyes. I open our psychic connection, but all I get is the sense of rapidly turning pages as she processes.

Follow your gut instinct. Troy's thought plants distinctly into my mind. Well, my gut tells me I have to touch this woman and know that underneath it all, we're still okay.

"I'd be happy to discuss it with you after we've kissed."

What the hell am I going to do with this woman who, in many ways, is my opposite? Finding her is like a poor man winning a lottery or a rich man discovering humility, but what do I do with this beautiful alien force that's now part of my life? I need to kiss her, touch her, confirm she's truly mine. Then we can deal with the differences between her strong emotional consciousness and my practical view of life that overshadows idealism.

I need to know that our differences bring balance to our relationship in much the same manner that her similarities to Troy bring balance to theirs. And my gut tells me she needs this reassurance, too. I give her my best imploring look and wait for her consent. Not a chance I'm making that mistake twice.

After a long, penetrating look, Troy says, "Oh, for gods' sake, you two, kiss and get it over with. We don't have all day."

"Fine." Ali holds up her index finger. "One kiss."

She's perched on the edge of the couch Troy's sprawled on, so it's easy to pull her up into my arms. She stiffens slightly. Ignoring her surprised rush of adrenaline, I tip her chin up with my finger and slowly lower my mouth to her lips, giving her plenty of time to stop me. I need to know that she needs this kiss as much as I do.

Instead, her lips part slightly, and the tip of her pink tongue swipes her lips. She doesn't touch me otherwise but returns my kiss with a hesitant mixture of gentle love and demanding lust that holds the promise of what's to come . . . after we work through our first fight.

Her body softens as she responds, and after a long moment, her arms slide up my bare arms, lightly tickling the hair on my forearms. She places those small elegant hands on my chest, lowers her head, and takes a long breath before sitting down, this time opposite me. Troy emotes so little, he could be asleep behind those sunglasses, but I'm keenly aware he's taking this all in.

Ali tops up her tea, keeping her gaze on the honey and lemon as she starts. "Tristan, I know I tend to go off on people when I feel I've been wronged, but I've had time to think about this." She throws a glance in Troy's direction, but he says nothing, only nods. I realize her discomfort is due to the diplomatic approach she'd take with a stranger. Troy had warned us exercising tact doesn't come easy for Ali. She's too much of a straight shooter. After straightening her spine and stretching her neck, she looks in my direction.

"Now is as good a time as any to talk about our limits. Spanking me as punishment is a hard limit for me. Doing anything to my body without my consent is a hard limit. I have the right to decide how you touch my body." Ali narrows her eyes, underscoring her edict.

"That wasn't a spanking, it was a love tap," I reply rather hotly. "Are you telling me I have to ask your permission each and every time I want to touch you?"

We're mates now, and that means lots of touching without consent. Her refusal to see reason pisses me right off. "If I follow your logic, I'll have to ask you for every fucking kiss, every fucking hug. Well, I—"

"We'd better call Cass in. The justices said he's a vital part of the team, and if we're setting limits, he needs to be part of the discussion," Troy says.

I throw Troy a look as he stops me dead in my tracks.

Remember our end game, Tristan.

Aleah grimaces, sucking in her full lips, and sighs, but nods. "I guess that makes sense." She sounds less than enthused at adding Cass to the equation, but that and Troy's reminder is enough to bring me back to my senses.

"Good idea. Maybe Cass can help you see some reason." I throw Ali a hot look and stalk across the large deck. Poking my head through the sliding doors, I bellow, "Cassiel, we need your ass up here now."

Despite Cass's calm and ruthless countenance, his seething emotions take the wind right out of my anger.

Steady. End game. Troy still knows how to calm my temper. He had ever since that time as boys when I'd backed him up against a wall, taunting him over some slight I can't remember.

"Go ahead. Hit me," he'd said, refusing to take the bait. Troy's calm intense gaze had drilled through my anger, and one message was clear: he wouldn't hit me first, but if I hit him, he'd flatten me. No question. I relax and open myself to Troy's certainty. *Now, we poke the bears.*

"It's about time. I assume this means you're ready to get some work done," Cass says.

"Good morning to you, too," Troy says. "Aleah was just about to tell us her hard limits. Go ahead, beauty." Troy throws an encouraging smile Ali's way. The dark look she pitches back tells him she sees through his innocent act but knows it's pointless to argue.

"Good morning, Cass. Did you want some coffee?" Aleah says.

I study Ali from behind my shades, interested in this hostess act. Troy had warned us Ali could be direct to the point of rudeness. Now, doubt dances with the confidence she'd had moments ago.

"No, I don't want any coffee. I've been up since dawn." Cass's stress on the last word lets us know he thinks we've wasted half the day. "Let's get on with it. Who called this little meeting of the minds?"

"I did," Troy says. "Ali wants to discuss her hard limits, so you need to be part of the conversation."

We all look at Ali, who's finding her teacup fascinating as she wrestles with a strong flight response. Every part of her screams to escape from Cass's intimidating presence as he towers over her, but she squares her shoulders, facing down her Goliath. I want to hold her and promise her everything will be all right, but Troy's insistent voice in my head holds me firmly back. *Let it play out.*

"So, what is it? Spit it out. We don't have all day." Cass is more of a bastard than usual. Something is most definitely up with him.

Ali clears her throat. "We were discussing consent as it pertains to touching my body."

"Touching you how? Is there something specific on your mind?" Cass plays at being reasonable.

After another slight hesitation, Ali says, "Tristan spanked me without asking me. I was letting him know that's a hard limit, and he was arguing with me."

"It was a love tap," I grumble.

Cass sweeps his hand through the air as if dismissing her complaint. "That's between you and your new *mate*. Why bother me with this? If Tristan decided you needed a spanking, you deserved it. We are sex angel lords, and if we deem it appropriate to punish our supplicants for the greater good, we administer such punishment. That's part of our job, our duty, and the way it's always been." Cass doesn't raise his voice, but the military bite in his voice comes through loud and clear as he utters this bald-faced lie. He's also not happy about my bond with Ali.

Ali is having none of his bitchy attitudes. Planting her hands on her hips, she faces him down. "I'm not one of your frigging supplicants, and Troy seems to think you need to be part of this discussion since it pertains to my limits. When it comes to my body, I have the right to say no. And spanking is a hard limit for me."

"Your rapid pulse tells me that's an outright lie, and it's

that kind of attitude that has us in this sorry mess," Cass says smugly.

"If my heart rate increased, it's because I'm pissed. What sorry mess are you referring to? Because if you're suggesting my love for your brothers is a problem, then you'd better go back to school. I would think, of all people, a sex angel would live by that commandment," Ali says.

"*Love* is what got us into this. That and this fucking hold you have on my brothers." Warmth and romance aren't Cass's strengths, and that part of his personality is front and center. If a relationship isn't strategically valuable, Cass isn't interested, and I've never known him to care about our relationships unless he perceives some threat to the family. But something about Ali's lit his fuse.

Ali's quiet for a hot beat before she spits out, "Meaning?"

"Meaning, you might be able to hide it from Troy and now Tristan, but it's clear you've used your Nephilim powers to put some sort of hold on them both. This mating brand wouldn't have happened otherwise," Cass retorts.

"What makes you so sure?" Despite the emotional distress flowing through me from Ali, she keeps her voice measured and controlled.

"Why else would Troy be compelled to give up everything he had to follow you to Earth from the forest? And if that wasn't bad enough, he suffered agony protecting you. His human vessel ate itself from the inside out, for gods' sake."

Ali winces but says nothing.

"But was that enough? No. Even in death, you wouldn't let go, using your Nephilim powers to cast some sort of spell on him. I see through this act of yours." Cass is in big brother protection mode.

He's being uncharacteristically irrational, and watching this rarely seen side of him might have been entertaining if I weren't dealing with Ali's resulting emotional fallout. She glances at me as if she feels my distress. Troy's voice drills into my head. *Shield!* With great difficulty, I push past the stream of emotions and picture Ali naked and spread wide open, head thrown back in rapture. It must do the trick because she turns back to Cass.

"So let me see if I've got this right. Your supposition is that I've known all along that I'm Nephilim, and I'm working on some nefarious plot for reasons unknown." Ali's voice catches, halting her speech. She calls on the strength of her will to capture and hold back the tears rising as anger bolts to the surface.

"That's not fair. You can't hold me responsible for something I have no control over. In fact, if anyone has a *nefarious* plot, it must be you boys." Ali points to her shoulder. "After all, you did say this is an angelic mating brand, and you're the angels in the bunch."

"Oh, you're a clever one, but you can't fool me," Cass says. "I'm onto you."

If I weren't sitting down, the wave of nausea that hits me would have knocked me on my ass. Troy swivels to a sitting position, arms on thighs, head bowed. I try to stand. I've got to stop this. Troy gives a quick shake of his head but doesn't look at me. *Hang on. She's strong. She'll be okay.* I take several deep breaths and sit. If Troy can withstand Ali's onslaught of emotion, I most certainly can. I trust Troy. He knows Ali, and he's got one of the best strategic minds when he decides to use it.

Ali rubs her forehead and sucks in a lungful of air, the only outward signs of her distress. "Look, can we call a truce, take a time-out, and circle back later?" She holds a small, tawny hand for Cass to shake. He looks at it as if it's covered with weeping sores.

"No, we do this now. This is not a democracy," Cass says. "It's time you three start listening to me. We are in danger of losing our lives, and your impulsiveness puts us in danger. As does your unwillingness to accept the truth about yourself. You like the idea of a spanking but if you prefer to live a lie, far be it from me to go against your will. After all, Aleah gets what Aleah wants. Any other hard limits you want to discuss?" Cass gives Ali his best "you can talk, but my mind's made up" look.

Several things happen simultaneously. Ali's vibrant skin tone turns gray, a series of cramps grip her GI system, and she claps her hand over her mouth. The pain she's in almost cripples me, but she's fleeing toward the inside of the villa.

Troy plants the image of Ali's beautiful body sandwiched between us, allowing me a modicum of relief from the onslaught of Ali's suffering.

"Now, you've done it." Troy's voice is laced with disapproval as he stands and turns to face Cass. "What are you going to do to fix this?"

Cass's barely restrained fury and indignation flash through me as he steps into Troy's personal space. "Oh, no, you don't, Troy. You're not dumping this on me."

Troy ejects his wings. "Afraid so, Cassiel. I don't know what bug crawled up your ass, but one thing I do know—you're the one who gave Aleah a sick migraine with your accusations, and you're the one who's going to make this better."

"Just how am I supposed to do that? You two are the ones with the healing powers," Cass retorts.

"There's healing power woven in the Double Diary, so I suggest you read it to her. The rest I'll leave to you to sort out." Troy massages his temple. "Now, if you'll excuse me, Ali's pain is causing a serious drain on my reserves, so I've got to put some distance between Aleah and me to regenerate. Finish what you started, Cass. Come along, Tristan."

If the situation weren't so serious, I might have laughed at the look on Cass's face. Usually, Troy shuns any leadership role, but when he does step up, people listen. I unfurl my wings and follow Troy as he flies toward the islands dotting the distant landscape. Despite my physical distress, the new place in my heart swells with anticipation and longing. I'd found my destined mate, and I can't wait to see what the universe and Ali's love have in store for us . . . Assuming Cass doesn't fuck things up.

Will Cass throw a wedge into Tristan and Aleah's fledgling bond? Can the mating bond survive without him? Grab your copy of *Cassiel* for a lot more sizzling fun and adventure with Aleah and her princes. Feed your fantasies!

Join Lilith's Smutty Readers Email List and get a free copy of *Mick's Mission*, a paranormal reverse harem romance!

lilithdarville.com/newsletter

Chapter One
Cassiel

Fuck! Fuck! Fuck! Aleah's rapid heart rate warns me she has her head in a toilet long before I reach her. The power to read the heartbeats of others comes in handy at times. If I didn't love my brothers, I'd kill them for putting our team in this position.

We're the three royal princes of Nirvana, called to serve the gods as sex angel lords. It's not a job, it's a vocation, although you'd never know it the way my brothers are behaving. Both are more than capable of shielding themselves from the negative effects of physical illness. My gut tells me Troy's not as affected by Aleah's sickness as he pretends to be unless you count being love sick. Whatever the two of them hope will happen by leaving me alone with Aleah simply won't happen. I know a problem when I see one.

I detour through the kitchen where Tristan put Aleah's medications. *Fuck.* Whose bright idea was it to put me in a caregiver role? Which pills should I give her? I take a chance and grab the anti-nausea tablets, pain meds, and a glass of water. By the time I reach the bedroom, Aleah's curled into a ball on the bed, eyes squeezed tight, and her small form takes me back to when she was a young girl in the forest. The corresponding tug on my heartstrings proves I'm not the cold-hearted bastard my brothers accuse me of being or that I portray.

"I brought your pills." I read off the names on the bottles for good measure.

I barely catch her muffled response. "One of each, please."

I shake a pill from each bottle into my palm then place them in the small brown hand that lies open on the bed. She dry swallows the pills refusing the water I offer. A strangled sound follows that I take to be thanks. I close the built-in blinds and light a candle to read by. Again, I curse the gods for being less than forthcoming about the angelic mating bond.

I settle on the bed beside Aleah without touching her, open the Double Diary to the bookmarked page and start reading aloud. I'm expecting the magic woven into the words to affect Aleah. What I'm not anticipating is their impact on me. The more I read in their diary, the more insight I have about what drew Atroyel to Aleah. The sexual and emotional passion they have for each other survived life's many hurdles and grew to a blazing fire. Their unconditional love for each other is evident even to a realist like me. Their outpouring of feeling flows over me like fine wine opening my palate to take in hidden undertones. It appears that Aleah took years to break through Atroyel's moody exterior, yet I have no sense of her berating or criticizing him. She seems to accept him for what he is.

Aleah seems to have shown Atroyel a way to express his feelings, and instead of weakening him, she's given him a way to face the world. As I read on, I can't remain blind to the gift Aleah's given Troy. Her love is pure and without artifice. The magic Atroyel wove into the words would reveal any hidden agendas. Her entries clearly show a depth of love for my brother that pierces my cynical core.

"Life with you hasn't always been easy, but it's always been real."
"I don't want you to feel regret. Not ever!"
"I'll fight for you until I'm forced to let go!"
"I fought to get you back."

As I read on, I'm left with so many questions: her feelings about motherhood, what had threatened their relationship, how had she fought to get Troy back? Their diary reveals a level of emotional exposure I rarely see between couples. They'd both risked fallout from leaving themselves so vulnerable to one another.

Slowly, Aleah's body uncurls as the words from the diary fall from my lips. While I read the words, she snuggles against me and rests her hand on my bare forearm. Electricity sizzles through me the instant her skin touches mine. My heart skips for a split second before I remember her rejection and remind myself of how she's disrupting our work. That puts things back in perspective, and I put the shock down to the quick movement of electrons in the air, nothing more.

Despite my best intentions to stay clear of her, my curiosity about this woman grows the more I read. I'm usually one for the big picture, but suddenly I want the details about what makes Aleah tick. I stop reading aloud for a moment and focus in on the entry dated September 1. Troy finds her to be distant, and who the fuck is Nick that he refers to? I push back the finger of jealousy that flickers as I read his name.

"I'm a mess, yet I'm strong and capable." I can't help but smile at her insight about herself. That hits the proverbial nail on the head when describing this fascinating woman. I quickly turn the pages searching for her hidden agenda. I'd learned through a millennium as a sex angel that most people have one, and I've seen the good, the bad, and the ugly. I have no doubt that if I look long and hard enough, I'll find hers, and the push-pull between her and Troy fascinates me.

When she writes about experiencing palpitations and tingles, my mind goes on high alert. This is the first indication of her powers breaking through the binding spell suppressing her magic. I read on, fighting harder and harder to convince myself my curiosity is strictly strategical. She's taped a sticky note from Troy over the end of one of his fantasies. For a reason I can't even begin to fathom, it's his sticky note that makes my heart ache.

Hi My Love!
My heart aches too, but that's not true. My ache is a little lower. You can pleasure yourself as long as you think of me. Gotta run errands—see you later. Thinking of you! Love Me.
:-)

I flip ahead several pages and notice sticky notes sprinkled throughout. As if sharing their love through the diary isn't enough, they have to leave each other sappy notes as well. Yet something in my cold heart yearns to have someone to exchange sappy notes with.

Morning Love:
Think of me as I do you! Again—smile—it's Friday. Soon Saturday...

Are you going to let me
PLAY?

To which she responds:

Am I ever! I've been waiting for this all week. Last night, I
had a prelude...

"I guess I'm not any good at come-hither looks." I glom
onto this first sign of artifice. She presents if as a flaw, but I
know better.

I close my eyes as the power of what these two share hits
me. Something makes Aleah stir, and she snuggles closer
against me tightening her grasp on my forearm. She sighs as
if taking comfort from my heat. Blue grace rises from her
skin coating mine, and I could swear there's a slight sensation of heat in my left shoulder. Slapping the fanciful thought
away, I get back to business. The sooner I figure out how
we're going to deal with the complications the mating bond
brings to our lives, the better for all of us. And one thing I
know for sure, Aleah will never be part of our team. I won't
allow it. I'm incredibly talented at spotting any skills and
strengths beneficial to helping us attain our mission, and this
woman doesn't have them. Instead, she's a distraction. I'd
been willing to overlook her intrusion for Troy's sake, but
now she's snatched Tristan and brings nothing but chaos.

Ali moans and moves restlessly beside me as if sensing my
thoughts. The interruption brings me back to the job at
hand, reading this damned diary. As I work my way through
another of Atroyel's convoluted passages, it doesn't surprise
me that he came up with the idea of writing a joint diary;
after all, word bestowal is his most potent power.

What's startling is the depth of sexuality, passion, and
commitment these two have been willing to explore, how

deeply they've exposed their soft underbellies. I doubt that I'd be willing to leave myself this vulnerable with anyone, yet I envy their deep and enduring bond. And now, the universe has given Tristan a matching gift, allowed him to share in their love. I shake off all this emotional foolishness and get back to the diary. The only love in the cards for me is the love I help create as a sex angel lord.

I need to focus on what I'm here to do and find out Aleah's weaknesses and triggers to teach her how to protect herself against Syrael. I'm not doing this for her; I'm doing it for my brother. Once we get rid of Syrael, I can get the hell away from this Nephilim and the irrational thoughts she provokes.

I run through what I've learned so far, and I have a lot of work to do. I think showing her how to protect herself against Syrael's manipulations will prove to be a more significant challenge than I imagined. Her self-esteem is far lower than her demeanor would suggest, and she has a large rejection complex and multiple hang-ups. However, these are the cards I'm dealt, so I'll play my best hand. I have to at least look like I'm trying with her. I won't give Atroyel any ammunition to put in that acerbic tongue. So far, the only area I have to work with is role play. Whenever I read about their fantasies and role-plays, more grace rises from Aleah. One thing is patently clear, my brother's fear of hurting his beloved has kept him from seeing what Aleah needs. *Fuck off, Cassiel.* I berate myself for all of this foolish talk. What goes on between those two is none of my business.

Aleah's next line, "I need your love! It makes me whole," does nothing to soften my hardened heart. I shouldn't begrudge my brothers a love like this . . . But I do.

But it's Atroyel's declaration that brings me to my knees.

My Love

*She was a lover whose mind never strayed far from
the scene.*
*All the power pieces concealed in me responded
fivefold.*
*Our open boldness of speaking out and then usually
acting it out was astonishing.*
*It got so that the mere touching of one another while
walking past each other could set off a confla-
gration.*
*As apprehension faded to trust, a cool sweetness
settled over us.*
Time, thank God, stood still.

I slam the book shut, unable to go on.

End of Sample
**To continue reading, be sure to pick up *Cassiel* at your
favorite retailer.**

ALSO BY LILITH DARVILLE

Wicked Angels Series

Dark Urban Fantasy Romance

Interconnected Standalones

Follow a team of fallen angels as they fight against human trafficking and navigate the blurred lines between good and evil. Set in Pandemonium, a notorious club where they blend in with humans, this heart-pounding series will leave you breathless. Don't miss out on this intense and spicy journey of redemption and second chances.

.

Rogue Angels Series

Dark Urban Fantasy Romance

Completed Series

Rogue Angels is a twist retelling of the Snow White fairytale. Enjoy an adventure with fated mates, midlife crisis, and evil demons. This story includes themes of love, sacrifice, and self-discovery.

.

Sexy Sins Afterlife Retreat Series

Paranormal Reverse Harem Romance

Completed Series

Warning: This series has one strong woman and four dangerously sexy immortal men. She's been their fated mate in every life they've lived and they refuse to live one without her. Read this series if you like why choose romance with a paranormal twist and hunky guys times four!

.

Masquerade Club Series

Dark Contemporary Romance

Completed Series

A contemporary saga with a side dish of spice and a second chance romance for two people you'll never forget. The Masquerade Club is exclusive and available only for the ultra-rich where all your dreams and fantasies come true. Join the party and fall in love with Connor and Katherine in this angst-ridden suspense-filled series.

.

ABOUT THE AUTHOR

Lilith Darville is a *USA Today* bestselling author of dangerously delicious romance, including sizzling paranormal reverse harem. With over forty years of storytelling experience, her stories are guaranteed to make readers flush and blush.

lilithdarville.com